PERILS OF
THE HEART

JENNIFER ASHLEY

LEISURE BOOKS NEW YORK CITY

To Forrest, with my deepest love.

A LEISURE BOOK®

November 2002

Published by

Dorchester Publishing Co., Inc.
276 Fifth Avenue
New York, NY 10001

ISBN 0-8439-5133-8

Visit us on the web at www.dorchesterpub.com.

ACKNOWLEDGMENTS

No one publishes a book without an incredible number of people who provide guidance and support. I would like to thank Kate Seaver for her interest in my book, and all the editors and production staff at Dorchester who make a printed book happen. I would also like to thank Yvonne, my agent, for believing in me even when I didn't.

I would also like to thank my parents, Gene and Carolyn, for always encouraging me to write, and to my friends and family who have lent me support and encouragement from the beginning: Leslie, Claudia, Chris, Elizabeth, Debbie, Magon, Nancy, and my wonderful in-laws Trudy and Al.

Last, the greatest thanks, of course, goes to my husband, Forrest, who has given me unconditional love and support throughout.

PERILS OF THE HEART

Chapter One

The Atlantic Ocean, 1790

"Miss Adams, I will *not* help you commandeer this ship," Evangeline said firmly.

The beautiful woman on the other bunk smiled. "Certainly you will, Miss Clemens. It is all arranged. You stepbrother has joined us and so must you."

Fear touched Evangeline's heart. "Well, I can be of no help to you. I know nothing about storming prisons and rescuing pirates. I know horticulture, geography, and social etiquette."

"And a fine lot of good they've done you. Look at you, dashing off to America to become a governess." Anna leaned forward, spanning the space between the narrow bunks. "Boston is dull, and governesses are duller. Come with me and see the world. Sebastian has many friends. Perhaps one will take a fancy to you, plain as you are."

"I have no wish to marry a pirate, thank you. Not if it leads to the rash actions you are taking at present."

Anna gave a throaty laugh. "I never said I'd *married* Sebastian. He's my lover, my dear, and languishing in a foul prison in Havana. I am going to fetch him."

Evangeline cringed back on her bunk, wanting to put as much distance between herself and the woman's evil as she could. "Well, I sincerely beg to be excused. You may put me off on a passing ship, if you like."

"And have you confess my plans to all who will listen? Not likely, Miss Clemens. Come with me. What kind of life can you have looking after some other woman's brats? Lieutenant Foster is with me. He will lead the crew in mutiny and sail the ship to Havana. Then we'll sell off the cargo for a pretty packet. You can take your share and buy fine clothes and return to Gloucestershire to rub your philandering Harley's nose in it."

Evangeline thought briefly of her betrothed, whom she'd found tumbling her maid, in Evangeline's very own bed, no less. Amid a haze of pain, she had cried off. Her mother and stepfather had raged at her. Harley was a perfectly good catch, they'd said, and all men had lovers.

But facing them the day she'd broken off her engagement paled against facing this beautiful woman, who was intent on bending Evangeline to her will.

"I am beginning to think I ought to have married Harley after all."

"Certainly you should have. Then shot him, taken a

lover, and lived off your widow's portion."

"Oh, of course. I ought to have thought of that."

Anna smiled. "You can make him pay, my dear. Sebastian and his friends will easily see him off if you like. Or they'll let him linger until he regrets every hurt he ever caused you."

The ship heaved on a swell and dropped suddenly, hitting the bottom of the wave with a hollow *boom*. Evangeline's stomach deserted her.

"Miss Adams, I cannot help you. If you wish to run to Havana and release your pirate from prison, it is your business. If my stepbrother wishes to help you, that is his. I wish only to reach Boston."

Anna's smile vanished. "You little fool. Did you suppose I'd outline my plans to you and let you walk away?"

"You—you may lock me in my cabin if you must. Though staying below still makes me a trifle seasick."

"Your only choice, Miss Spinster, is to help me— willingly or unwillingly. Willingly, I let you live. Unwillingly, I don't. If you like, I can shoot your stepbrother first and let you watch him die."

Evangeline saw certainty in Anna's eyes. Her stepbrother, Thomas Edgewood, had become infatuated with the woman from the moment they'd met her in Liverpool. He'd been most pleased when they'd discovered she was the third passenger who would travel on the merchant vessel *Aurora* bound for Boston. Evangeline hadn't liked the voluptuous woman with the cold eyes, but Thomas had fallen quickly for her false charms.

Anna had shared a cabin with Evangeline and had

tried to befriend her. Evangeline had not entirely trusted her, but she'd never dreamed the woman would try to instigate a mutiny, of all things.

Tonight, Anna had walked back to the cabin with Evangeline, closed the door, and announced her impossible scheme to help the first mate, Lieutenant Foster, take over the merchantman.

Evangeline's fear swelled and expanded, then broke. A strange calm stole through her, the same calm that had come upon her the night of the fire at Tottenham Grange when she'd rushed to the third floor to assist the two terrified maids trapped there. She remembered with clarity prying open the shutters, ordering the girls onto the waiting ladder, and descending after them. She'd collapsed once she'd reached safety, coming back to herself a day later to find her father's house in charred ruins.

The chant, *survive first*, had drummed through her head then, and it beat through her head now. Survive first, reason a solution later.

She lifted her chin. "Very well. What do you want me to do?"

Anna explained her plan. Evangeline stared at her in dismay. "You want *me* to divert the captain's attention? How on earth am I to do that?"

"Easily, my dear. Lieutenant Foster has many men loyal to him. You distract the captain for a quarter of an hour, and Foster begins the mutiny. It will all be over quickly."

"But I will never get near the captain. He shuts himself away from his passengers and has a guard. I will be of no use to you, after all."

"Don't be silly. According to Mr. Foster, the captain is a man of precise habits. He retires to his cabin at nine every night." She took a gold pocketwatch from her bosom and opened it. "Which was half an hour ago. His cabin boy brings him a decanter of brandy at five past. After that, he is left alone until he retires to bed. And do not worry about the guard. He will be taken care of."

"How? Are you going to kill him?"

"Drug him," Anna answered—too quickly. "Honor bright. All you must do is occupy Captain Blackwell's attention while we round up those who will help us. It will be over before you know it."

"Then what will you do to the captain?"

Anna shrugged. "If he does not concede then we will—" She caught Evangeline's eye. "He will be imprisoned, then released when we land."

"Do you swear to that?"

"Oh, for heaven's sake. Yes, I swear it."

Evangeline reached under her pillow and pulled out her red-covered book of devotions. "Swear on this. I'm afraid I cannot take the bare word of a liar and a mutineer."

Anna sighed and rolled her eyes, but she placed her hand on the book. "I swear. There, are you happy?"

Evangeline tucked the book back under the pillow. "I still cannot imagine how you suppose I will distract him. What conversation could I make that will hold his attention?"

5

"You unworldly chit. You will not *talk* to him. You will seduce him."

Water dashed against the hull with a sound like sand on glass. The lantern creaked on its chain. Evangeline pressed a hand to her chest. "Me? Seduce him? You must be joking."

"I am in earnest. You will do it."

"I cannot, I assure you. You ought to do the seducing. He will not even notice me."

"I would do it myself, but I don't trust Foster entirely, and I want to stay near to him. Believe me, you are a secondary measure."

"It's likely he will simply laugh and send me away."

"Nonsense. Lieutenant Foster told me the captain has been at sea a long while and does not have a regular mistress in port. Likely anything female, even one as plain as you, will catch his attention."

Evangeline shook her head. "I assure you, I do not know the first thing about seducing a gentleman."

"You must make a bit of effort, that is all." Anna yanked a strand of Evangeline's hair from its tight braid. "That will help. And take off those spectacles."

Evangeline squeaked and shoved them higher onto her nose. "Good heavens, no. I cannot see a foot in front of my face without them."

"I suppose they do give you an innocent look. At least show him some bosom."

She caught the edges of Evangeline's Pierrot bodice and jerked open the top hooks. Cool air touched Evangeline's modest breasts, pushed as high as possible by her stays.

"You are hopelessly small. But some gentlemen will

take any bosom, in a pinch. They're fascinated by the things."

Evangeline jerked the placket together. "Well, they have never been fascinated by mine."

"Then this will be your chance to shine, my dear. You and the captain will be alone. Pretend you are overly warm, and undo another hook. Or that you have an itch." She drew one curved nail along the neckline of her blouse, pressing the decollatage slyly to one side.

Evangeline gulped. "I—I don't think I can do that."

"My dear, it will be simplicity itself. With his bed close to hand, and you so eager—"

"His *bed*?"

"Don't be silly. We will be finished long before that becomes necessary. Come along, it's almost time."

Evangeline rose, her knees shaking. "Notwithstanding the presence of the bed and the merits of my gender, I am skeptical about my powers to distract him."

Anna pushed her toward the cabin door. "Dangle your tits under his nose if you must. That will awaken him."

"I very much doubt it."

She reached for the cabin's door. Anna's hand clamped down on her shoulder, fingers biting like claws. Her hot spittle touched Evangeline's ear. "Know this, Miss Clemens. If you warn him, if you breathe a word of what we are doing, I will shoot him in the belly and throw him to the sharks. Do you understand me?"

Evangeline looked into her cold, evil eyes, and read truth there. "I understand."

They emerged onto the deck and crossed to the short stair that led down to the captain's cabin. The chill sea wind whipped Evangeline's narrow skirts about her ankles and dragged tendrils of hair from her braid. The ship, rocking under the clear night sky, reflected the peacefulness of the relatively calm sea, but the crew spoke in hushed voices, as if sensing catastrophe about to strike.

In the stern, on the command deck, Lieutenant Foster leaned negligently on the rail. He watched Evangeline and Anna cross the deck below him, but made no sign of acknowledgement.

They descended the stair, out of the wind. Evangeline peered down the short hallway that ended at the captain's cabin. The polished walnut door with its brass straps looked more daunting than had Miller's pond the winter Silas Burns had dared her to dash across its thin ice. She remembered her terror when the ice had crackled and groaned under her feet, crumbling away to nothing and plunging her into icy water.

The same sensation overwhelmed her now. She knew in her heart that Anna would most likely kill her, and Thomas, too, if she refused this impossible task. Cool dispassion seemed to separate Miss Adams and the rest of the world. The woman had no honor.

Inside the passage, the guard whose duty it was to keep the crew and passengers from irritating the captain lay slumped on his side, eyes closed.

Behind her, Anna gave Evangeline a hard shove. "Go on."

Drawing a breath, Evangeline stepped over the guard and walked swiftly down the corridor. Grasping the brass doorhandle with her slick palms, she opened the door and stepped into the captain's cabin.

8

Chapter Two

Austin Blackwell, captain and commander of the merchant vessel *Aurora* out of Boston, heard his cabin door softly open and close.

Without looking up, Austin moved his dividers to another point on his chart. "Yes, what is it?"

Silence met his question. The only person allowed into the cabin, unannounced, after nine was Cyril, the lad who cleaned Austin's boots and brought him his meals. Cyril had already delivered the brandy, punctually at 9:05, and gone away. But Cyril was a mischievous lad, often at odds with the cook. Several times he'd crept to Austin to sheepishly confess his misdeeds and ask the captain to soothe the cook's temper.

Austin was not in the mood for Cyril's troubles. The closer the *Aurora* drew to Boston, the more uneasy he became. He ought to rejoice as the journey neared completion, bringing to an end his unwanted mission. But his instincts would not let him relax. If his enemies were to strike, they would strike soon.

He raised his head. "I said, what is it?"

His hand froze, the dividers dangling. The intruder was not Cyril. A tall young woman in a shapeless gray gown and spectacles stood with her back against the door, her hands behind her.

He recognized her as one of the passengers. Every merchant vessel took passengers, as room permitted. Three people had joined him in Liverpool: Miss Clemens; her stepbrother, Mr. Edgewood; and the overly voluptuous Miss Adams. Austin had kept his distance from them, as he usually did with passengers. He relied on his first officer to keep them entertained, and above all, out of the way.

Now his curiosity stirred. Was *she* the British agent sent to steal the papers? In English hands the documents he carried could do untold damage to his fledgling country. The American states were still vulnerable to those determined to see it restored to George III's rule. His mission was to keep the documents safely out of their possession.

He hadn't wanted the task. This voyage was to be his last, the end of his wandering days. He would become a partner in the shipping company and stay at home, perhaps to at last discover the peace that had eluded him all his life. He needed that peace, longed for it to soothe his bruised and battered soul.

Captain Gainesborough, Austin's commander and one of the few men Austin could not refuse during the war, had chosen him to deliver the sensitive papers into the proper hands. His mentor trusted him implicitly, and Austin had no intention of betraying that trust.

He wondered briefly at his enemies' choice of agents. Miss Clemens seemed harmless enough. Why not the provocative Miss Adams?

Too obvious, perhaps. Miss Clemens might slip in under his guard, where Miss Adams would definitely arouse his suspicions. Or perhaps they'd simply been desperate and sent the first person they could lay hands on.

Austin put down his dividers, leaned back in his chair, and took a moment to study his adversary. She was tall, and, though a bit on the slender side, well formed. Her narrow skirt lay flat against long, slim, shapely legs. A mass of golden hair coiled in a heavy braid around her head, not all of it staying put. Enchanting little curls hung about her face and teased her inviting white neck. Her eyes behind the spectacles were gray, not slate-gray, but the clear and liquid color of diamonds.

"What are you doing in here?" he asked, his voice quiet. "Davis should have announced you."

She started. "Yes. Of course. I do beg your pardon."

Her voice, even trembling, was whispery soft, warm as sunshine. It caught his thoughts, wrapping around his buried desires. Deep inside him an alarm like the bell that announced the changing watch clanged a warning.

He rested his elbow on the arm of his chair. "Very well, you have my notice. What do you want?"

Her mouth opened and closed. Her tongue darted out to lick her lips. "Oh, yes. Indeed. You must be very

11

busy. You are—you are looking at the charts, are you not? Can you—that is, will you show them to me? Show me where we are, I mean?"

He hesitated one moment, then motioned her to him. "Easily done. Come here."

She looked dismayed, as if she'd planned to rob him of the papers while taking root against the door. But he wanted the opportunity to study her more closely. She intrigued him. Besides which, he wanted her hands out from behind her back, to see what weapon, if any, she held there.

She dragged in a breath, like a swimmer preparing to plunge into icy water, and scuttled across the few feet separating them. Under the low-swinging lantern her hair blossomed into burnished gold. The bodice of her dull, gray spinster's gown parted still more, tantalizing him with hints of the delights inside. Austin imagined himself dipping his hand into that bodice, fitting her lovely globe into his palm.

He shook off the vision with difficulty, trying to suppress the warm stirrings that had begun within him. He did not have time for passion. Every attachment he'd formed with a woman, including his own wife, had turned catastrophic. For a long time now, he'd habitually pushed aside any thoughts of lust simply out of self-preservation.

Now those thoughts trickled through him and threatened to become a flood.

He touched his finger to the chart. "We are here."

She rested her hands—empty of weapons—on the desk, and leaned down to look. A lock of her hair caressed Austin's fingers. Silken warmth rubbed his skin, and the stirrings below multiplied. The subtle scent of her filled his nostrils, flowed over his brain and nudged his senses awake.

"It looks different than a regular map," she said. "How can you tell what everything is?"

Austin jerked his hand from under her hair. "The lines are latitude. Here is our position, according to the compass and sextant and what I can deduce from the time."

"I see. How far are we from Havana?"

"Havana? A long distance. Why?"

Her gray gaze flicked to him. The mirror told Austin he had little to worry about under a woman's scrutiny, but he became suddenly aware of his defects: the scar that creased his cheekbone, the minute lines about his eyes, the color of his hair—perhaps she would dislike dark brown laced with red.

"I—that is, it is all so fascinating, is it not? All these charts and things. Do you know, I had never been on a sailing ship before this voyage, and yet, I long to stay on this ship forever. I suppose you feel that way, too. That is why you are a captain."

"Perhaps. But I plan to retire after this voyage."

"Oh, how sad."

Her simple exclamation awakened a voice buried deep inside him. The voice told him he would be miserable landbound for the rest of his life, that he would yearn for the sea and its freedom, always.

No, I am tired. I deserve to rest.

Alone. In his cold house on Beacon Street, away from everything he had ever loved. His wife had lived in that house, and had hated it.

He let coolness enter his voice. "You should retire, Miss Clemens. No doubt you find life at sea wearying."

"Not at all. In fact, I feel more lively than I have in many a year. It quite agrees with me, though I was queasy at first."

He shoved back his chair and rose. "But it wearies me. Perhaps I wish to sleep."

"Oh. I beg your pardon, I hadn't thought of that. Do you wish to? Sleep?"

Austin let his gaze rove to his bunk, low and narrow under the sloping port wall of the cabin. "I had thought of going to bed, yes."

Her cheeks pinkened, like ripe, dusky peaches in snowy-white cream. She glanced once at the door, then swallowed hard. "My, it is warm in here, is it not?"

He had thought the room rather chilly, except for the area around his thighs. She fluttered her hand in front of her face, her movements jerky, then she yanked open a hook of her bodice.

The heat in his loins raced to fill his entire body. He knew she'd come to rob him, to seduce him into a stupor so she could search his cabin or convince him to hand the papers over to her. He should stop her, send her on her way.

But she paralyzed him. Her beauty, at once both subtle and breathtaking, held him mesmerized. So he stood, tensely watching her.

She fumbled at another hook. It caught. She yanked.

He went to her. "Please. Allow me."

Her lips parted, her eyes widening like a startled dove's. His pulse beating hard, he reached up and unfastened the hook. Her breasts rose swiftly, splaying the

14

bodice open to reveal a chemise of white cambric, tied with a ribbon. The round, dusky tips of her breasts, lifted high by her stays, pressed against the thin fabric.

"How beautiful," he whispered.

"What is?"

"You. Do you wish me to go on?"

Her voice shook. "Go on?"

He smoothed a loose tendril of hair from her forehead. "You play the innocent maiden so well. You have enchanted me, my sparrow. Shall we continue on the bunk? It might be more comfortable."

"Your bunk? I thought—I mean, oh, yes, of course."

He cupped her shoulders. Need throbbed through him, demanding that he take her. If she had come to seduce the papers from him, let her seduce him. He could laugh and send her away later, empty-handed. An hour with her might be worth it.

From out of the depths of his memory came the voice of his mentor. Captain Gainesborough had stood in Austin's Beacon Street sitting room the day before the voyage, his gray head nearly touching the chandelier in Austin's sitting room. Tall and lean, Gainesborough had been easily distinguished on the deck of his frigate during the naval battles of the War of Independence. If the American navy hadn't disbanded after the war, and if the Americans had adopted all the ranks of the English, Gainesborough would be a commodore or even an admiral by now. But Americans had believed those ranks sounded too "royal" so Gainesborough had retired a captain, if a highly respected and senior one. Now a partner in the shipping company Austin also had joined, he served as a go-between between shipping interests and the new American government. He let the government know the problems and concerns of the merchant traders; they occasionally asked him for his naval expertise on some problem. "Those papers, my boy," he'd said, "could mean the difference between peace and prosperity, and disaster. You must protect them with your life." And Austin had stood before him, ramrod straight, and answered, "I understand, sir."

Cold reason smote him. She was subtle, and she had certainly cast her spell on him. She might be even more dangerous when she'd seduced him in truth, leaving him helpless and begging for more. The papers had to be protected, even from himself.

He leaned down, letting his voice grow chill. "I have a better idea, Miss Clemens. Why don't you tell me exactly why you came here and what you want? If you do not tell me too many lies, I may only lock you in your cabin. If you lie too much, I'll throw you in the brig. Now, which is it to be?"

Her face flooded with color, and she whirled from him, clutching her placket. "Oh, I knew my bosom would not entice you. You knew why I came all along, didn't you? And you let me go on and on. You must have been laughing all the time."

He clenched his hands. "Not laughing, no."

"Are you going to put me in the brig?"

He hesitated. This little sparrow would perish in his brig, sleeping on rope hammocks and dining on hard tack and water. But he ought to make good his threat and lock her up. His secrets would remain safe, and his sanity, too.

"Not if you tell me the truth. Were you sent here against your will?"

"Indeed. I knew it would never work. Silly to think a man such as yourself would ever be tempted by me."

Good lord, how could she doubt she was anything but beautiful, sensual, intriguing. . . .

"How do you know you have not enticed me?"

"Because I am hopelessly plain, my bosom hopelessly small."

"Who has told you that?"

She paused. "Everyone, I suppose."

He watched her a moment, trying to decide if she were a good actress or if everyone who had ever met her was impossibly stupid.

"Will you allow me to judge for myself?"

"For—for yourself?"

He went to her. Gently he took her cold hands and moved them away from her bodice. She watched him, transfixed, as he unfastened the remaining hooks and pulled the placket apart.

Creamy breasts, round and smooth, rose with her breath. Her skin was pale, almost translucent, the scent of her intoxicating.

He cleared his throat. "I assure you, this bosom is a thing of beauty."

"You truly think so?"

The shy question made him suddenly, and hotly, aroused. "Indeed. So lovely I long to see more of it."

"Perhaps you have simply been at sea too long. Perhaps you haven't seen a bosom in a long while."

Austin choked back a laugh as he grasped the chemise's ribbon. "I had a wife, miss. And I have had—"

He stopped. "I have seen bosoms. Yours compares favorably."

She slanted him a smile that fired his blood.

The ribbon unraveled from its bow, and the thin fabric loosened. Austin carefully parted the chemise. His breath caught.

The garment's lace formed a fitting frame to her breasts, ripe and sweet, smooth like white satin. The pink nubs tightened and narrowed, and he imagined tantalizing them with his tongue.

"Now then, miss," he said with difficulty. "Let us discuss why you believe your bosom inadequate."

"Harley did not like it." Her voice was barely a whisper.

"Who?"

"Harley, my fiancé. I found him on my bed with my maid. She had a large bosom."

"He did not like this?" He brushed her skin with the backs of his fingers. "What a fool. I hope you cried off."

"I did. My stepfather and mother were very angry."

"The loss is Harley's entirely."

"You are kind to say so. I did not know you would be kind."

Kind? She called this *kindness*?

Austin slid his arms around her waist. Her bared bosom pressed his waistcoat, and his clamoring need tightened in response.

Perhaps he *had* been too long at sea. Austin did not have a mistress in every port, as some ships' captains had. His few liaisons since his wife's passing had never lasted. In each case, the lady hadn't liked his leaving her alone for so long. His first mistress had dallied with

18

her footman in his absence. He'd discovered them to-gether when returning home unexpectedly one eve-ning. The next lady had screeched at him to give up his career for her; the third had merely tired of waiting for him and left. Life at sea, he'd decided, precluded long affairs, and after the disaster with his wife, he'd never wanted to marry again.

He hated short intrigues, and yet here he was, ready to take this charming young woman into his arms. He'd make love to her thoroughly and skillfully then have her lead him back to whoever had sent her. He would make sure his enemies knew that their attempt had failed.

The next attempt would be more dangerous.

Austin cradled her head in his palms, and her silken hair trickled through his fingers. His blood beat hot. She had such an odd mixture of innocence and sensuality. It intrigued him, whispered to him to have more of her.

He bent and brushed his tongue across her parted lips. Her sweet breath washed over him, hot moisture beckoning him. He covered her mouth with his. Her warm lips responded clumsily to his pleasuring, her kiss unpracticed.

This woman had no experience of men. His hands sensed it, his mouth sensed it. But he wanted her. Lord, how he wanted her. He wanted her to sigh in his arms, to beg for his kisses. He wanted to take her to his bunk and teach her how to love him. He would make her understand that scheming to steal the papers was use-less. She'd never get them, but she could stay with him and learn to be his lover.

He nipped her silken lobe. She moved against him,

giving a little whimper that drove him wild.

"I've gone mad," he whispered. He swirled his tongue around the sweet shell of her ear. "You have driven me mad, my siren."

She did not answer. She sagged in his arms, her eyes half-closed, her spectacles askew. Wisps of her glorious hair straggled across her cheek, dipping down into the bared heaven of her breasts.

Never mind the bunk. Austin swept the charts and sextant from the desk. He lifted her and set her hips on the edge, then lowered his head and kissed the side of her breast. His lips brushed soft delight, the scent of her beating on his senses. Back to her mouth now, to pleasure the hot sweetness of it, to—

Someone scuttled across the deck overhead. The sound worked its way through Austin's desire, and he raised his head. No matter his task—even one as compelling as Miss Clemens—he was always aware of the sounds of his ship: of the hull creaking, the occasional thump of boots overhead as the officers and men went about their watch, Lieutenant Foster's barked order for a minute change in course. Sounds so familiar he heard them without listening. His mind checked them off of the orderly list in his head, his awareness flowing to every corner of the *Aurora*.

His awareness told him that something had changed. Speed and course had remained constant, but the character of the ship had altered. The running feet overhead held agitation. Davis had let Miss Clemens straight through, and she'd—

She'd only arrived ten minutes ago. But enough time to throw him off the scent.

He turned to the door. "Davis!"

Silence.

If the man had been at his post, he'd have answered. And if something untoward were happening above, Davis would have given the alarm.

"A moment, Miss Clemens." He stepped away, as if he were leaving her in his drawing room while he rung for tea.

He had taken two steps when Miss Clemens seized his arm. "Please, you must not go out there."

He looked down into eyes that had become pools of terror. Her breasts hung, firm and tight, against her open chemise, the nubs still pointed with arousal.

"I *must not*?" he repeated. "Why?"

"I cannot tell you."

He jerked from her grasp. "Davis!"

She caught his arm again. "Please."

He whirled and seized her shoulders, lowering his face to hers. "What is happening on my ship, siren? Tell me now, and I might show you mercy."

"Please, no, she'll kill you!"

"She?"

"Miss Adams."

His need dissolved into pure and overpowering rage. Damn her and her innocent gray eyes and her sensual body that had awakened his from long and tormented sleep. His desire almost sobbed in disappointment, but he clamped down on it, sliding into the iron control that habitually ruled him. He gripped her by the elbows and backed her across the floor until her heels met the desk with a bump. He bent over her, a parody of the passionate way he'd held her only moments ago. "Explain, Miss Clemens. Why will Miss Adams kill me?"

"I cannot tell you."

He made his voice deadly quiet. "You will tell me, siren. Or we will discuss this in the brig, where your innocent act will not save you. Do you understand?"

Chapter Three

Evangeline gazed up into the molten fury of his dark eyes. A moment ago, those eyes had promised her untold pleasures. Now they held the hardness of an executioner's stare.

She'd thought him handsome, with his strong cheekbones and firm mouth and eyes the color of night. The lantern light burned red streaks into his dark hair, which he wore pulled back, sleek and tight against his head. Fine lines from squinting into the sun on the sea fanned the corners of his eyes. A thin, white scar creased his cheekbone, and for some reason, she'd had the desire to trace it with her tongue.

She'd also sensed deep passion in him, pressed down behind his stern exterior. But his anger had swept that passion aside, as a tidal wave sweeps away all unfortunate craft in its wake.

23

"Please. She said that if I warned you she'd shoot you and throw you to the sharks."

"And if you do not tell me, I will send your lovely body to their waiting mouths."

"My—my body isn't lovely."

"That is your opinion."

"Please, I do not want to watch you die."

"You would rather die yourself?"

Evangeline hesitated. He possessed the strength to easily lift her over his shoulder, carry her up on the deck, and fling her into the sea. He'd do it cheerfully, dusting off his hands and thinking it a job well done. But Anna's threat haunted her.

"I think I would rather, yes."

His smile was cold. "Your bravery is admirable. But I do not intend to let Miss Adams shoot me, whatever her reasons."

His mouth nearly touched hers. Her lips still burned from the heat of his kiss, from the taste of brandy on his tongue. When Miss Pyne had boasted that all the young ladies who finished her select academy would be ready for life, the good lady could not have anticipated anything like this. Evangeline had not been prepared for the sensations that had torn through her body when he touched her, when he whispered that she drove him to madness.

Now his voice held quiet menace. "Here is how we will proceed, Miss Clemens. I will ask you questions, and you will answer each one truthfully. Shall we begin?"

Evangeline stared up at him mutely.

"Excellent. First. Is Davis dead?"

"I don't know. Miss Adams said they drugged him."

"We shall see. And Miss Adams wants—" He paused. "What exactly does Miss Adams want?"

"Your ship."

His brows shot up. "My *ship*? The entire ship?"

"Yes."

He frowned, and she sensed her answer had taken him by surprise. "For what purpose?"

"To sail it to Havana."

"Havana?"

"Yes. That is why I asked how far it was."

"Why the devil does she want to go to Havana?"

"To rescue Sebastian."

He clenched his teeth. "And who is Sebastian?"

"Her lover." She bit her lip, then blurted, "He is a pirate. In prison. In Havana."

His body relaxed a fraction. "I see. So the foolish woman has chosen to take *my* ship on an equally foolish errand."

"I assure you she is deadly serious. She will kill you if you resist her."

"No doubt." His hands loosened, sliding to her shoulders. "And your role in all this is—?"

"To distract you. To give her time to arrange things."

"Ah. You played your part remarkably well." He traced her cheek, but his touch was cold. "Does Miss Adams have an accomplice? Besides your good self, I mean."

"Lieutenant Foster. And my stepbrother."

"Hmm. He truly is your stepbrother, I presume?"

"Thomas? Yes. Why wouldn't he be?"

25

"Because if Miss Adams is chasing across the Atlantic to rescue her paramour, perhaps you accompany her with yours."

She started. "Good heavens, no. I do not have a lover. I should not even know what such things mean."

His eyes went flat. "You do the maidenly act very well. I can almost believe you are an innocent. Except that you came here fully prepared to become *my* paramour."

"Only if it were unavoidable."

"And it almost worked, did it not?" he asked, his voice deadly soft. "You had me wrapped around your finger with your seductive smile, and your charming eyes, and your lovely, lovely breasts, bared for my delight. When had you planned to spit me out, my dear?"

"I don't know what you mean."

He gripped her jaw and forced her face upward. "You are dangerous, siren. With your maidenly airs and those spectacles, a man might feel safe with you—just before you tangle him in your lies."

What on earth was he talking about? "Please don't mock me. I know I did wrong, but I had no choice."

"I? Mock you?"

She stared at him numbly. His fingers hurt where they clamped her jaw.

"You need watching, Miss Clemens. The best place to keep you for watching is in my brig, but I don't have time to convey you there now." He straightened, releasing her. "Remain here until I return."

Her fear surged. "You cannot go out there."

"This is my ship. I will not cower in my cabin while Foster and a love-sick pirate's woman try to take it over."

"She said she would let you go if you did not fight. She promised me."

He crossed to a cabinet, opened it, and drew out a pistol. Lantern light slid over his hair as he bent his head to prime the weapon. "Did she, indeed? Forgive me for not taking her at her word."

Evangeline pulled her chemise together and retied the ribbon with clumsy fingers. "I will pray for you, captain."

He glanced at her sharply. "If you wish. But stay here. I will decide what to do with you later."

"If you come back," she whispered.

He gave her a hard, tight look. "I always come back."

He turned away and opened the cabin door. A gust of chill air rushed over her, bringing with it the sharp smell of the sea. She heard shouts overhead, but the passage was quiet.

Without looking at Evangeline, he strode from the cabin and closed the door, leaving her alone.

Davis was dead. Austin straightened from the lad's cold body, fury pounding him. The young sailor lay still, eyes closed peacefully. He had not struggled. Perhaps they had meant only to drug him, with opium or laudanum, but had given him too much.

He didn't believe that.

Apart from Davis's body, the passage remained empty. And silent. From the deck above came shouts, frantic running, high-pitched laughter, and a man swearing mightily. But no one moved toward the stair that led to Austin's chambers.

Austin tightened his grip on the pistol. He thought of the woman in the cabin behind him, and his anger beat strong and hard. He had been so certain she'd come for the papers—they preyed on his mind so that he saw danger from no other quarter. Perhaps Foster's mutiny also had to do with the papers; perhaps the lieutenant used Miss Adams's quest for his own purpose. Either way, Austin would stop them. He had promised to deliver the documents to his mentor in Boston, and deliver them he would.

He moved to the end of the short corridor and ducked into the shadows beside the stair to wait there until his breathing stilled. He had never lost control with a woman in his life. And yet, he'd been ready to take Miss Clemens, a woman who barely knew how to kiss, in a mad frenzy.

He still wanted her. His blood burned, his mouth held the taste of her, his fingers itched to know every curve of her body. He wanted her and a part of his mind spun out ideas of ways he could have her. She might be a deceiver, but that didn't make her less enticing, less enchanting, less desirable.

But anger burned as hot as his desire. He would deal with Miss Clemens once he defeated Foster and the mutiny. She would pay, oh, dearly she would. She'd woken in him a great longing that he'd thought he'd subdued years ago, all to make sport of him. Oh, yes, she would pay.

Austin inched his way up the ladder, holding his pistol ready.

Above, chaos reigned. Miss Adams, a smile on her beautiful face, stood not far away watching as three sailors beat one of the lieutenants with cudgels. Miss Clemens's stepbrother, Mr. Edgewood, a weedy young man with protruding eyes, skulked nearby, gazing idiotically at Miss Adams.

Lieutenant Foster held the wheel on the poop deck, imperiously surveying all before him. Near the mainmast, a sullen group of sailors and officers clustered under the guard of another lieutenant and several seamen. The group must be those who'd taken a stand against the mutineers.

Other sailors worked the lines, heaving and bending to move the sails. Austin glanced at the stars. They'd changed direction now, heading south, southwest. Toward Havana.

If he could gain the main deck without being detected and inch to the port side, he'd have a clear shot at Foster. The man commanded the mutiny, whatever Miss Adams thought, and, with him dead, it would be easier to regain control.

A numbness stole over him, one he'd felt as a young lieutenant in the war against the English, the first time he'd ordered his cannons to fire at a British frigate. He remembered watching blankly as flames licked the ship, sending it crumpling into the sea. Men had fallen, burning, from the rigging to the uncaring ocean where they'd died. Austin and his shipmates had lived.

He moved stealthily from the stair, crouching behind a stack of kegs, keeping to the darkness. Not far away, sailors grunted and strained against the ropes, faces drawn. Others laughed among themselves around a barrel of rum they'd broached.

Idiots. Foster knew nothing about running a ship. Routine and clockwork and tight discipline kept boredom down, disease at bay, and drunkeness to a minimum. The lieutenant would have chaos on his hands in no time. Austin hadn't wanted to take Foster as his lieutenant in the first place—he'd never liked the man—but he'd been overruled by the company. Well, they'd paid the price in the life of Davis and other good men, as well.

He studied the group of resisters and found his own hand-picked men: Osborn, his coxswain; Lieutenant Jameson, young Seward. Good. He could count on them. This was Lieutenant Seward's first voyage, but he'd already proved he had mettle.

Slowly Austin rose to his feet. The sailors, busy tying off the sails or getting sodden drunk, did not notice him. He brought up his pistol, extended his arm, and sighted.

A sailor opened a lantern, and the golden light gleamed on the barrel of Austin's pistol. Miss Adams whipped her head around, her eyes widening. She shouted.

Damn.

Foster turned, saw, moved. Anna Adams raised a pistol and pointed it straight at Austin.

Everything slowed. Austin knew he could hit Foster now, without missing. But Anna Adams's shot would kill Austin an instant later. Or he could dive for cover and lose his chance to rid the mutiny of its leader.

Lieutenant Seward saw him. His young eyes widened.

Austin made his choice. He fired. The ball hit Foster hard, not in the chest, because the man dodged, but in the clavicle. He stumbled, tried to right himself. He stumbled again just as the ship bucked high out of the water. Foster lost his balance. He grabbed at the rail, but his hands slipped and his legs buckled. He wavered on the rail, then slowly, slowly, pitched over the side. His screams echoed back on the cold wind.

Anna Adams shrieked, and fired.

Chapter Four

Another shriek rent the air.

Miss Clemens bolted from the stair and careened into Miss Adams just as the pistol went off. The shot cracked, then the gun bounced onto the deck and skittered crazily across the wet boards. The fired ball whizzed past Austin and out to sea.

"You promised," Miss Clemens cried at her. "You swore on a *Bible*."

Miss Adams backhanded Miss Clemens across the face, sending the taller girl tumbling to her knees.

Austin drew his knife from his boot and sprinted across the rocking deck. He seized Anna, jerked her back against him, and jammed the knife against her throat.

Thomas Edgewood gave a cry of dismay and clumsily tugged a pistol from his pocket.

32

Austin pressed the knife harder against Anna's white skin. "It's her life if you fire, Edgewood."

"Let her go, you bastard."

"No. Drop the gun."

The young man stared, his mouth trembling, then he slowly tossed his firearm to the deck.

Out of the corner of his eye, Austin saw Miss Clemens start to crawl toward the fallen pistol. He planted his boot on her thigh, pinning her down.

"Osborn," Austin called to his coxswain. "Get the weapons."

Osborn, a short young man with red hair, simply walked away from the mutineers. He reached the pistols and retrieved them both, then gave Edgewood's gun a look of disgust. "Not even properly primed, sir."

"An excellent confederate you chose," Austin said to Miss Adams.

She glared at him and snarled a filthy word. Only a fool like Foster would fall for this woman. She was like a rotten apple—firm, ripe flesh on the outside, black corruption on the inside.

Austin threw her at Edgewood. At the same time, he hauled Miss Clemens to her feet and dragged her with him toward the command deck. He shoved her up the stair to the deserted poop deck, then swarmed up the ladder behind her. He pushed her onto the bench under the rail, then, with his foot, stopped the wheel that had been left spinning after Foster's fall.

His men cheered.

Anna screeched, "What are you waiting for? Take him!"

The mutineers wavered. Osborn acted. He shouted

orders to the men who had remained loyal to the captain, and they quickly obeyed. Weapons were jerked from hesitant hands, turned round and trained on the insurgents.

A band of Foster's men attacked. The battle was short and ugly. Osborn, Seward, and Jameson wove in and out, fighting with swords and cudgels. Many of the mutineers switched back to Austin's side, turning on their fellows. In the middle of it all, Edgewood tried desperately to drag Anna to safety.

Austin had the reputation for running a tight ship, and his discipline was legendary. But he had always been fair, and his men knew it. No man suffered punishment undeserved, he was more than generous with rations, and he made certain his crew was always well-rested and alert. His reputation served him well now, as his men responded quickly to Osborn's commands, subduing the uprising in short order.

By the time Austin had fought the rudder back into place, the mutiny was over. Jameson jogged to the foot of the deck and shouted up to him. "That's the last of it, sir."

"Well done, lieutenant. Let it be known that anyone who fought for me will be rewarded."

"And those who did not?"

"Pick out the men who were simply too afraid not to mutiny and confine them to quarters. Put Foster's dogs in the brig."

"Yes, sir." He glanced at Miss Clemens, who was clutching the rail and staring around her with wide eyes. "What about the ladies? And Mr. Edgewood."

Austin slid his gaze to Miss Clemens. She returned

the look, her chin lifted, as if defying him to throw her to the sharks as he'd threatened. "Lock Miss Clemens in her cabin. Put Miss Adams in Mr. Edgewood's. Take Edgewood to the brig. It might make a man of him."

Jameson laughed. "Aye, sir."

"Search their baggage, their cabins, and their persons for weapons or anything else suspicious, then take all of their belongings to my cabin. Get Seward to search the ladies."

Jameson chewed his lip, as if debating whether to speak. Austin had heard the whispered jokes about young Lieutenant Seward, but he had decided to take no notice. The lad had given him no trouble thus far.

In the end, Jameson only nodded. "Aye, sir."

"Go with him, Miss Clemens."

She rose, her lips parted. She hadn't yet managed to do up her bodice. Two hooks hung from the wrong loops, and the placket gaped open.

Jameson went a fine shade of pink. He coughed. "If you'll just come this way, miss."

She switched her gaze to Austin. "Will you return my things after you've searched them?"

"No."

"But—"

"I said, no."

"Not even—"

His control snapped. "Miss Clemens, get off my deck. I am tired of you. You will be confined to your cabin until we reach Boston and I decide what to do with you. Until then, I do not want to see you, or hear from you. Do you understand?"

She looked at him a moment longer. Her face was

streaked with dirt, her spectacles spotted with tar and seawater. She was nothing like the voluptuous beauty who had seduced his first lieutenant into mutiny. But danger radiated from this meek-looking girl, smiting him like the pistol shot that hadn't reached him. He sensed that he was not finished with her; that she would reach out once again and endanger his ship, his mission, and his sanity.

She opened her mouth as if wanting to speak, then she snapped it shut. She gave him a shaky salute, then turned and scuttled down the stairs to Jameson.

Austin forced himself not to watch her go. His blood still pounded from her sensual and unpracticed kisses, her warm breath, the silken smoothness of her breast. Suppressing the mutiny hadn't erased the new and hot sensations that swamped his body.

He suppressed a groan as he began to correct the ship's course. He'd weathered bad storms at sea, but he'd never had to face anything like the diamond-gray eyes of Evangeline Clemens.

Evangeline took great gulps of dark sea air as she stumbled up onto the deck. Bright moonlight bathed the ship, and she sought the deepest of shadows as she scuttled to the rail.

For two days, she'd remained locked in her cabin. In the tiny confinement, her seasickness had returned. She'd been barely able to keep down the broth and hard biscuits that Lieutenant Seward delivered to her twice a day. This afternoon, she'd asked the polite, boyish lieutenant if she could take the air on deck. He'd promised to speak to the captain, but hadn't returned to tell her the verdict.

Evangeline had tried to sleep, then given it up and paced back and forth in her cabin. But because she could only take three steps either way, that simply made her dizzier. That's when she'd discovered that her cabin door hadn't been fastened all the way.

Through the tiny crack in the door she could see that the latch sat just barely on the catch. Without stopping to think, she pried a loose nail from her bunk, and set to work on the lock.

The nail made scratching noises on the wood and metal as she tried to knock the latch aside. The noise sounded so loud to her own ears she feared a passing officer would hear. He'd slam the door, lock it, and report the incident to the captain. Then Captain Blackwell would toss her into the brig. She imagined dark cages filled with straw and rats. The other mutineers would be there, leering and pawing at her through the bars.

But no officer came to investigate.

After sawing back and forth for a long time, the latch suddenly fell from the catch. Evangeline discarded the nail and slid the door open.

The common area outside her cabin contained a polished table and chairs in the center and cabinets along the walls. The cabins of the officers circled the small area on three sides. But the room was deserted. Evangeline crept through it, her shaking legs barely able to hold her, and climbed out onto the deck.

Even if Seward caught her and spirited her back to her cabin, the effort was worth it. The night was clear;

the stars blazed in a smudge across the black sky. The foam off the ship's prow glowed with pearl-like opalescence. Clean air filled her lungs and made her heart beat stronger.

The ship sailed high on a swell, then boomed back down into the ocean. Spray shot up, stinging her chafed hands and face. She clutched the rail, and laughed.

A hand clamped hers, hard, to the rail, pinning her fast.

"What are you doing here?"

Evangeline twisted around. Captain Blackwell loomed above her, moonlight making sharp shadows of his square face and hard brow. His eyes were as black as the night.

"If Seward let you up here, I will have him toting water for the rest of the voyage."

"I picked the lock."

The chill in his eyes grew more pronounced. "Do I have to nail your cabin door shut to keep you in?"

"I only needed air. I was seasick. Lieutenant Seward said he would ask if I could come above."

"He did. I denied the request. You told me you'd gotten over your seasickness."

She shook her head. "I had recovered. Only, confined in the cabin, with no air, and the ship rocking all the time the queasiness returned." She felt dizzy just thinking about it.

"So you took it upon yourself to release yourself."

"Only for a bit of air. There's no harm done."

"The last time you crept about my ship where you pleased, my crew mutinied. I have every interest in seeing that you stay put."

"Five minutes, that is all I ask, Captain. Let me enjoy the breeze for five minutes, and then I will go back to my cabin. I promise."

His eyes narrowed. "I do not trust your promises. You look at me with your shining eyes and I want to believe every word you say."

She swallowed and looked away. His hand remained on hers, heavy, trapping her. Despite the fresh air, her lungs were tight, her heart constricted.

"What will happen when we reach Boston, Captain?" she asked.

"To you, you mean?"

"To the mutineers. And my brother. And Miss Adams."

"Trial for the mutineers and Miss Adams. They might be lenient with her because she is a woman, but I will have her arrested and charged with the rest of them. Your stepbrother is only an idiot. I'll recommend he be returned, in disgrace, to England."

"And what about—" her voice went small. "Me?"

He was silent a long time, and in his silence she imagined she heard the clang of a cage door as it slammed shut in the darkness.

"I have not decided yet. I haven't made up my mind if you are truly an innocent spinster, or if you are a consummate liar and an accomplished actress."

"I *am* a spinster. I'm going to Boston to become a governess."

"A governess?" He gave her an incredulous look. "Did you truly believe, Miss Clemens, that you could board my ship, take part in a mutiny, then stroll away to become a governess?"

She bit her lip. "The mutiny was not exactly in my plans."

"And who is the family foolish enough to employ you?"

"I do not know, yet. My cousin, Mrs. Farely, wrote that she would arrange it. No doubt she will have a position for me when we reach Boston."

His dark brows drew down over his nose. "I will send her a message that you no longer require a position. If you stay confined to your cabin and stop letting yourself out to roam free, I will simply put you on a packet bound for England with your stepbrother, and return you home."

Pain smote her heart. "Oh, no. I cannot return to England."

"Why not? Are you escaping the law?"

"Good heavens, no. I left England because I have no prospects there."

She felt again the bitter sting when her stepfather had shouted at her that a plain woman like her, already on the shelf, would never find another gentleman interested in marrying her. She'd been a bloody fool to dismiss Harley, no matter what he'd done. Her mother had sat silently, never saying a word against her husband.

"No prospects for what?"

"Marriage. Anything, actually. My parents were quite angry with me when I cried off with Harley. He wasn't much of a catch, but he'd have taken over the keeping of me, you see."

A spark glowed deep in his dark eyes. "And they let you run off alone with only your idiot stepbrother for protection?"

"Yes."

He put his fist under her chin and tilted her face upward. "You expect me to believe you? English families guard their daughters more closely than gold. And yours simply let you walk away?"

Tears welled in her eyes. She tried to blink them back. "They were glad to be rid of me."

He gazed at her for a long moment, then said softly, "You are very good."

"I—beg your pardon?"

He grasped the line above her, closing the gap between them. His warmth and the smell of him covered her body.

"You are so innocent and charming. Those spectacles and your unworldly air make a man want to leap to your aid. How many others have you snared?"

The rail dug into her back. "I don't know what you mean."

His pulse beat in his throat, and his eyes held black heat. "Do you know why I confined you to your cabin? So you will not turn those soft eyes and that sweet voice on another of my men, and have him eating out of your hand. You are on my ship, and will obey me, and me alone. Am I clear?"

"Perfectly." Her heart beat swiftly. His nearness sent a wash of confusion over her. His touch burned her blood, making it race hotter than ever. But she could not let him see that he affected her so. She must remain on guard against him. He had the power of life and death over her, and she'd seen he was not afraid to use that power.

She firmed her mouth. "Perhaps *I* should be clear,

captain. It is true I must do as you say—you are the captain, after all. But I will not like it."

"I don't give a damn if you like it. So long as you do it."

She gave an awkward salute. "Aye-aye, sir."

He gazed at her for a long time. Moonlight danced on his dark eyes; a smoldering fire within them answered it.

"Damn you."

His arm snaked around her back, and he leaned down and covered her lips with his own.

Chapter Five

His kiss was hard and warm and *hungry*. Evangeline clutched the rail behind her, its rough wood splintering her palm. He bent her back, the iron band of his arm pulling her against his hard chest. The molded muscles of his thighs crushed her hips into the rail. The sea wind blew against her back, chilling her, but his warmth engulfed her. Hot promise sent her blood searing through her veins and pounding heart.

He smelled of the wind and the sea and maleness. His tongue dove into her mouth, strong velvet and heat. His lips bruised and crushed. She was drowning in him; he dissolved her like a warm spring rain washes away melting snow.

Her hand ached, his arm cut off her breath, but his lips slid, hot, across hers, exciting her. She moved in response, timidly tasting his mouth.

43

He groaned deep in his throat. Then slowly, very slowly, he eased his mouth from hers.

"Siren, you hurt me."

His hand splayed on her back, his fingers digging into her ribs. Her hard stays kept him out, but the pressure of his touch burned her through the layers of fabric and bone.

"I don't want to hurt you," she whispered.

"I want . . ." His voice broke. He pried her hand from the rail and placed it on his shoulder. "I want you to hold me while I kiss you."

She nodded.

He bent to her again. His devouring mouth slid over hers once more, his kiss consuming. Shyly, she slid her hand to his back, and rested her other hand on his waist. His muscles, hard and supple, moved beneath her palms.

"Yes," he whispered against her lips. "That is what I want."

His body was warm through his coat, the wool rough against her skin. She had never touched a man before. He was so large, and so strong. He kissed her hard, holding her tight against him, but she felt, under her hands, that his strength was leashed for her, that he had not released his full power.

Her heart beat faster as she imagined what he would be like if he undammed his strength and let it flow.

A shrill cry sounded from high above. Evangeline gasped and jerked her hands from his body.

He stilled. The flame in his eyes dampened swiftly, and he shoved her away from him, the cold captain returning.

44

The watchman on his platform high above the main-mast shouted again. "Sails astern!"

Lieutenant Osborn materialized from the shadows. Lantern light glinted from the spyglass in his hand. "We've spotted a ship behind us, sir. A frigate. English, with all guns showing."

"How far away?"

"On the horizon, sir. We'd not have seen her if the moon weren't so bright."

Austin snatched up the spyglass and strode toward the center of the ship, Osborn in his wake.

"Seward," he bellowed as the lieutenant emerged from the forecastle. "Take her below."

Seward looked from Evangeline to the captain, his boyish face troubled. He jogged to her. "Sorry, miss. You have to come with me, now."

Evangeline shivered, suddenly cold, as she watched Captain Blackwell climb the ladder to the command deck. The heat of his mouth still seared her, and she felt something change within her.

Seward waited. She forced herself to turn away and go with him around the lines and windlasses and hurrying sailors.

As they descended the stairs, he said, "I tried to convince him to let you on deck, but he would not agree. I'll leave the latch loose again, if you like, but I don't dare do it too often."

"English," Austin confirmed.

Through the spyglass, he saw it clearly. The moonlight glowed off the frigate's sails and glittered on her guns, two decks of them. A chill touched him. A frigate

45

had no reason to travel with gun decks open unless its commander anticipated a fight. But no other boat marked the horizon. The frigate sailed toward the *Aurora*, malice in every cannon.

"What orders, sir?" Osborn asked.

Austin lowered the spyglass. "We keep sailing, and we watch. We're too fully loaded to outrun them, and she outguns us."

"Will they try to board us, do you think?"

"They have no reason to. We are a merchantman keeping to agreed sea lanes. The war is over."

"Not for everyone," Osborn said grimly.

Austin silently concurred. English frigates had the habit of regarding American ships as so much booty. American merchantmen had been boarded, the crew press-ganged, the cargo stolen. Illegal, yes, and the British crown promised reparations, but little happened.

He thought of the papers locked away in his cabin, the letters that haunted him like a perpetual itch between his shoulder blades. Here he sat in the open water with a quarter of his crew locked in the brig. Once again he wondered if the mutiny had been part of a larger plot to steal the papers. Miss Adams might have been an unwilling dupe in a plan led by—whom? Foster? Or some other player who hadn't yet made himself known?

In any case, an English captain would be overjoyed to find the papers in his hands. He'd be given an admiralty on the spot. And Austin, who knew too much, would most likely be shot or hanged.

"We watch," he repeated. "We're carrying half a shipload of brandy. If they give us trouble, we'll set the kegs alight and fling them at them."

Osborn gave a short laugh, then he turned away and shouted orders to the waiting sailors.

"You were on the deck, tonight."

Miss Adams's voice floated through the wall between her cabin and Evangeline's, as clear as if the boards between them didn't exist. "I heard you working the lock. How ingenious of you to escape."

Evangeline leaned her head against the rough wall. The boom of the hull hitting the water shuddered through the wood at her back. Her mouth still hurt from Captain Blackwell's brutal kiss, and she still felt the impression of his body beneath her hands.

His eyes had told her he wanted her, but she'd seen the anger and coldness in him drive away the wanting. He was a captain first. His longing would not stop him from punishing her for nearly losing him his ship. He would carry out his threat and either have her arrested or sent back to England.

"But how foolish of you to get caught," Anna went on. "Especially before you could free me."

"I was not trying to escape. I was ill, and wanted the air."

"Stupid girl. You ruined your chance."

Evangeline glared at the wall. "Where am I to escape to? We are in the middle of the ocean."

"You leave that to me. I have many, many friends."

"Captain Blackwell isn't likely to let a *second* mutiny occur."

Anna's voice went cold. "You pried your way out

47

once. You do it again, and open my door, too. If you don't, and I find my way out first, heaven help you."

"But if you remain locked in your cabin, you can hardly be a threat to me."

The voice on the other side of the wall lowered to an evil hiss. "Do not be too certain that I am confined forever. I have escaped from sturdier prisons than this."

"More's the pity," Evangeline said, and put her pillow over her head.

Austin descended the stairs to his cabin, his thoughts troubled. He'd told Osborn he would rest so he'd be refreshed by the time the frigate drew near enough to be a threat. In truth he wanted to move the documents to a safer hiding place, in case they were boarded. If the worst happened, he'd simply put the documents in his pocket and jump into the sea with them.

The day after they'd sailed from Liverpool, Austin had, in the privacy of his cabin, broken the seals and read the papers within. The documents consisted of an unfortunate letter, written by a high member of the English admiralty, to an English loyalist, the cousin of a lord, in America. The letter suggested establishing a popular uprising in the new nation, to bring down the weak government and restore British rule. Folded within the letter was a list containing the names of prominent people in Boston, New Haven, and Philadelphia, whose wealth and influence could make the plot reality.

The letter had been stolen by a gentleman who monitored such things for America. Austin had been ordered to meet the gentleman in Liverpool and to carry the documents back to Boston.

Austin opened his cabin door. He halted in the doorway, his gaze taking in the neat cabin, the charts spread across his desk, the unmade bunk. Nothing looked amiss.

But he knew, as instinctively as he knew the set of every sail above them, that someone had searched his cabin. Things had been moved and replaced, not in quite the right order each time. Someone had been looking for the documents. The searcher hadn't found them, because Austin knew their hiding place and needed only one glance to see they hadn't been disturbed.

He'd foiled the intruder. But he leaned against the doorframe in disquiet. Someone knew the existence of the documents, and someone had looked for them— coinciding neatly with the appearance of the English frigate.

Evangeline heard the lock of her cabin slide back, and the door creak open into darkness. She sat upright in bed, groping for her spectacles and shoving them onto her nose.

Lieutenant Jameson, carrying a barely lit lantern, stood on the threshold. Behind him shone the cold eyes of Miss Anna Adams, and the single candle gleamed on the length of the pistol in her hand.

Chapter Six

Anna stepped into the cabin. "We are leaving, Miss Clemens. The lieutenant has kindly offered to assist. He believes it wrong for women to hang, you see."

Jameson's whisper was hoarse in the darkness. "And he will hang you, miss. He's a hard man to cross."

Evangeline stared from one to the other. "That is ridiculous. If we attempt to escape, he'll certainly hand us to the magistrates."

"You are a fool if you believe he has any leniency in him. He forced his attentions on you and clouded your brain."

Jameson's eyes blazed anger. "And I will make him pay for that, miss. For every way he's hurt you."

Behind him, Anna flashed her a wicked smile, and Evangeline realized Anna must have spun him a pretty yarn. Probably punctuated with sobs and sighs and the heaving of her large bosom.

"Come along, Miss Clemens. Our salvation in the form of a British vessel has come calling, and we are going to make for it."

"How? And why should I go with you?"

"As for how—the lieutenant will row us over. As for why—well, you don't want to be hanged, do you?"

"Leave me here. I'll take my chances."

"Nonsense, my dear friend. I need you."

For some other plot, or perhaps as a convenient hostage. She remembered the chill in the woman's voice when she promised untold horrors if she got free before Evangeline did.

Anna moved the pistol. She pointed it, not at Evangeline, but at Jameson. Evangeline understood. If she did not do as Anna commanded, she would kill the lieutenant, a poor idiot whose only fault was to believe in Anna.

"Oh, very well. Step outside and let me dress."

"No time. We must go now."

"I cannot possibly run about the sea in my chemise."

"You will have to. Lieutenant, fetch her."

Jameson started for her. Evangeline threw back the covers. "No need. I will come."

Jameson quickly averted his eyes. Evangeline scrambled out of bed, trying to think. She must get the captain's attention, or at least make Jameson change his mind. "Let me cover my feet at least." As she spoke, she drew her small boots from under the bunk and pulled them on.

Jennifer Ashley

"Hurry," Anna hissed.

Evangeline made for the door, her flimsy chemise floating around her. She tied the ribbons tightly closed as they moved into the cold passage.

"If I go with you," she said severely to Anna's back, "do you promise to leave Captain Blackwell, and his ship, and Mr. Jameson alone?"

"My, you are demanding. I want nothing more to do with this hideous vessel. And Mr. Jameson and I have made an agreement. He will not come out of this the loser." She shot Jameson a promising look, and Jameson cleared his throat.

"Quiet now," he said, and they emerged from the passage and slipped into the shadows of the deck.

Austin tucked the packet into its new hiding place, and arranged things so the casual observer would notice nothing.

He went to the windows that lined the stern and looked out at the lightening sky. A few hours would tell him if the English frigate would threaten them or simply pass by.

But thank God the frigate had come along when it did. His body tightened as it remembered the feel of Evangeline in his arms, her satin lips beneath his.

Seward must have seen him kiss her, and Osborn. Never in his life had Austin lost control with a woman. He'd always firmly reined in passions and emotions, never allowing desire to interfere with the business of command. Now red-hot heat seared through his veins, like the lava flows on volcanos he'd seen in the Pacific. He'd voluntarily stood two watches since he'd met the

52

little siren, forcing the cold wind to dampen his wayward thoughts.

If only she wouldn't go on about how much she loved the sea. He saw the joy in her face as she stood at the rail, reveling in the roll of the waves and the salty ocean breeze. Despite her seasickness, she spoke of how restful she found life aboard ship, and Austin's heart stirred in response. A joy he'd learned to suppress started to awaken, and he sought to stamp it down again.

The sea had destroyed his life. Once upon a time he'd loved sailing, the freedom and never-ceasing wonder of the world unfolding at his feet. But he'd wearied of it. The sea had ended his marriage and left him lonely and bitter. He'd tried to bring his young and beautiful wife on his voyages, but she'd hated it. She'd hated the seasickness, the endless ocean, the boredom. On her last voyage, in her loneliness, she'd developed a passion for one of his lieutenants. In fury, Austin had dragged her back home.

She'd never consummated the desire for his officer, but the incident made her decide she didn't want Austin, either. Austin had wanted to give her a child, but she refused him. Unwilling to be attached to a woman who wanted nothing to do with him, he sought a separation, and was granted it. He gave her a house and an income, and left on a voyage that would take him around the Horn and out into the Pacific, giving him time to forget the humiliation of his failed marriage.

During that long trip, his wife, alone in Boston, had taken ill, and had died before he'd reached port again.

The sea had torn them apart, but he'd taken refuge

in it, volunteering to take dangerous routes and dangerous cargo, running blockades the English tried to set up during the war, and evading press gangs and pirates. He'd gloried in his adventures, ignoring the burning pain of his destroyed life.

But he'd tired of that, as well. Going home to Boston, taking up with women here and there, brought him no relief, and he'd returned to the sea again, weary now, going through the motions.

Until the siren Evangeline Clemens stood on his deck and gazed at the crashing waves with loving eyes, her laughter delighted. She saw all the magic, the joy, the wonder that he'd lost. That joy radiated from her, bathing him in a moment of magic that he'd not felt in many a year.

He'd wanted to embrace that magic, that wonder, and he'd gathered her to him and kissed her, tasting her excitement, pulling it into himself.

Dawn broke to outline the frigate, quite close now. The rising sun sent a golden glow over the elegant ship. No denying its beauty. Austin had served aboard such a frigate during the war against his English counterparts. Frigates ran swiftly, decks broken down to render it a clean, gun-heavy fighting machine. Elegant, simple, deadly.

But he would not turn tail and run. Part of the purpose of the merchant and exploration voyages after the war was to prove that American vessels had a right to the sea lanes and free trade. A frigate had no reason to pursue a ship full of French brandy and farm equipment bound for Boston.

The sun sparkled and danced on the waves, dazzling

his eyes. Across that golden sea, a tiny, dark boat skittered toward the frigate, black in the bright morning light.

Every muscle in Austin's body tensed. He could see the silhouette of oars rising and dipping into the water as the boat grew smaller by the second.

Rage streaked through him. He wheeled around, crossed his cabin, flung open the door, and stormed up to the deck. He emerged into the dawn wind, cold and biting, then plunged down the stairs to the officers' and passengers' cabins.

Quiet reigned here in the morning, as all the officers but Jameson were on duty. But the quiet this morning had a different tenor, and he saw why immediately. The door of Miss Clemens's cabin stood open. The blankets on her bunk had been hastily thrown back, but her dull gray gown still hung neatly from a peg on the wall.

Miss Adams's cabin lay similarly empty, as was the cabin of his newly promoted first lieutenant, Jameson.

The tiny boat bumped the frigate and leapt backward with a sickening lurch. Evangeline shivered in the ice-cold wind.

Anna waved a friendly greeting to the faces that peered at them over the side, confident of her welcome. During the trip over, Evangeline had toyed with the idea of pushing her and Mr. Jameson overboard and struggling back to the *Aurora* alone. But she knew she'd never prevail against them both, and she only had the remotest idea of how to row a boat against ocean waves and make it go where she wanted it to. She supposed she could have leapt overboard herself, but the icy waters would have meant her death.

Survive first, the familiar refrain whispered. She would survive and find a way to escape Anna and journey safely to her cousin in Boston. Evangeline would make the captain of this vessel see Anna's true self, and then Evangeline would be free to follow her own course.

A net slid over the side of the frigate, and with it, several sailors, climbing like spiders toward them.

Jameson dropped the oars and seized Miss Adams's hands. "Take care, my love."

Evangeline struggled to keep her balance. "Aren't you coming with us?"

"My duty lies on the *Aurora*."

"Captain Blackwell will toss you over the side."

He acknowledged that with a nod of his head, then returned his adoring gaze to Miss Adams. "But I have gotten you away from him. That is what matters."

Miss Adams leaned forward and gave Jameson a lingering kiss on his lips. "You are a good man."

"I will see you in Paris, love."

"Likely she'll shoot you in Paris," Evangeline muttered. Anna sent her a sharp look, but Jameson, besotted, didn't notice.

The sailors reached them. The familiarity of their white and blue English uniforms startled her.

"Steady, miss." A youth grinned at her, gap-toothed, but with rough good nature. His accent put him from her own native Gloucestershire, a strange bit of home in this wilderness of sea.

He and another sailor assisted her onto the net, and

helped her to climb upward toward the decks. The rope cut her hands, the planking beneath it rubbing her fingertips raw. The wind yanked her long braid of hair, and dislodged locks of it stung her face.

The sailors guided her ascent with strong hands under her arms. She acutely sensed the *Aurora* behind them, could almost hear Captain Blackwell's bellow of rage as he watched them crawl aboard the English ship. Any moment now, he'd come about and train his guns on them—two precise shots and she and Miss Adams would be no more.

She made it to the railing without any such incident. Brawny hands reached for her, sailors lifting her up and over the rail to the sturdy deck. She collapsed to her knees, shivering, and someone draped a blanket around her shoulders.

She looked up to see the ship's captain in the circle of men. Short and heavy, his dark hair gray at the temples, he had little of the dignity and prowess that Captain Blackwell possessed.

The voluptuous torso of Anna Adams appeared at the rail, and the sailors surged forward, reaching for her far more eagerly than they had for Evangeline.

Anna arrived breathlessly on the deck, her glorious hair tumbling riotously around her face, her bodice gaping to show a promise of her lovely bosom. The captain stepped forward. He took Anna's hands and raised them to his lips.

"Well met," he said.

Anna Adams flashed him a brilliant smile. "Lovely to see you again, Mortimer."

Evangeline buried her face in her hands, and groaned.

"Hard about!" Austin bellowed as he sprinted for the upper deck. The pilot at the wheel, Lornham, stared at him, then looked down at the wheel as if checking to ensure they'd been going the right way after all.

"That's an order. *Do* it."

Startled, Lornham cranked the wheel and shouted orders. Sailors swarmed on deck, grabbing lines and whirling pulleys to realign the sails for the abrupt change of course.

Osborn peered at him, his young face puzzled. "Sir? Don't we want to avoid the frigate? Why are we going *toward* it?"

Austin clutched the rail as the ship lurched. His anger carried such force he imagined the polished wood crumbling beneath his grip. "Your fellow officer, Jameson, has absconded with the female prisoners. We are going to retrieve them."

More stares.

"But—"

"You wanted to say something, Osborn?"

Osborn flushed under his tan. "Sorry, sir, but isn't it good riddance? They were a handful of trouble. Let the English captain be burdened with them. They're English, ain't they?"

Austin's hard, hot rage had cooled into something more deadly. In the empty cabin, he'd lifted Miss Clemens's discarded glove, smoothing the soft kid with calloused fingers. He'd envisioned the slim hand that fitted inside it, the fingers that had timidly touched his side when he'd bent to kiss her.

He'd flung the glove onto the bunk and strode out of the cabin. She'd not get away from him so easily.

The other men on the command deck waited for his answer, clearly in accord with Osborn.

"They outgun us sir," Lornham, the blond, leathery-faced pilot ventured. "You said so yourself. And they are much faster. What is the point in pursuing them?"

"This is not a debate, gentleman. This is an order. To be obeyed unless you want to join your shipmates in the brig."

Osborn and Lornham shared an uneasy glance. "Yes, sir."

Seward stepped forward. "Sir?"

Austin bent his glare on him. "What is it, Mr. Seward? Do you want to voice your objection, as well?"

"No, sir. I concur with you. Miss Clemens will be in great danger. We must get her back."

Austin gazed him for a long moment. The officers turned surprised looks in the young man's direction.

"I am pleased you agree," Austin said in cold, clipped tones. "My first officer's position seems to be vacant again. Fill it, Mr. Seward."

Seward's eyes widened, astonished. "Sir?"

"Are you questioning my decision?"

"No, sir. I mean, yes, sir. I mean—" He saluted. "Thank you, sir."

Austin pivoted on his heel and strode to the port rail. The frigate now lay broadside to the *Aurora*. Its sails had shifted, and its prow pointed south, southwest. Making for Havana, Austin had no doubt.

He smiled grimly. He knew the western Atlantic better than any man. He did not have to chase the frigate. Despite his ship's heavy cargo, he knew enough tricks to put the *Aurora* in Havana well before the English frigate, ensuring he could plan an interesting surprise for the other crew. As for the papers hidden in his cabin, they'd be even safer with what he had in mind than they were now.

Chapter Seven

"He's cut west again, sir," the lieutenant reported, standing stiffly in the entrance to the ward room. Captain Mortimer Bainbridge of the English frigate looked up from the head of the table.

"Then he's broken off his pursuit. Good. Though how he thought he'd catch us, I do not know. Poor bastard must be touched."

Evangeline idly drew her spoon through the bowl of warm stew. She'd eaten hungrily at first, cold and weary, but now she listened intently.

The lumps of potato and carrot floating in her bowl blurred. Captain Blackwell had gone. The dark-eyed, handsome, hard-faced captain had vanished from her life.

Anna sat to Bainbridge's right. Even her gown had managed to tear becomingly. The bodice drooped down one shoulder, exposing a small bit of her white breast.

The captain's men had found Evangeline a coat to wear over her flimsy chemise. She'd had to fold the overly large sleeves back to keep them from dragging in the stew. She imagined that the shapeless coat, her bent spectacles, and her snarled hair only made her look like a half-drowned rat, not a spectacular heroine like Anna Adams.

She'd learned as she ate that the bizarre coincidence that had brought Anna's lover, Captain Bainbridge, to their aid had not been coincidence at all.

"I followed your instructions to the letter," Captain Bainbridge said as the lieutenant who'd brought the news saluted and departed. "The *Aurora* wouldn't give herself up to you?"

"The captain proved—difficult." Anna's eyes narrowed as if Captain Blackwell had personally displeased her.

"Any man who wouldn't fall to you must be a fool. But there's no accounting for these Yanks."

Anna pressed the captain's hand. "I am pleased you were on hand to take care of me, Mortimer."

"I would not leave you out here alone. We will rescue Sebastian. Have no fear."

Evangeline blinked. "You know about Sebastian? And you are helping her?"

Captain Bainbridge looked up in surprise. "I was the one who discovered where he lay imprisoned. I agreed to help Anna find him months ago. Why shouldn't I?"

"Indeed. Mortimer has lent me great assistance in the search for my dear *brother*."

Brother? Oh, good heavens. "You are a fool, Captain. This woman plays you like a marionette on strings. Sebastian is her lover, not her brother, and a pirate to boot. I cannot think what she intends for you after you find him, but were I you, I would fear for my life and my ship."

The room went silent, save for the creak of the hull and the sputter of the lanterns. Evangeline waited for Captain Bainbridge to express dismay and outrage and to call for his men to throw Anna into the brig.

Anna smiled coldly. "My poor, dear friend. She is quite out of her mind."

The captain stared at Evangeline in fascination. "Is she? Good lord, what happened to her?"

"The captain of the merchantman used her most cruelly. She broke under his forced attentions and went raving mad."

Bainbridge's face whitened. "The monster. Thank God you got away from him. He didn't touch *you*, did he?"

"I managed to evade him, my darling. But he took out his frustration on my friend. Poor child. You simply cannot heed a word she says."

Evangeline looked back and forth between them, her mouth open. Then she put her elbows on the table and glared at her stew. "Oh, for heaven's *sake*."

They pulled Jameson aboard before the *Aurora* turned and streaked for the west. As Jameson gained the deck, Austin grabbed him by his sodden shirt and threw him against the mainmast.

Jameson righted himself, his eyes defiant. "I surrender, sir."

"You'll do a damn sight more than that. You'll do slave labor for me for years before you make up for what you've done. What in the name of seven hells were you thinking?"

The wind jerked a hank of Jameson's dark hair free of its queue to snag on his cheekbone. "I could not let you go on hurting them, sir."

"What are you talking about? Who was I hurting?"

"The ladies, sir. I understand you confining them, but not brutalizing them. Sir."

Austin stared. "Brutalizing? What the devil are you yammering about?"

Tears sprang to Jameson's eyes. "Why do you make me say the words, sir? You—you raped Miss Clemens. And beat Miss Adams. I cannot—" He blinked, the tears glittering on his lashes. "I could not stand idly by."

Austin cursed freely. "And what idiot told you this rigmarole?"

He knew the answer before Jameson even opened his mouth. "Miss Adams told me. Sir."

Austin looked at him for a long time. Jameson tried to meet his gaze, but dark eyes flickered and dropped. Young, gentle, naive Jameson. A damned good sailor and lieutenant, but a sight too gullible.

Austin switched his gaze to the poop deck. "Seward!"

"Sir?" His newest first officer looked down, hand on the railing.

"I told you to let no one near Miss Adams but yourself."

64

"I did not, sir. I delivered her meals alone. No else saw her."

Austin snapped his attention back to Jameson.

"My cabin is next to Miss Adams's. We—we spoke through the wall."

Damn it all. "I should have gagged her, too. She worked you for a fool, Jameson. I never touched either of them."

Austin's face heated as he heard himself voice the lie. He'd kissed Evangeline, kissed her like a lover would kiss his woman. He'd begged her to touch him, had crushed her to him and taken her mouth and tasted her sweetness.

Jameson drew himself up. "I *saw* you, sir."

Rage flared through him like a torch through kindling. "What you saw—" His voice caught. "No, you are an idiot, Jameson. You have delivered a dove into the nest of a viper, and I will fight the entire British navy to get her back. Do you understand me?"

His lips white, Jameson nodded. "Yes, sir."

"You're stripped of your duties and confined to quarters. And if anything happens to Miss Clemens, if so much as a hair on her head is harmed, you will pay for it for the rest of your life."

Jameson looked into his face and recognized truth. He swallowed. "Yes, sir."

"I know you are a reasonable man, Captain Bainbridge." Evangeline clutched the railing as the frigate heaved. Warm wind whipped her hair from its braid, and the sun prickled hot on her skin.

The English captain allowed her more freedom than

had Captain Blackwell, letting her up on deck to take the air whenever she liked. She was instructed to stand in a corner near the poop deck, out of the way of the sailors, but at least she could emerge from below when she wished. The refreshing warm wind, the nourishing stews, and the relatively large first lieutenant's cabin afforded her, had driven away her seasickness. But it had not eased her fears.

Anna had well and truly snared Captain Bainbridge, and he fell all over himself to do her slightest bidding. For the last seven days, they'd rushed southward, the rising heat proclaiming their latitude. The sailors seemed to obey the captain's orders readily enough, though Evangeline wondered what on earth they thought of their commander relinquishing his ship to the woman who held him captive.

"What you say cannot be true, Miss Clemens. I have known Anna—Miss Adams—for a long time."

"You have been her lover. You know she is not virtuous."

The captain turned faintly pink. "Miss Adams has had an unfortunate past. She has told me all about it. But I intend to marry her when we return to England."

"After we rescue Sebastian."

"After we rescue *her brother,* yes."

Evangeline gathered her patience. He absolutely refused to believe Sebastian was anything but Anna's darling younger brother. "And what of me?"

"Eh? What of you?"

"Did you plan to let me off at port in England with good wishes for my health? I who have run mad from torture?"

66

He looked at her uncomfortably. "You will be escorted somewhere safe, have no fear. Er, returned home."

Evangeline stared out to sea, watching the green depths under the warm clouds. "No, Captain, what will happen is this. Anna will rescue her lover, Sebastian, a notorious pirate. She will murder you, or have you murdered. Then she'll take your lovely frigate, filled with guns, promising your sailors untold riches if they follow her. She will probably shoot the ones who won't. She will run about terrorizing the seas, stealing ships and cargo right and left. *That* is what will happen if you do not lock her in your brig and turn this ship around." She sighed. "Captain Blackwell had the right of it. But he should have locked her in a cage—even with the rats."

Captain Bainbridge was silent a moment, then he spoke gently. "I do not wish to upset you, Miss Clemens. But I have seen unfortunates held captive by men such as Blackwell, men who performed unspeakable acts on them, as he did to you. Often these poor prisoners develop a strange and terrible bond to their captors, and they wish to remain with them, no matter how horribly they are treated. I can see that such a thing has happened to you, and I am pleased I have gotten you away from him. You will be returned home, Miss Clemens."

Evangeline let her breath. Anna had imprisoned *him*, and he was too blind to know it.

"Well," she sighed. "I hope Sebastian decides he wants to stay with *his* captors. It would save us all much trouble."

*   *   *

67

Austin Blackwell lowered his spyglass and frowned at the blank horizon. Wind warmed by the tropics whipped his long hair and scoured his skin. He could have been no more than a day ahead of the frigate. Where was she?

Perhaps Anna Adams had changed her mind and decided to leave Sebastian behind and roam the seas— with Evangeline. He gritted his teeth.

No, the prison that lay near the harbor in Havana, cut off from the rest of the settlement by one long arm of inlet, contained Miss Adams's pirate. He'd inquired. One Sebastian Longe, an innocuous name, but one with many grievances against it, was confined here.

At age fifteen, Sebastian had murdered a dock worker in London then taken a job aboard a ship to escape the law. In Lisbon, he'd gone ashore with the cook to purchase supplies. He'd killed the cook, stolen the money, and gotten away. Since then, he'd gone from one crime to the next, finally turning to out-and-out piracy. He'd stolen a ship, murdered half the crew by gleefully marching them overboard, and sailed away. The Spanish navy had caught up to him six months ago, salting him away in the prison in Havana, planning ultimately to hang him.

He was there, and his lover Anna would come to claim him.

With Austin waiting at the doorstep.

He raised his spyglass again. Evangeline floated out there, somewhere. He wondered if she'd been sent to "distract" the English captain while Anna plotted to break into the prison. The thought of Evangeline smiling her crooked smile at the English captain and fumbling at the hooks of her bodice streaked rage through his body.

He lowered the spyglass. God help the English captain when Austin found him.

On the twelfth day at sea, a finger of land appeared to the west. All day the low-lying green sliver grew larger off the bow and to starboard. Evangeline emerged late in the afternoon and watched it with dwindling hope. She'd failed to convince Captain Bainbridge of the folly of his actions. She'd argued that he would be relieved of command, and possibly hanged, for breaking course to free a criminal from prison. The captain seemed not to care. He'd replied that rescuing an Englishman from the hands of the Spanish was a good day's work.

Anna emerged from below, the lowering sun gleaming on her fiery hair. She sauntered down the deck to observe two sailors loading one of the rowboats with provisions for storming the prison.

Evangeline tried to cheer herself. Perhaps the prison guards would object to Anna trying to free a notorious pirate. Perhaps they'd capture her and lock her up, as well.

Unless the master of the prison guard was yet another of Anna's lovers. Evangeline clenched the rail and tried not to think of such things.

The sun dipped to the horizon. The headland grew larger, green and damp and misty. They slid close enough along it to make out sandy beaches lying white against the green. A beautiful place, Evangeline thought wistfully. The kind of place Captain Blackwell would explore. She imagined him striding up and down the beach, barking orders to his men, or standing, straight and quiet, to drink in the beauty of it.

The sun slipped farther down in the sky, which flushed a brilliant red, dotted by low clouds that caught the light and turned lemon yellow. The headland curved away. A long stretch of land appeared beyond it. She concluded from the sailors' shouts that they had reached their destination. Havana. Lights played up and down the coastline—outlining the prison, the town, marketplaces, the homes of ordinary people.

She'd been an ordinary person once, Evangeline thought, a young lady trained at Miss Pyne's academy, ready to marry and settle down to begin her nursery. Her entire life had cascaded out of control the bright afternoon she'd returned to her chamber and found Harley rolling on the bed with her maid, his face buried firmly in her large breasts. Evangeline had thought it strange that jealousy had not flooded her, nor rage. Her only emotion had been fear. One sinking thought had filled her mind—*What am I to do now?*

That moment had led to this one. Now she stood on board an English frigate in her underskirt and chemise, covered only by a man's coat that did not fit her, preparing for an expedition to storm a prison in Havana.

Perhaps to die there. Evangeline knew that when Anna Adams had no more use for her, she would kill her. She would die, alone and friendless on the wide seas, with few to mourn her passing.

She wondered if Captain Blackwell would know, and if he would care. For twelve days and nights, she'd thought of the rough passion of his kiss, and ached for his embrace. She remembered the raw urgency in his

70

whisper, the feeling of his heart beating hard under his ribs. He'd awakened something in her that was new, questing, needing, and it would not go tamely back to sleep.

The wind pulled strands from her carefully wound hair and brought to her the smell of brine and the odor of civilization—fires, food, refuse. She lifted her chin. She would not slip into self-pity. She would *survive*. Anna Adams would not win. Evangeline would see to it, somehow.

Anna saw her and beckoned to her. Evangeline had not obeyed Anna's commands since boarding the ship, but curiosity stirred. She left her corner by the poop deck and stepped around lines and windlasses to the small boat.

A rowboat, like the one that had brought them to the frigate, had been raised to hang alongside the deck. Two sailors, one middle-aged with shiny skin stretched over hard bones, and one younger, with a quick eye and gap-toothed grin, carefully laid small, round black spheres into the boat. Small barrels of gunpowder followed.

Anna smiled. "Do not worry. There will be enough room for you."

Evangeline pulled the rough wool coat closer. "There is no need for me to go ashore."

"But you will be so useful, my dear. You are small and quick, and can lay charges on the walls."

"Lay charges—"

"A simple exercise. The lads here will show you how."

Evangeline imagined herself in a muddy, dug-out tunnel, trying to carry a squat keg of gunpowder that might explode at any moment.

"And if I refuse, you will shoot me? Why not simply shoot me outright, because I will certainly not help you."

Anna's eyes glinted. "The poor girl. Always imagining I will harm her."

"Are you going to shoot these two gentlemen, as well? Or will you at least allow them to row you back to the ship?"

"My dear, you are having one of your raving fits again. You must have a lie-down, until we—"

A shout from the poop deck cut her off. Captain Bainbridge sprinted from his cabin, swarmed above, and snatched a spyglass from an officer. The older sailor loading the gunpowder squinted into the dying light and spat a filthy epithet.

Anna followed his gaze. The color drained from her face.

Evangeline turned. She gasped.

In silhouette against the crimson and indigo sky at the entrance to the harbor rocked the stocky shape of the American merchantman, *Aurora*. Two sleek, lean American privateers floated behind it, twin decks of guns gleaming in the sun's last rays.

Chapter Eight

The English frigate erupted in noise. Captain Bainbridge bellowed orders for his pilot to come about. Sailors swarmed up the rigging, moving sails, winding ropes. Slowly, the ship backed away from the rows of deadly guns.

Evangeline clutched the rail, her heart beating wildly. *He'd come back.*

The older sailor laid down his keg of gunpowder and turned to join his fellow sailors. Anna stepped in front of him. "Go on loading the boat. We'll need it."

"That's two armed ships, ma'am," he said. "Primed and ready. We'll go down in one blow."

"Do you think I care about what happens to this ship? Load it. Sebastian will deliver you far more wealth than you'll ever see in the king's navy."

The sailor stared at her, his light eyes blank. Then he

gave a shrug and retrieved the cask of gunpowder. The younger sailor wavered a moment, then followed the older man's lead.

"Hurry," Anna told them. "Bainbridge has moved the ship out of range."

"*We'll* be in range if we row to shore, ma'am. They'll shoot us right out of the water."

"Don't be ridiculous. It will be pitch dark in a moment, and no one will see us. They'll be aiming at the lights of this ship."

On the poop deck, Captain Bainbridge trained his spyglass on the three prowling ships. The lieutenant shouted more orders. The sailors winched ropes and hauled lines, muscles standing out on their bare arms.

Light flared from the American ship, a blinding spot of brilliance. Moments later, the muffled *boom* of the cannon floated across the water. The flare died as the last of the twilight faded from the sky.

Anna grabbed Evangeline and threw her toward the rowboat. "We go now."

Evangeline did not resist. She climbed quickly into the little boat, finding a place to squeeze herself between the gunpowder casks. Her heart thumped. It was a mad way to escape. If one small spark, one stray flame touched them, this little boat would light the sky for miles.

But if she could get off this frigate and somehow get herself to the *Aurora* or to the American ships, she might have a chance. Captain Bainbridge thought her mad. Captain Blackwell thought her a mutineer. Neither wanted her. But she would feel a sight safer locked in Captain Blackwell's brig than resting in Captain Bainbridge's cabin. No telling what Anna would do when she returned with Sebastian in tow.

The older sailor helped Anna aboard and the younger began working the pulley to lower them all over the side. In the chaos of the deck, no one heeded them.

The rail slipped from view as the boat creaked and jerked downward, foot by foot. The frigate's side heaved next to them, wood stained and smelling of water and salt. The young sailor grunted as he worked the rope, the overweighted boat straining the pulleys above.

Water ran under them, lifting the little boat high. The sailor cut the rope, and they slapped into the trough of a wave.

"Hurry," Anna snapped.

Both sailors took up the oars and bent their backs. Anna scrambled into the stern to navigate. They crept from the great shadow of the frigate out into the black water, not a lantern to light their way. The wind, cooled by the ocean and the night, swamped them; the smell of brine and the tarry stink of the frigate was engulfing.

No one pursued them. Evangeline clutched the side of the boat and sent a few prayers heavenward. The lights of Havana hovered to the left and south; the American ships and the *Aurora* hung to the north. They'd have to slip between the English frigate and the Americans to gain shore.

Spray stung her face, raw on her wind- and sun-burned skin. She, who'd prided herself on neatness, now traveled the open sea in a chemise and man's coat, her hair in tangles, her hands and face chapped.

She curled her toes in her sensible boots. If Miss Pyne could see her now—

But no. Miss Pyne would have swooned outright long ago, when Anna had proposed the mutiny on the *Aurora*, and probably would still be sunk in that swoon. Miss Pyne had trained her young ladies only to expect the conventional from life, and to be indignant when the extraordinary thrust itself upon them. In Evangeline's opinion, Miss Pyne needed to adjust her curriculum. Perhaps she'd write a letter suggesting such a thing upon her arrival in America. If she ever arrived in America.

The small boat floated undetected between the American and English ships. The ships' lights shone bright, but the little boat went unnoticed under the cover of darkness. Of course, the darkness also could hide things like rocks and other lightless craft, Evangeline thought nervously. She expected at any moment the row boat would blunder onto something, and break apart with a squeal and a groan.

They probably wouldn't simply sink. The impact would produce a spark, and they'd all go up in a spectacular firework.

If she were brave enough, she could light the gunpowder now. She, the two sailors, and Anna Adams would be no more. Or she could rush past the straining, rowing sailors, and topple Anna into the sea. Of course, the sailors might then simply topple *her* into the sea and row back to the frigate. She held onto the gunwale and gritted her teeth.

A burst of fire flared into the night. Evangeline squealed. The younger sailor cursed. The cannon ball sailed from the English frigate and struck the water many yards short of the *Aurora*.

One of the American ships turned ponderously. Flickering sparks of red marched in a line down her gun decks. Evangeline imagined the sailors waiting behind those torches to light the deadly cannon.

"Keep going," Anna ordered. "That shot came nowhere near us."

"Beg to differ, ma'am," the older sailor grunted, but he kept rowing.

Slowly, slowly the American ships turned. The boat slipped behind them. The Americans blocked their view of the English ship, cutting off the light and the frightening glitter of waiting guns. The *Aurora*, on the other hand, began to move toward shore.

Anna's voice grated. "He'll have to row ashore just like us, and he can't possibly get there before us. Row, damn you!"

The boat skipped and slid across the water. The air warmed. The smells of the city she'd detected earlier, the comingling scents of fire, mud, and humans, floated stronger now on the damp wind. The *Aurora* silently moved toward the harbor.

The shore grew larger. The beach spread itself before them, the white of the waves glistening under the darkened sky. The sailors rowed them toward a small inlet that the younger one pointed out. The little boat bounced on the waves, heaving and falling, until Evangeline had no doubt they'd capsize.

The rowboat at last reached shallow water, and the two sailors leapt out to drag it onto the sand. Anna stood up, studying the land. Evangeline looked at her set face, sharp and cold, and wondered how anyone could think her beautiful.

"The English captain's putting to shore," Lornham announced. "Trying to slip by. I saw one boat go over a while ago. He's putting over a couple more now."

"Shall I tell the gunmen to fire, sir?" Obsorn asked eagerly.

Austin turned back from the rail, his blood pounding. "Miss Clemens is on that ship. I want warning shots only. Signal the English captain I want to talk to him."

"Hang on, sir. He's signalling us."

They turned back to the rail. A series of light flashes blinked from the English frigate. A simple code. "Stand down."

"He has balls doing that, sir," Seward said behind him. "One up against three."

"Two. This isn't a warship."

Lornham gave a sudden yelp. "Sir. You'd better look at this."

Austin strode to him. Lornham held out the spyglass, and pointed. "There. I saw it when the Englishman signalled at us. On the water just beyond our frigates."

Austin raised the spyglass and trained it on the black waters. He saw nothing but darkness. Impatiently, he moved the glass, searching for what had Lornham so concerned.

One of the American ships fired another warning shot. In its glare, Austin found what he was looking for. A tiny boat was being pulled onto the beach. The brief light flared on the red hair of the woman in the stern and shone on the spectacles of Evangeline Clemens.

"Turn this ship, Lornham," he said quietly. "Get behind the privateers. If the English captain wants me I'll be on shore."

Lornham looked startled, but nodded. "Yes, sir."

"Seward. You're with me."

Seward snapped to attention, his eyes glowing. "Yes, sir! We'll rout those English dogs, sir."

"Just get Miss Clemens back safe, Seward."

"Right, sir." He grinned.

The pink stucco on the prison's walls peeled here and there to reveal rough, muddy brick beneath. The arched gates at the front of the prison were lit with torches, but the walls behind them lay bathed in darkness.

Evangeline tramped behind the lead sailor and ahead of Anna, her back aching from the load she carried. The prison seemed deserted. Evangeline had pictured it swarming with guards, grim men waiting to shoot down any who even thought to escape. She also expected prisoners, perhaps chained together and shuffling through a paved yard, shame in their eyes from their past misdeeds. But darkness and silence prevailed.

Anna stopped against the back wall. The smells of damp, mud, and brine assailed them, and Evangeline's boots sunk into the muck.

Anna pointed. "Here. Pile up half the charges and fuse them."

Evangeline carefully set the tiny bombs that Anna had made her carry against the peeling wall. Her hands shook. Anna hoped to cause chaos, she'd said, to draw attention to this part of the prison while the four of them slipped in the front. Evangeline feared they'd bring the whole prison tumbling down into rubble. Sebastian would be buried, as would all the other poor unfortunates inside.

The older sailor began to coat the little hollow with gunpowder. He unwound a fuse and laid it in the nest of bombs. The deadly heap was stark black against the pink of the wall.

The young sailor trotted back from his lookout point. "That merchantman's putting boats to shore. He'll rouse the place, even if he don't find us."

"Then we will have to hurry. Come on." Anna seized Evangeline's wrist and pulled her along the weed-choked wall and around the corner. The sailors came behind. "Light the fuse."

The older sailor shook his head. "We ain't far enough away."

"Light it!"

He glared at her. She pulled a pistol from her pocket and shoved it in his face.

He looked at her for a long time, then, with a resigned shrug, knelt, struck a spark with stone and steel, and lit the fuse.

Anna darted away. Evangeline stumbled behind her. The two sailors passed them at a dead run, their faces white. They had all nearly reached the front of the prison when a huge *boom* nearly knocked Evangeline flat. Her ears rang, and a shower of pebbles, stucco, and mud rained down on them.

Anna laughed, an evil sound. "Let your captain lover chase us through that."

"He isn't my—"

Anna dragged Evangeline into the shadows. The two sailors ran on, disappearing into the darkness.

Shouting rose from the prison and suddenly, the place did swarm with guards. They poured out from the front of the prison, dashing toward the rear wall where the charge had exploded.

Anna jerked Evangeline to face her. "You're going inside."

"Me? Why?"

"You will lay more charges in the guard's quarters. That should clear them out, and I'll retrieve Sebastian."

Evangeline set her mouth. "I will not be party to killing innocent guards."

"They are not innocent, my girl. They've got Sebastian, and they'll not hesitate to kill us." She draped the chain of small grenades around Evangeline's neck like a diabolical necklace. "Lay the charges in the hall and run away."

"How do you know you won't blow up Sebastian?"

"Because I know exactly where they're keeping him. I've planned this for months. You needn't worry about that."

"And if I refuse to help?"

Anna knotted a line of fuse onto the smallest bomb. "Then I will kill you, you stupid girl. Now, inside with you."

"You are going to kill me anyway."

"Nonsense. You help me get Sebastian out and I'll reward you. Promise."

"Your word is worth nothing."

"That's where you're wrong, my little friend. Some promises I *do* keep. Remember that."

She shoved Evangeline toward the archways and disappeared back into the shadows.

The mud-colored pavement echoed Evangeline's footsteps back to her as she scuttled through the open wrought-iron gate. Across a small courtyard, a narrow doorway led into a cool, tunnel-like passage. She peered into it fearfully, but it was deserted.

She lifted the chain of bombs from around her neck, and laid them on the bricks in the courtyard. Sweat slicked her palms as she tugged at the fuse on the lead one, but it was fastened too tightly for her to unravel or break.

She left them. If Anna blew the bombs here, they might hurt fewer people. The vile woman would no doubt murder everyone inside just to free one man. She groped for the cool reason of her survival chant, but her thoughts flitted and danced and her legs shook.

She scurried into the passage. At the end of the cool hall stood another door, this one thick and heavy and pinned with large wooden bars fit into slots in the walls. To the right, a narrow corridor ran into darkness. At the head of it, a smaller, ordinary door stood ajar, light slanting from it.

She pushed this door open to reveal a small, windowless room. Three men sat around a wooden table onto which cards and counters had been tossed, as if the explosion, and then her entrance, had interrupted their game. Two of the men, black-haired and in rumpled white tunics and black trousers, started up, hands on holstered pistols.

The third man, blond and sporting a black eyepatch, remained seated. His mane of dirty yellow hair straggled to his shoulders, and his face was lined with stubble. His shirt of threadbare linen gaped open to his waist, revealing a rather hairy chest. He stared at her with his one eye.

"Good lord," he said in perfect English.

The guard's face relaxed, and he took his hand from his pistol. "Señorita?"

"Please, you must get out. I have put bombs in the courtyard. She's going to set them off!"

They stared back. Oh, dear. Miss Pyne's academy had given her an excellent training in French, but Spanish had not been looked upon as a language a young lady needed to know.

"You must run. Run! Boom! Boom!"

One guard chuckled. The blond man, not laughing, spoke a string of words at them, quickly, fluidly.

Their smiles faded. They looked hesitantly at the third man, exchanged a glance, then pushed past Evangeline and ran out of the room.

Evangeline turned to the third man. "You must go, too. Run!"

His brows rose nonchalantly, as if she'd simply announced she'd found a cockroach outside. "Who the devil are you, girl?"

"I am Evangeline Clemens. Are you Sebastian? Anna came to rescue you. She sent me to blow up the guard's quarters. She didn't know you were here."

"I see."

"And even if she has destroyed my life because of you, it's not your fault. I can't leave you in here to die."

He cocked his head. "How kind of you."

"Please. There isn't much time."

"I understand your urgency, miss, but . . ." He raised his right hand. A manacle encircled it, and a chain led from this to a ring in the wall.

"Oh, dear."

"The keys are on that table."

He gestured with a long-fingered hand. A ring of iron keys, left in the guards' haste, lay haphazardly on a table near the door. Evangeline snatched them up.

"Which key is it?"

"They are hardly likely to label them. Bring them here."

Holding the clanking ring high, Evangeline trotted to him. He took the ring from her and fitted one key into the manacle. It did not work. Patiently, he tried the next one. "Who are you, my brave rescuer?"

"I told you. I am Evangeline Clemens. From Little Marching. In Gloucestershire."

"I see." The third, then the fourth key did not work.

Evangeline wrung her hands. "Hurry!"

"You may run, my rescuer. You do not have to wait for me."

"That would be—" She stopped. Why should she care about a murderous pirate who was Anna's lover? But something inside her would not let her leave this chained man to his doom. She'd get him out, shove him toward Anna, and run the other way.

The fifth key did not work. Impulsively, Evangeline reached for them, but he pulled away.

"If you drop them, we must start all over again."

She gave him an anguished look. He smiled faintly

and bent over the keys again. Under the filth his blond hair looked to be thick and wavy, and his one good eye was clear blue. When he cleaned up, he might be almost handsome. For a pirate.

She thought of Captain Blackwell's dark hair, warmed red by the sun, and the smoldering fires in his black, black eyes. He was out there. She knew in her heart he'd come to stop Anna, and probably hadn't spared a thought for her. If he'd already captured Anna, out in the night, he would finish his business and sail away again, leaving Evangeline behind.

"Please hurry," she whispered.

"Ah." Key number eight worked. He broke the manacle open, let it drop to the floor, and rubbed his wrist. "Now, my rescuer. Where do we go?"

"She'll blow up the courtyard at any moment. Is there another way out?"

"Come with me."

He rose and took her hand. His fingers were steady, though Evangeline's shook uncontrollably. She expected him to stop and pocket the gold coins that lay upon the table, cackling in pirate satisfaction, but he ignored the money and made for the door.

He took her not toward the entrance or the stout door, but farther along the narrow passage. The corridor slanted downward, becoming almost a tunnel. Loose bricks loomed here and there, and she tripped and flailed, clinging to the man's hand for support. The light from behind grew too faint to be useful, and soon they moved in pitch darkness.

After a time, he stopped. "Here."

Evangeline put her hand out. Instead of rough stone, she touched the cold iron bars of a gate.

Keys clinked, and she realized he'd brought the ring with him. He began the tedious process of fitting each key, one at a time, into the lock.

A loud bang sounded behind them, and the passage filled with dust. Pebbles flew at them. She yelped and flung her arm over her face.

The pirate touched her arm. "Are you all right?"

She coughed, brushing crushed brick from her hair. "I must say that your Miss Adams is a stupid woman. She might have killed you."

He did not answer. His touch vanished, and the patient clink of keys began again.

Just as Evangeline reasoned that this gate must open with another set of keys entirely, hinges creaked. "This way out," he said, his voice cheerful.

He took her into a tunnel equally as treacherous. After a time the dry dust underfoot became crunching rock. The passage began to slant upward, and the smell of mildew, damp, and sea grew.

A tiny light stabbed into the darkness. Evangeline shut her eyes momentarily as even the faint glow seemed blinding after the complete darkness in which they'd been traveling. A door, she thought, her heart lifting. A window?

They trudged toward the light. The pirate seemed to have no doubt of where he was going. The light grew and became a square. Warm, tropical sea air reached them.

But the door or window she'd hoped for turned out to be a grating in the ceiling. Which was locked.

"Climb onto my shoulders, my rescuer." The pirate put his hands on her waist. "I'll pass the keys up to you."

"No. Wait—"

Her breath cut off in a squeak as he slid his hands to the outside of her thighs, placed his head between her legs, and rose, lifting her high on his strong shoulders.

He pushed her skirt from his face, and chuckled. "I will tell no one I was here. Do you have a brother, my dear?"

"A stepbrother, but Captain Blackwell has imprisoned him for mutiny."

He gave the tiniest of starts, then chuckled. "Are you a mutineer as well?"

"Almost. But I kept Anna from shooting the captain, so he allowed me to keep to my cabin instead putting me in the brig."

"I see."

The cold ring of keys touch her fingers. She picked one out by feel and guided it to the lock above her. It would not turn. "Drat. I wish the guards had been kind enough to explain which was which."

"Yes, they should make prison breaks more convenient. Have I expressed how grateful I am that you came along?"

He spoke like a gentleman, urbane and quiet, as if they chatted together in a shop or at the vicarage.

"Do not thank me, sir. Thank your Anna. I would have preferred to stay on the frigate. And I would have truly preferred to remain on the *Aurora* with Captain Blackwell in the first place."

"The captain who locked you in your cabin for mutiny?"

"Yes."

"If you wished to remain aboard the *Aurora*, why did you lead a mutiny?"

Another key did not work, and she grunted with frustration. "I did not lead it. Anna did. She forced me to help her."

She thought of Captain Blackwell's hot and hungry kiss, his teasing playfulness when he unhooked her bodice, his warm breath on her bared bosom. Her face heated.

"And the captain imprisoned you?"

"Indeed. He was very angry. I cannot blame him." His deep rage when he'd realized she'd betrayed him still chilled her.

"I can blame him. You are far too forgiving. Shall I run him through?"

"Indeed, no," she said in horror.

"Very well." He sounded puzzled. "I will let him live if you wish it."

Her fingers shaking, she thrust another key into the lock. This one turned. The grating swung outward with a groan.

The pirate seized her by the waist and eased her to the floor. As Evangeline shook her skirt out, he raised his arms, jumped, and caught the edge of the opening. He hoisted himself upward and through the square and was gone.

Her heart sank. Of course. She'd released him; he did not need her now. He would shut the grill and leave her in here for the Spanish guards to find. If the prison did not tumble down upon her head from Anna's ex-

plosives, they'd lock her in chains for helping the notorious Sebastian escape.

The blond man's face appeared at the opening. He
extended his long arms down to her.

"Give me your hands."

She reached up to him. He leaned down, slid his
hands beneath her arms, and hoisted her upward. His
grip strong and sure, he pulled her through the opening.

She landed on hard ground, and sat up, scrubbing
the dust from her skirt. "Where are we?"

"Too close to danger. Come."

He jumped to his feet and helped her to hers. They
had come out near the corner of the back wall that
Anna had blown up. A hole in the stucco gaped there,
but the prison showed no signs of collapsing. The thick
walls held.

To the front of the prison, men fought, hand to hand,
sword to sword. Pistol shots sounded in the darkness.
Evangeline made out Spanish guards, crew from the
English ship, and—her heart thumped—Captain Blackwell's men.

"Anna will wait for you over there." She pointed into
the darkness toward the spot the English frigate's boat
had gained the beach. "Go on."

"You're coming with me."

She shook her head until her hair stung her face. "No.
Never again."

"I'll not leave you in such danger, my rescuer."

"I would rather remain and take my chances with the
guards."

His face went stern. "No you wouldn't. They'd eat you
alive."

"At least I would be alive."

He stepped in front of her. She thought he'd argue further, but suddenly he bent, wrapped his arms around her legs, and lifted her over his shoulder. "Oh, no you don't," he said. "I'd have to rescue you all over again, and I'm in no mood to be a hero."

She beat her fists against his back. "Put me down. I want to go to the *Aurora*."

He did not heed her. He jogged away from the walls, while she kicked her heels, and the night swallowed them.

Chapter Nine

From her position upside down against the pirate's back, Evangeline heard the waves slapping the shore and smelled the sea, sharp and clear. Anna's voice, shrill and cruel, floated on the warm breeze. The older sailor answered her, staccato and angry.

Then Anna cried out. "Sebastian! This way, my love. Hurry!"

Evangeline's captor hurried. Sand scattered from under his boots, stinging her face. The rowboat came into view, then her handler skidded to a halt and bent forward, sliding Evangeline off his shoulder. She let out an "eep!" as her feet touched the ground.

The wind tore the clouds apart, and the moon shone down, brighter than the torchlight at the prison. Anna glared at the blond man, raking her gaze up and down him. "Who the devil is this?"

The gentleman pressed his hand to his chest and made a courtly bow. "Lord Rudolph Wittington, at your service, madam."

Anna screamed through her teeth.

"But he told me he was—" Evangeline stopped. No, he had not. She'd asked if he as Sebastian, and he'd not answered.

Anna swung on Evangeline. "You stupid fool." She tore the keys from her hand, swung on her heel, and ran back toward the prison.

Austin scrambled up the wooden ladder, slipping on water and seaweed, and leapt onto the dock just as a second explosion sounded at the prison. He peered into the glare of fire and smoke and dust, and swore heavily. Evangeline was in that hell somewhere, perhaps already dead. Or perhaps she was busy seducing a Spanish guard at Anna's command. Damn, damn, damn.

The wharf teemed with chaos. Men in black and white shouted to each other in Spanish. Men and lads in English naval uniforms ran among them, cheerfully pummeling them and the Americans, alike. The Americans fought back just as cheerfully. Not quite a war. More a barroom brawl. Only the Spaniards were not enjoying themselves.

He wondered briefly what the mood had been on the English frigate when they'd spotted the two privateers looming behind Austin. He hoped that all aboard the frigate had simultaneously needed to use the head.

He had served alongside captains Lawson and Bancroft in the American navy—after the war, Austin had joined the shipping company at Gainesborough's suggestion, and Lawson and Bancroft had turned to lucrative careers as privateers. Without a navy, the new country encouraged bold captains to harass those who would harass Americans. Austin personally knew five captains who liked to mill about the Caribbean, trying to blockade the English ships that were trying to blockade American trade. Austin had hoped to find at least one of them near to Havana; his luck gave him two in the forms of Lawson and Bancroft. *Help you harry an English ship?* they'd asked eagerly. *Lead us to it!*

Seward scrambled to the dock behind him. He had a knife in his hand and his eyes gleamed with eagerness.

Austin drew his own rapier. "Steady, lad. You're my first officer. I cannot afford to lose you."

Seward looked disappointed. "Yes, sir."

"If you find her, get her into the boat, and send someone to find me. Don't let her out of your sight."

"Yes, sir." Seward saluted and jogged off into the fray.

As Austin reached the end of the dock, the fracas overtook him. He dodged through the fighting, fending off those who tried to engage him. Men melted from his path, grins fading to alarm under his glare.

He made it off the wharf, and started across a brick-paved street to the stretch of beach beyond. Far ahead, under the bright moonlight, a long boat lay stark against white sand. Near it, a stocky man in English uniform waved his arms at the red-haired woman who sprinted toward him with a hulking man in tow. Anna and her pirate.

Where was Evangeline?

As Anna neared the signalling Englishman, fire spurted suddenly from her hand. The reverberation of the shot reached Austin a second later. The Englishman stiffened, as if in astonishment, then he crumpled and fell slowly to the sand.

Austin began to run toward them.

"Sir!"

Seward cut him off, waving his knife. "I found her, sir!"

"Where?"

He gestured with his knife. A man and a woman, hand in hand, emerged from the darkness and ran toward the wharf. The woman was small, slim, her loose brown hair streaming behind her. Moonlight and fire-light glinted on the lenses of her spectacles. She was dragging a large muscular man with blond hair and an eye patch behind her.

Austin gained the wharf. Evangeline wore the thinnest of skirts, which clung to her bare legs, outlining them from calf to hip. A large blue seaman's coat covered her torso, above which the bows of her chemise peeped.

He stepped in front of her and she barrelled straight into him. He caught her in the crook of his arm.

Her diamond eyes behind the twisted spectacles regarded him in gladness. "Captain, it's you."

She was warm and supple in his arms. His mouth craved hers, demanding that he curve over her and relieve his frustrations even here for all to see. He would taste the spice of her, feel her cushioned against him, as he slowly took her mouth.

He set her down with a thunk. "I have a boat at the

94

end of the wharf. Do you think you can manage to gain it without mishap?"

"Yes."

He turned away. "Escort her, Seward."

"Sir."

She clutched his arm. "Wait, you must help this gentleman. He was locked in the prison."

Austin regarded the blond man. Tall, half-dressed, his hair hanging in a dirty hank, he gazed back at Austin with a cocksure look in his one eye.

"Criminals are locked in that prison. Why should I help one to escape?"

"Because I rescued him. He is English. And a lord."

The man grinned. "Which to an American makes me no less a criminal. I am Lord Rudolph Wittington, sir." He held out his hand.

Austin ignored it. The surname Wittington was on the list of names that lay hidden in his cabin. George Wittington, cousin to the marquess of Blandesmere. Lord Rudolph, with his courtesy title, was no doubt the marquess's son.

Seward glowered at him, clutching his knife.

Wittington let his hand drop. "I dare say I can convince the English frigate's captain to take me if you've no room."

"Oh, no, you mustn't," Evangeline broke in. "Captain Bainbridge is well and truly under Anna's thumb. He is in love with her, the poor fool. He does as she commands."

"Anna is that red-haired harpy we met on the beach?" Wittington asked.

"Indeed. She came here to free her pirate, Sebastian.

95

I thought you were Sebastian, you see. Even if you weren't, I could not leave you chained to the wall to be blown up by Anna's bombs. So you cannot return to the frigate—"

Austin cut her off. "The English captain is dead. I saw her shoot him."

Her jaw dropped. "Oh, the poor man. He did not deserve that."

Austin seized her chin and tilted her face toward the light. "What is all over your face?"

"Gunpowder most like."

"Damnation."

"It's all over me, actually."

Austin had a sudden vision of her in his cabin. He would peel away the layers of her clothes as he sponged the lethal powder from her damp body. "God's teeth."

"She is brave, my rescuer," Wittington said. He laid his hand on Evangeline's shoulder. "Is this the chap who locked you away for mutiny, my dear?"

"Yes. This is Captain Blackwell."

"Indeed?" He held Austin's gaze, measuring him. "Perhaps we can discuss the situation, captain. Gentleman to gentleman."

Austin measured him back. An aristocrat's son, far from home, sequestered in a Spanish prison—for what? "I would be happy to. Once we've reached Boston."

"Excellent." The man swung around and began sauntering toward the boat. "You do not have to prepare special quarters for me, Captain. String up a hammock anywhere."

A gentleman of his wealth and standing would normally merit the cabin of an upper officer. Austin, by etiquette, should offer him his own or his first lieutenant's cabin, or one of the empty passenger cabins.

Which would put him right next to Evangeline.

"I'll find you an empty spot in the forecastle with the crew."

Wittington stopped, surprised, then grinned and kept walking.

Evangeline watched him go. Austin itched to throw her over his shoulder and plant his palm on her round backside. "Get to the boat, Miss Clemens. Go with her, Seward."

Seward hesitated. "Are you sure about that Englishman, sir? Shouldn't we leave him?"

"I'd rather keep an eye on him and not have him strike a bargain with Anna. We'll treat him as a guest, but watch him. I want a report twice daily on everything he does and everything he says."

Seward touched his forehead. "Aye, sir."

He hurried away, Evangeline trotting ahead of him.

Austin lingered, watching the English and American sailors fighting each other. No doubt in time, they'd stop and get roaring drunk, probably linking arms and singing together. He saluted a lieutenant of the American privateer, who raised his saber and returned the salute.

Austin made for the boat. He reached the ladder just as Evangeline started down it. The wind billowed her flimsy skirt upward, giving the world a glimpse of a long, slim leg, a lovely thigh, and a round, firm hip. He bit back a groan.

Wittington reached up and lifted Evangeline into the

boat. He helped her to a seat and sat down next to her. Right next to her. Hips and legs touching.

Austin dropped into the boat and made his way to the stern. "Take us out, Mr. Thomas. Give the signal to withdraw."

"Aye, sir."

Seward took up an oar, still glowering at the Englishman. Wittington slid his arm around Miss Clemens's shoulders.

"Are you all right, my rescuer?"

She smiled at him. As the small boat slipped into the harbor, Austin toyed with the idea of using his rapier.

Evangeline landed, shivering, on the deck. A wave had splashed over her on the long ride to the *Aurora*, drenching her thin skirt, which the wind now pasted to her legs. She huddled into the coat, longing to be warm and dry.

Wind-disheveled, his shirt soaked with grime, the English lord climbed over the rail after her. Evangeline understood her mistake in thinking the man a pirate. He looked the part, tall, hard-faced, and unkempt. The eyepatch finished the picture.

Captain Blackwell swung onto the ship with lithe grace. He stood slightly taller than Lord Rudolph and was a little wider of shoulder, but otherwise, both had muscular frames and were broad-shouldered, narrow-waisted, narrow-hipped.

Lord Rudolph had a flyaway mane of yellow hair; Captain Blackwell's nearly black hair was tied into its usual queue, though a few strands straggled down his neck. Lord Rudolph had an open face and an affable smile, as if nothing in the world bothered him very much, not even being held prisoner thousands of miles from home. Captain Blackwell's face was closed and forbidding. He commanded and he knew it. He could smile—she'd seen the heart-stopping curve of his lips before—but he did not give that smile freely.

He wasn't giving it to her now. He was regarding her as if she, and not Anna, had instigated all those explosions on shore.

"Go to my cabin and get warm, Miss Clemens. I will speak with you there."

She touched her forehead. "Aye-aye, sir."

"And stop that."

Mr. Seward and the coxswain both grinned, then looked innocent when Captain Blackwell fixed his eye on them.

"Show Wittington to the forecastle, Mr. Seward. And have someone find him some clothes."

"Aye, sir."

Seward scurried away. Wittington followed, after a lingering glance for Evangeline and a distrustful one for Austin.

The captain growled. "Why are you still standing there, Miss Clemens? Do you want consumption?"

"Of course not—"

"Then get below."

He spun on his heel and stalked away, his shoulders squared. He snapped orders as he went, and men scrambled out of his way.

Evangeline made her way to the stern, dodging sailors who were running to obey his snarled commands. She climbed down the stair to the passage to his cabin, happy to be out of the open air. While it was warm in these latitudes, the wind was chilly on her wet limbs.

The young guard who'd replaced poor Davis opened the door for her, giving her a cheerful smile. She scuttled inside, and he closed the door behind her, leaving her alone.

She shivered, trying to get warm. The harbor lights appeared in the black glass windows across the stern wall; the ship was turning. Amid the gold and yellow lights of the town, the burning prison glared like an angry fountain of hell.

She wondered if Anna had found Sebastian, and how many people she'd killed to get to him. She said a silent prayer for Captain Bainbridge. The man had only been guilty of blindness. Anna had much to answer for in his death.

The lantern above swayed as the ship came about. Another lantern glittered on the floor, the candlelight dancing through its lattice and glass. The cabin was as tidy as she remembered it, with the desk empty and the bunk made up neatly.

At the captain's order Mr. Seward had gathered all her things and brought them here when he'd first confined her. Her dresses, her underthings, her nightrail, her stockings, her book of devotions. A very embarrassed Mr. Seward had also turned his back while she'd removed her gown, and then patted her chemise-clad torso all over, to look for weapons. He'd been very polite and had not touched her in any unseemly manner.

She would need some clothes to change into once she washed herself. She pattered to the cabinets and began to search for her belongings.

A second later the cabin door banged open. She whirled around, startled. The captain strode in. He took one look at her, flicked his gaze to the open cabinet behind her, then strode to her and slammed it shut.

The boy called Cyril scuttled in, carrying a basin of water. He set the bowl in the hole cut for it in the washstand, and ducked out again.

Evangeline looked up into his furious black gaze. "I was looking for a gown. You took all of my clothes. I will have to have something to wear."

He reached past her, snapped open a cupboard high above her head, and jerked out a gray worsted gown. He tossed it onto the desk. "After you've washed."

"I'll need—um—underthings, too."

He reached up again and tugged out her finest skirt of white cotton and a chemise of almost sheer gossamer adorned with bows and lace. She'd worked the finery on that for a long time, first in anticipation of her wedding day, and then to console herself after Harley's betrayal.

She never imagined a man would hold it up to the light and gaze first at it, then at her, his eyes smoldering like fires in the night.

He laid it on her gown. "This one."

"I will ruin it. I have things that are more practical."

"I want you to wear it."

She swallowed. "Very well."

He pulled clocked white cotton stockings out next and ran them slowly through his fingers. "There is a shop in Boston, where my w—" He stopped, his eyes going remote. "They make fine stockings. You will buy some there."

"I'm afraid I haven't the means—"

"I will buy them for you."

He laid the stockings on top of her underthings and dress, then closed the cabinet above her head and latched it securely. He looked down at her, emotions she could not read flicking across his face.

"Where did you get that thing you are wearing?"

Evangeline looked down at her torn chemise. The lace that had once adorned it now hung in tatters. "They would not let me dress."

"I meant the coat."

"Captain Bainbridge told one of his men to give it to me. A small fellow, very wiry." She looked at the sleeves, folded back twice upon themselves. "It still doesn't fit, does it?"

He made a slight noise in his throat. Evangeline looked up in surprise, but he'd turned his back and moved to the desk. "Tell me about this Captain Bainbridge. Why did he decide to keep you?"

"He didn't, exactly, but he didn't know what to do with me. He loved Anna. He came to help her try to take over the *Aurora*."

"The idiot."

She shook her head. "He couldn't help himself. I observe that gentleman have little sense when they go nigh her. Except you, of course. Why could you resist her, when so many others couldn't?"

He leaned against the desk and folded his arms. "You didn't answer me. What did Captain Bainbridge want of you?"

"Of me? Nothing. It was Anna he wanted. He looked upon me as an inconvenience. As do you."

"Inconvenience? Yes, I would say you were an inconvenience."

"Then you ought not to have come after us. You must be days off your schedule, miles out of your way."

"Yes."

"Why did you bother? Or did my stepbrother beg you to find me?"

"I did not ask your stepbrother his opinion."

"He is all right, isn't he? May I see him?"

"Later." He pushed himself from the desk. "After you've cleaned yourself up."

Evangeline glanced down again and sighed. Where the coat gaped open her skin was gray with gunpowder. The stuff clung to her forearms, her collarbone, and even to the soft roundness of her breasts.

She heard another soft noise, almost like a groan, and looked up. The captain was watching her this time, his eyes stark, his jaw hard.

"I couldn't help it," she said. "She made me carry the cask, and I got wet getting up on the beach, and it was so warm . . ."

The ship lurched suddenly, the calm waters of the harbor giving way to open sea. Evangeline lost her balance and went sprawling.

"Dammit Evangeline." Captain Blackwell caught her by the elbows and shoved her hard away from him. She landed against the cabinets, the latches digging into her back. He yanked the top from the lantern on the floor and pinched out the flame.

She stared. "Why did you do that?"

"You are covered with gunpowder, and you almost

103

tumbled head-first into the lantern. Why are you smiling? Do you find that amusing?"

"No. It's just that you spoke my given name. You called me Evangeline."

He paused a heartbeat. "What of it?"

"I liked your voice when you said it. As if you were talking to *me*, not an aging spinster."

"You are not an aging spinster."

"I like your name. Austin Blackwell. It's strong."

His eyes went flat. "Oh, no you don't, my little siren. That seductive look will not work this time. Tell me what happened on that English ship. Start with when you decided to run off to it and finish with when I met you on the wharf."

"What seductive look?"

"The ship, Miss Clemens."

She blinked. "It was quite dull, really. Except for Anna and the captain. And the two sailors."

His voice cracked. "What two sailors?"

"The ones she bribed into rowing us to Havana. She promised them great wealth, the poor fools. I hope they're safe."

"I don't give a damn what happened to them."

"It wasn't their fault they fell to Miss Adams. You can't blame them."

"I can and I do. Now, please begin at the beginning."

She opened her mouth, then closed it again. "Oh. I've just realized. I was in Havana."

Sparks glinted in his eyes. "Yes."

"But I saw nothing. Only the beach—in the dark—and the prison."

"You expected a grand tour?"

"You can be cavalier because you've sailed the world. I've only known Gloucestershire and Liverpool the day before I boarded your ship. I was in Havana—and I missed it."

He clenched his hand. "I am not turning my ship around so you can shop in the market square."

"But wouldn't it be lovely? All that balmy air and wares laid out the like of which I've never seen before? A missed opportunity is the saddest thing, Miss Pyne says."

He looked utterly lost. "Miss Pyne?"

"Of the select academy for young ladies. Her training is why I am able to offer my services as a governess."

"God's teeth, Evangeline. You will never become a governess."

"But I must—"

He made an impatient gesture. "You've been running about the open sea in your chemise and a sailor's coat, living on an English frigate without an escort, storming a prison and running about with that half-dressed Englishman—"

"And I showed you my bosom."

"There is that, as well."

"And you kissed me."

"On deck, in full view of my crew."

Her face heated. "Oh, dear."

"I'm inclined not to give a damn. But all of it has put an end to your governess career."

"Before it even started. I suppose now you'll give me to a magistrate. And I'll have the opportunity to witness my own execution." She swallowed. "But I will not be able to tell anyone about it."

105

Jennifer Ashley

The ship hit another swell, rising to what felt to be a great height before plunging downward again at an alarming rate. The hanging lantern swayed and creaked, its light burnishing fiery streaks into his damp hair.

"I have decided not to hand you to a magistrate. I will return you home. To England."

"I do not want to go back to England."

"You'd rather face a magistrate?"

"Indeed, no—"

"Then I will return you home."

In disgrace. Her mother and stepfather would not want her back. They might not even let her come home. She wondered briefly if a quick death at a hangman's rope would not be better than a slow death as an un-wanted spinster, alone and starving for what she had only glimpsed. A tear trickled down her cheek, and then another. She tried to blink them back.

"Oh, dear."

"Evangeline, you slipped between three ships doing their best to shoot each other, stormed a prison, res-cued a man, and fought your way back without turning a hair. And the thought of returning home makes you cry?"

She swiped at the tears, their salty wetness stinging her windburned skin. "Everyone said what a useless weight I was on my stepfather's back. He and my mother were happy to be rid of me. I can only imagine what they'll say at my return—"

A wave broke against hull, spattering the windows like a sudden rain. She sensed him move to her, his steps firm and silent. His breath brushed her cheek. "Don't cry, my sparrow."

"I can't . . . help it."

He slid his arms around her. "Shhh."

She leaned into his warmth. His clothes smelled of wind and salt and smoke from the fires on shore, and the wild masculine tang that was his own. He was so large and strong. He could do anything. He was powerful and daring and cunning. A bit bad-tempered at times, but the weight of command sat heavy on his shoulders.

She let her hands rove up his back to those broad shoulders, where responsibility rested. His muscles moved beneath her fingers. The ship rocked, but Austin Blackwell stood like a bulwark, holding her steady against the tossing of the sea. Under her ear, his heart beat steady and even.

"Are you going to kiss me?" she whispered.

He tilted her face to his. His dark eyes filled her vision. "I am. I can't resist your call, my siren."

Chapter Ten

Her scent filled him. Her sweet breath touched his mouth as he leaned to take her red, ripe lips.

He recognized that he wanted her and that he could not control this wanting. It grated at him and made him stand watches in the middle of the night, welcoming the cold spray that pelted his burning skin. It compelled him to turn his ship and pursue her down the western Atlantic, ready to throw his mission to the wind.

Almost.

Maybe she was in truth an English spy, twining him in her net of desire and then running away so he *would* pursue her and endanger delivery of the papers. Or maybe her objective had been to retrieve the English lord she'd dragged back to his ship. Perhaps Austin had played right into her sensual hands.

No. She was an innocent. His lips told him that. She

kissed him in soft delight, her caresses clumsy and un-practiced. She squirmed in his arms, and the movement melted her hips to him. An innocent who knew seduction. Who had taught her to sigh that little sigh that brushed his skin, to trace the muscles of his arms with her fingertips, to curve her body against his, in an excellent imitation of surrender?

Whenever Austin caught up to the man, he'd kill him.

He moved his lips to the tears that wet her face, then to her temple, her forehead. He kissed her eyelids, soothing them shut.

Her chemise hung in a ruin, the ribbons that held it closed shredded and useless. He untwined the ribbons easily, pushing back the thin cotton and the remnants of lace. Her white skin, darkened with deadly gunpowder, beckoned his fingers. He traced patterns on her damp collarbone, brushing away the gray coating.

The chemise slid down, catching on the sleeves of the coat. The satin of her breasts rose to meet his cupped hands, the points of them caressing his palms. He kissed her lips, her throat, the crease of her breast against her arm.

"You unmake me, Evangeline." He licked her throat. "You do it on purpose, don't you?"

"Um," she whispered, eyes closed.

He nipped her earlobe, sliding his hands under the chemise, molding his touch to the curve of her waist, before moving down to her back and her cool, smooth, round hips. She wriggled and murmured, pressing against his hot arousal, which laughed at him and told him that standing watches in the freezing rain were no match for *this*.

The bunk would be a tight fit. But there was always the desk. He hadn't had the chance to fully explore that possibility the night she'd come to seduce him. He could seat her there and slowly wash the gunpowder from her long, curved body. He groaned.

"Austin, please kiss me again."

"Yes." He sought her lips. "All night, my siren. Forever."

Her mouth opened for him, letting him into her delights.

The strident tones of Albright rose on the other side of the door. "First Lieutenant Seward to see you, sir!"

Cold reality slapped him. He raised his head, gasping for breath.

Dear God, she'd done it again. She wrapped him around her fingers and teased him and begged him until he forgot who he was, what he was doing, and where he was going.

She blinked at him in alarm. It was those spectacles. They fooled him every time into thinking she was innocent, a maiden who knew nothing of her own charms. They made him forget her lies and half-truths and blatant evasions.

He yanked the chemise over her breasts and jerked the coat closed.

"Enter," he said between his teeth.

Seward stepped into the room, his face guileless, his arms full of cloths. "I thought Miss Clemens would need some soap and clean towels."

Evangeline moved to him, joy in her eyes. "Yes, indeed, Mr. Seward. Thank you."

He smiled at her. "I'm pleased you have come back,

miss. I hope Miss Adams is justly punished for trying to take you from us."

"Then *you* believe she kidnaped me."

He turned puzzled eyes to Austin. "Of course we do. Don't you, sir?"

"Are you finished, Seward?"

Seward stared at the towels he carried. "Oh." He dropped them on the desk. "Yes, sir."

"We will let Miss Clemens wash in private. Out."

Seward looked from Austin to Evangeline, brow puckered. "Yes, sir." He departed, casting Austin a doubtful look.

Evangeline stroked the towels, her expression happier than when he'd kissed her.

"A supper will be served in the ward room in a half hour's time. If you come late, you will miss it."

She looked up, eyes shining. "Then you will not be confining me to my cabin?"

"That remains to be seen. If you steal one of my boats or my lieutenants again, or if you and that Englishman get up to any nonsense, you're going in the brig with the mutineers."

"I assure you, Captain, I will give you no trouble. You cannot imagine how pleased I am to be on the *Aurora* instead of with Anna and her murderous pirate, even if I was on an English ship. I know rescuing me was not in your plans, but I am most grateful to you for letting me back aboard, even if I am an inconvenience."

God help me. "Twenty-eight minutes, Miss Clemens. Or you get nothing."

He flung himself out of the cabin and slammed the door.

111

* * *

Forty-five minutes later, Austin gazed at the assembled party in the ward room: five officers, Lord Rudolph, and Evangeline. Snowy linen adorned the table, dampened so that the heavy silver plates would not slide as the ship pitched. A cutlery box was fixed to the wall next to the captain's chair to hold the forks and eating knives until the party needed them.

After leaving Evangeline, Austin had gone to the bow, as far as he could get from his cabin without actually jumping into the sea. He'd closely inspected the windlasses and lines in the bow, to the consternation of the sailors there, while trying not to imagine water dripping from her bare limbs, her clean chemise clinging to her damp body, her white stocking sliding over her slim foot and round calf . . .

The officers and servers stood to attention as they waited for his signal to sit. Evangeline stood behind her chair, neat and prim in a gray dress with two lines of pink lace marching down the bodice. The ship's carpenter had straightened her bent spectacles and behind them, her eyes glistened clear and gray. She'd dressed her hair, pulling it into a modest knot beneath a lacy, feminine cap.

She was a far cry from the ragged nymph in his cabin. When she'd parted the coat to reveal her torn shift, the damp cloth pasted to her gunpowder-smudged skin, he'd gone instantly hard. She must have known it, the little wretch, and used it to her advantage.

Austin gave her a stern look, which she did not see because she was smiling across the table at Lord Rudolph Wittington. He made a curt gesture and the assembled party took their seats. Cyril set a tumbler of port at Austin's place.

One of the officers led them in a brief prayer of thanks for the meal, then the men tucked in as if they hadn't seen food for a fortnight.

"A good evening's work, I'd say, sir." Osborn said. "I'd give anything to have seen those English dogs' faces when they came around the headland and saw those two American ships."

Evangeline gave him a prim look. "Their language was unfortunate."

Osborn and the others roared with laughter. Austin sipped his wine in silence.

Seward turned to her eagerly. "Tell us what happened, Miss Clemens. How did you come to be blowing up Havana prison?"

Lord Rudolph had apparently commandeered some officer's civilian clothes. He wore the embroidered waistcoat and velvet coat with slight disdain, as if he were used to much better. He slanted a glance across the table at Evangeline. "Yes, do tell us your story. How did you come to rescue me?"

Evangeline's cheeks pinkened. A fallen strand of her gold-brown hair drew Austin's gaze to the long curve of her throat. He watched her swallow a sip of wine and traced its path to the dip between her breasts.

He'd licked that lovely throat in the cabin. He'd wanted to devour her, and that desire hadn't changed. Never in his life had he lost control of his physical reaction to a woman. The movement in his breeches signaled that he'd lost control of it again.

She set down her glass and began her tale, hesitantly

113

at first, then warming to it as the men hung on her words. She told them everything, beginning the moment Anna Adams had entered her cabin and ending the moment Austin had boosted her over the rail of the *Aurora*, his hand on her round little backside.

She told his officers and Wittington everything, where she hadn't imparted one word to him.

Wittington raised his glass. "To my rescuer. The bravest woman I know."

Good-natured laughter followed; glasses were raised.

Austin eyed the marquess' son. He'd trimmed and combed his unruly yellow hair, catching it back in a tail. Even with the eyepatch, some women might call him handsome. Evangeline certainly favored him with her admiring attention. She offered Wittington her crooked smile, her gray eyes flashing.

"But we have you safe and sound now." Seward patted her hand. "We so worried about you."

Lord Rudolph guffawed. "You're smitten, Lieutenant."

A man down the table snickered. Austin shot him a quelling glance and the man turned the laugh into a cough.

"She reminds me of my sister, my lord," Seward said.

"Your sister?" Lord Rudolph sent Evangeline a knowing wink.

"Yes. She died shortly before the *Aurora* sailed from Boston."

The teasing twinkle in Lord Rudolph's eyes died. "Ah, I do beg your pardon. Hard luck."

The other gentlemen at the table made murmurs of sympathy, and looked at him in new respect. Evangeline squeezed his hand.

"You never spoke of this," Austin said.

All eyes turned to him in surprise. He took a sip of port, hiding his irritation.

"You should have told me," he said.

"I didn't like to, sir. I did not want you to think I could not perform my duties."

Evangeline frowned in Austin's direction, reproach-ful. Hell and damnation.

"She must have been a fine young lady if she was anything like Miss Clemens." Lord Rudolph lifted his tumbler again, saluting Evangeline. She smiled at him.

Austin pictured himself seizing Lord Rudolph by the collar and tossing him into the sea. The man would make a satisfying splash.

Now Seward was holding forth about his sister. Evangeline kept patting his hand, gazing up at him with com-passion. The others listened with interest.

Someone had control of this table, this room, this conversation, and it wasn't Austin.

For two weeks, the *Aurora* sailed north, heading for America and Boston. The air grew cooler and rains came, often confining Evangeline and Lord Rudolph to their cabins or the ward room. Austin allowed Evan-geline to go on deck when she pleased, but he insisted Seward or young Albright escort her each time. For her safety, he said.

Even escorted, she loved to stand in the bow and look into the wind and the waves and wonder what was to come. Austin had spoken of sending her back to England. She would have to think of a way to prevent that. She wanted to move on, to go forward, not back to her old life and sorrows.

As for Austin, he had not said one word to her since she'd taken supper with him and his officers the night she'd come back on board. She often saw him on deck, giving orders to his men or studying his sextant, or writing notes in a book that a sailor held for him when he didn't need it, but he rarely spared her a glance.

He did not speak to her, and he did not speak to Lord Rudolph. He became as aloof as he had been before the mutiny, when he all but ignored his passengers.

Perhaps it was just as well, Evangeline told herself as the days went by. Every time she saw him, she went hot with confusion. She relived in her memory his searing kisses, his hands reaching inside her clothes to touch her skin, the hungry need he whispered to her. Her own hungry need answered, sending her tossing and turning every night and searching for a sight of him every day.

Lord Rudolph, on the other hand, was a genial companion. He often stood on deck with her and Seward, or played cards with her in the ward room during the rain. He told her stories of his travels, regaling her with tales of lands far away and people exotic and strange. He spoke of Chinese ladies who could fight with feet and fists alongside men, of Siamese ladies who could bend their bodies into fearsome contortions, of Polynesian ladies who tattooed their faces. Miss Pyne would have been shocked. Evangeline was delighted and curious.

Of his life in England he said very little. When she

asked direct questions, he found ways to change the subject.

She found it easy to talk to him about herself, however. She told him of her life in Gloucestershire, of her father's death, and of Harley and her decision to leave home and go to America. His indignation over Harley and his praise of her courage to travel to a new country in search of happiness warmed her.

The days slid by one after the other, but Evangeline found the monotony restful. No more mutinies, villainesses, or prisons to storm. Only three events marked the journey, which was otherwise quiet: the arrival of an American ship to tell them of Anna Adams, an attempt on Austin's life, and the problem of her book of devotions.

Chapter Eleven

The American packet caught up to them three days out of Havana. A faster ship than the heavy *Aurora*, it appeared astern in the morning, and by late afternoon had come alongside.

Evangeline and Lord Rudolph watched from the rail as, after a series of signals and good-natured shouting, a boat was lowered over the ship's side, and three men rowed to the *Aurora*.

Captain Blackwell strode down from the command deck to greet his guests.

A short man with unruly red hair, a boyish grin, and captain's insignia on his coat clapped him on the shoulder. "Blackwell. Well met. Thank you for that invigorating game in Havana. I haven't had that much fun in years."

"Glad to be of service."

"The hell you are. I want the whole story. Who was that woman with the fireballs? I've never seen anyone so ruthless. She cut a swath straight through a patch of poor Spanish soldiers, leaving a bloody trail in her wake. The woman needs hanging."

"Is she on her way to her hanging?"

The American captain looked uncomfortable. "She got away from us."

Austin's eyes glinted. "One woman evaded two ships filled with guns?"

"One woman and her murdering pirate. He was a huge, ugly mother's son, laughing like a maniac as he shot at my men right and left. They made it to the English frigate. Then they started throwing the men overboard."

Evangeline clutched the rail, thinking of the English sailors in their familiar uniforms, and the one who'd spoken with a Gloucestershire dialect.

"We hauled them out of the sea and put them ashore. They said she gave the men who wouldn't follow her pirate a choice—to be shot in the stomach or to go overboard. They were madder than hell to be rescued by us. We thought about press-ganging the English bastards, but we let them go."

"Decent of you," Lord Rudolph drawled.

The American captain glanced his way and raised his red brows. "Who's this, Blackwell?"

Lord Rudolph stepped forward and extended his hand. "An English bastard."

"He's Lord Rudolph Wittington," Austin said shortly.

The captain shook his hand, and cocked an eye at Austin. "Friend of yours?"

119

"I'm taking him to Boston."

"We can get you there faster," the captain offered.

"Thank you, no. I've grown fond of the *Aurora*, and I doubt I'd enjoy a journey with a captain who likes the idea of press-ganging Englishmen."

Austin shot him a sharp glance, but his expression betrayed nothing.

"Wittington," the red-haired man mused. "I know a George Wittington in Boston. Relation of yours?"

"My cousin, I'm afraid, if it's the same George Wittington."

The captain gave a short laugh. "My condolences."

"He is only a second cousin, but yes, he is an ass."

Austin cut in. "Which way did the English frigate go?"

"Eh? Oh, she ran due south. Probably thinks there are better pickings in the Caribbean. Lawson is after her, and he's signaled others to follow. I've been warning all ships to avoid her as I sail. I'm afraid if the woman is caught, Lawson may not be able to keep her alive for a trial."

"I don't give a damn what happens to her. As long as she stays away from my ship."

The captain's brows shot up, but he shrugged. "As you like. Now, I came all the way from my ship, Blackwell, because I know you always stash away some of the best brandy money can buy. Take me below and give me some."

Austin gave him a ghost of a smile. He gestured for the man to follow him, and led him and his two men toward the stern. He did not ask Lord Rudolph or Evangeline to join them.

"Why did you do that?" Evangeline asked when they were alone at the rail again.

Lord Rudolph gave her a blank look. "Do what?"

"Become all English aristocrat. You looked like one of those caricatures in my brother's magazines. I half expected a balloon with words to come out of your mouth."

He chuckled. "It impresses the Americans."

"Why did you really do it?"

He lost his smile. "It amused me."

Evangeline gave him a puzzled look. He shrugged and sauntered away. She followed him to the opposite rail where he directed her attention to a school of flying fish, lifting their white bellies to the afternoon sun, and refused to talk about anything else.

"The American captain was right. This brandy is fine." Lord Rudolph Wittington crossed his legs and sipped from the goblet Austin had given him.

They sat together in Austin's cabin, Wittington in the one chair at the desk, Austin on a folding chair he'd taken from one of his cabinets. It was three days after the American packet had sailed away into the setting sun, shouting advice and good-byes and cheerful insults.

"I have been lacking in manners. Captains should extend courtesy to their high-ranking guests."

Wittington gave him a look. "You're a bloody liar, Blackwell."

The folding chair creaked as Austin leaned back and stretched out his long legs. "I am a bad liar. But if you

121

knew I didn't invite you here out of courtesy, why did you accept?"

"I was curious. And you tend to throw people who disobey you into the brig."

He spoke glibly, but his one eye held wariness. Austin sensed his tension all the way across the rocking cabin. "The brandy is French. Not easy for Englishmen to get these days, unless it's smuggled. I bought it in Paris. I thought you'd enjoy it while you told me your story."

"Ah, my story. I imagined that's why you lured me here."

"The story of why you were in the Caribbean and how you came to be a prisoner in Havana. The story you seem at great pains not to tell anyone. You haven't even relayed it to Miss Clemens."

"How the devil do you know that? You haven't so much as spoken to her in a week."

Austin shrugged and didn't answer.

"You're a tricky bastard, Blackwell." He took a slow sip of brandy then let the glass dangle from his fingers. "I hate to disappoint you, but I don't have much of a story. I was in the wrong place at the wrong time. That is generally what happened."

Austin cradled his goblet in his palms. "What were you arrested for and what was your sentence?"

His lips curved. "I feel disinclined to answer, Captain. Even if this is excellent brandy."

"Aboard ship, the captain's word is law. His orders are obeyed, and punishment meted out, if not. Ships remain civilized under that system."

"And many captains use it as the chance to be martinets. God help a crew whose captain has a streak of cruelty. Your own crew seem content, so I put you down as a martinet without the cruelty."

"I don't punish without cause. But I do it."

Wittington set down the goblet and regarded him without expression. "I am not one of your sailors or officers."

"You are here under my auspices. At Miss Clemens's request."

"I know. I am forever indebted to my rescuer. I find it interesting you took me on for her sake."

"I was tempted to leave you to the wolves. It is your choice, Wittington. You can spend the remainder of the voyage comfortably or you can spend it uncomfortably."

Wittington laughed. "As guest or prisoner, you mean? And you'd do it, too, wouldn't you? I've heard all about the mutiny and how you put it down by shooting your first lieutenant. Your brig has a dozen men in it regretting their hasty choice to overthrow you. Plus a few more disgruntled ones tucked away here and there. And none dare to rise against you. I'm not sure Miss Clemens is safe here."

She wasn't safe, but not in the way Wittington meant. Austin had forced himself to stay away from her, and it had been the hardest thing he'd ever done. But he had to stay away. She was driving him mad.

"We digress. Why were you a prisoner in Havana?"

Wittington lifted his goblet. "I see it is fruitless to evade you. I know you won't believe me, but I truly was in the wrong place at the wrong time. I took a turn in an alley, and found myself intruding upon an altercation. Two fellows were amusing themselves murdering

123

a third. When I tried to intervene, the two gentlemen fled, and I was left with bloodstained clothes and the body of a dead man. The constables arrested me on the spot, and I was taken away to await trial, no doubt to hang. I know that the man who passed for their magistrate didn't believe I did it, but they were happy to have someone to blame. They allowed me to send for my own representation, and so I was awaiting them." He took a sip of brandy. "I imagine they will be surprised when they arrive and find me gone."

"You seem calm for a man who narrowly escaped death. Even on the docks, you behaved as if you were out for an evening stroll. Or is that simply your cool English manner?"

"I never had the slightest doubt I'd be released. My father is the Marquess of Blandesmere, a man of much influence, especially in the ongoing struggles against the French. He's not likely to allow his only son and heir to die in a Spanish-governed prison for a crime he did not commit."

Austin crossed his booted ankles. "You are lucky, then. Many men in that prison will never again see the light of day, unless Miss Adams managed to blow down all the walls. You were strangely lucky again to not be in your cell when Miss Clemens rushed in. She'd never have found you, else."

"It was pure luck, I admit. The guards took a liking to me, because I spoke Spanish well. They also had a weakness for wagering at cards. Since that is also a natural weakness of Englishmen, we rubbed along well."

"Mmm."

He could be what he seemed, a pampered, wealthy

man's son, swaggering about the world, confident he'd get out of any trouble he got himself into. Austin had met such men before.

"Why were you in Havana at all?"

He shrugged. "Thought I'd have a look at it."

"While you were in the Caribbean for? . . ."

"You are persistent, Captain. Very well, I had business to look into."

"Most Englishmen confine their business to Jamaica and other English-held colonies."

"Mine happens to be a little more broad."

Austin set down his goblet and steepled his fingers. "Most Englishmen don't have a fluent command of Spanish."

"There's no mystery about that. As a lad, I had a tutor who'd lived most of his life in Spain. He taught me the language."

Damned bland-faced, smooth-tongued lordling. Did he keep his exploits secret to taunt Austin, or did he hide something Austin truly needed to know? Was the man a harmless dilettante or something more dangerous?

"When we land in Boston, I will seek out a ship returning to England and put you on it. No doubt you'll want to return home right away."

The fatuous smile faded. "I am in no hurry. Put me ashore in Boston and forget about me, Captain."

"Why?"

"I'd like to see the sights."

"There is little to see."

"Oh, come now. Boston has become famous. The cradle of the rebellion."

"It has nowhere near the magnificence of London."

He gave a short laugh. "I think you are jealously guarding your city from me, Captain."

Austin regarded him in silence for some time. "You don't play the ingenuous idiot very well, Wittington. I suggest you drop it."

Surprise flashed in Wittington's one eye, then his smile turned cynical.

"But *you* play the game very well. I salute you." He hefted his glass at an ironic angle. "Ask me no more questions so I do not have to come up with more stupid lies. My business will in no way harm you, your cargo, your crew, or your passengers. Leave it at that."

"Promising no harm does not mean you are harmless."

"I am not. But then, neither are you."

Austin drank his brandy again, knowing he'd get no more from the Englishman. This time.

"Let me ask a question of you, Captain. Miss Clemens. What is she to you?"

The answer to my dreams. The thought flashed through Austin's head, unbidden. It startled him, but he knew it for truth. Her gray eyes and crooked smile had left an imprint on him that would not easily be erased.

"She is a passenger. Bound for New England."

"Are you her lover?"

Austin sat up straight, rage climbing.

Wittington held up his hand. "Wait. Do not run me through yet. I mean no offense to her. I simply want to know where things stand."

"They stand nowhere. And if you plan to seduce her, I will fling you overboard."

126

"Calm yourself, Captain. I have no illicit designs upon my rescuer. She is a courageous and lovely young woman. I have every wish to keep her from harm."

"She will not come to harm on my ship."

Not if he had to lock her in his own cabin and guard the door himself. She'd stirred passions within him he hadn't known existed. With her, loving would be intense and powerful. They would share a desire that would shake the skies.

Which was why he put the entire distance of the deck between them whenever he saw her.

"She has already been forced to assist a mutineer, then was abducted to another ship and returned to you covered in gunpowder. I think you've taken care of her poorly."

"The person who did her harm is far from here."

"Ah, yes, the splendid Miss Adams. I met her briefly. She made my blood run cold. According to Miss Clemens, she twines men around her finger as easily as string. I admire you for not succumbing." He lifted his glass in mock salute.

"She is obvious."

"To a perceptive man. But I'd rather speak of Miss Clemens. What is to become of her?"

Austin sat back. "She has a cousin in Boston. Apparently this cousin has arranged a governess position for her in a wealthy household."

Wittington blanched. "A governess? My rescuer? I'll never let her go to that horrible fate."

"In America we don't believe working for a living to be a horrible fate."

"That is why we consider you barbarians. Miss Clem-

127

ens is not an American. She is English born and bred, and I'm damned if I'll let her become a governess. She'll be little better than a servant."

"You have no say in the matter."

"Of course I have say. I am her countryman. I met her stepbrother once in London. He is an idiot, and not fit to take care of her. When we reach Boston, I will arrange passage back to England for her and accompany her myself."

Austin clenched his hand around his glass, wanting to leap from his chair and dare Wittington to take Evangeline anywhere. "Her family engaged her to a philandering fool, and grew furious when she jilted him. They don't want her back. And I don't much want them to have her."

"I agree that her family has not done well by her. She told me the story of the disgusting Harley. If I ever meet him, I will certainly call him out."

He spoke coolly, the English aristocrat loftily dismissing his inferiors.

"And you would take her back to the people who so humiliated her?"

"You misunderstand me, Captain. I will take her home with *me.*"

Austin's jaw hardened. "The hell you will."

Chapter Twelve

"Calm yourself, Captain." Wittington gave him a lofty smile. "My mother would welcome her with open arms, especially when she discovers Miss Clemens pulled her son's worthless balls from the fire. She will sponsor her, give her a Season. If anyone can make Miss Clemens a good match, it will be my mother." A dry note entered his voice.

"You intend to marry her off to some English fop?"

"I assure you, my mother knows the best people. She will find Miss Clemens a man of breeding and good character. Do you not think she deserves a reward for all she's done? With a good marriage, she will become mistress of a prosperous household and hold much influence in society."

Austin tried to envision Evangeline, her hair neatly coiffed, standing quietly by her husband's side as she

129

greeted guests in their well-appointed mansion.

No, Evangeline was not made to stand tamely while others talked over her gowns and her hair. Those faceless, cold English could not know that she was more beautiful in her torn chemise, with her hair tangled, her face smudged. That she laughed wildly as the ship rode the waves, that she escaped from deadly danger to mourn that she had no opportunity to see the sights of the place she'd escaped from.

"She will fare ably in Boston," he said.

"As a governess? Or married to some bank merchant—or perhaps a ship's captain?"

Austin didn't flinch. "She would not be shamed married to such a man."

"She deserves far better. A bank merchant is far cry from a baronet, or viscount, or even a marquess' son."

He shot Austin a smile. Austin gave him a flinty stare.

"As long as she is on this ship, Miss Clemens is under my protection. She has expressed a wish to join her cousin in Boston, and I will take her there."

"I propose to let her make the choice."

"When she reaches Boston. For now, you will leave her alone. If you pester her before we dock, I *will* throw you in the brig."

Lord Rudolph showed his white teeth. "It is crowded, your brig. Let me remind you that I am an Englishman, and the son of a peer of the realm."

"Which means damn-all aboard my ship."

Their gazes locked. After a time, Wittington looked away and drained the last of his brandy. "I would love to get you inside the House of Lords one day, Captain. What havoc you'd wreak."

Austin got to his feet. "My cook does a splendid poul-let. It will be served to my officers in the ward room soon. You must be hungry."

Wittington set down his goblet, and rose. "I under-stand you perfectly, Captain. Thank you for the brandy. Good evening."

He made a slight bow. Austin returned a cold nod. Lord Rudolph pulled open the door and exited into the passage. Albright closed it for him.

Austin took up his own glass of brandy and drained it. There went a man with no good on his mind.

He'd be damned if he let Wittington take Evangeline back to England. Austin's own solution had been to ship her back, but now he wanted her nowhere near England. Not if Wittington would be there.

She could stay in Boston, if not as a governess, then he'd think of something. He would ask Captain Gaines-borough for suggestions. If Evangeline truly was an En-glish agent, it would be as well to keep an eye on her. If that meant letting the siren seduce him to his doom, he would just have to live with that.

"Captain, I must speak with you." Evangeline shouted up at the poop deck.

The broad back of Captain Blackwell did not turn. He went on staring through his spyglass at the vast, empty ocean.

She fought down the lump of trepidation in her throat. She had asked Mr. Seward to intercede for her on this problem, and he'd reported back that the cap-tain refused to budge. So, while Lord Rudolph occu-pied himself with something in the forecastle, she

131

summoned up her courage to confront him herself.

She waited until a sailor had clambered down on the run to obey an order, then she took hold of the slippery handholds and climbed the steep ladder to the upper deck.

She had only been on this deck, near the wheel, during the mutiny, and then she'd been terrified. She remembered huddling on the bench while Austin quietly returned the ship to his command.

From here, she could look over the broad length of the ship, from end to end. The masts towered overhead, the creamy sails snapping taut in the wind. Myriad ropes criss-crossed each other in fantastic patterns, and the wind moaned through them like a storm buffeting the eaves back home. The expanse of ocean unfolded to the stern, and the ship dragged a white V of foamy water behind it.

From his position at the wheel, Lornham noticed her, but said nothing. Osborn saw her, shot his brows up, then turned away, his mouth twitching.

Evangeline marched to Austin and planted herself behind him. "Captain, I must speak with you."

He whirled. His eyes held a blank, chill anger that made her take a halting step back. His gaze was remote and withdrawn, as if he'd never met her before.

She stuck out her chin. "This is important, Captain, or I'd not have—"

"Seward!"

The young lieutenant scrambled up the ladder, the strong sunlight glinting on his hair. "Sir."

Austin made a curt gesture and turned away. "Take her off."

Seward bit his lip. He watched his captain's back a moment, then faced her unhappily. "I'm sorry, Miss Clemens. Let's—let's go below and have some coffee."

Austin would not even look at her. Evangeline's feet urged her to flee, to abandon her quest. It would be much easier to go with Mr. Seward, to sit in the ward room and drink warm coffee while she told him her troubles and he made her laugh.

She balled her fists and marched past the distressed Mr. Seward to halt again at Austin's back. "I am not one of your sailors to order about, Captain. You have avoided me for nearly two weeks, and I am going to say what I need to say."

He spun, his eyes no longer remote. Sparks of rage flew from them.

He came for her, his large body moving fast. Evangeline squeaked and scrambled out of his way. At the top of the ladder, she made herself turn and face him.

"You do not frighten me."

Her trembling legs made her words a lie.

He leaned his hands on the top of the ladder to either side of her, enclosing her in the parody of an embrace. "No one comes on this deck without my permission. You do not have my permission."

"I only want to ask you a question."

"Not on my deck."

She raised her chin and met his eyes. He glared back at her, all his power brought to bear.

"You cannot bully me. I am not part of your crew."

"Take her down, Mr. Seward. Now."

Seward's worried face peered around Austin's arm. "Miss Clemens. Please?"

Jennifer Ashley

Evangeline looked from him to Austin's granite expression, and her limbs quavered. "Very well. I am going. But only because I do not want to get Mr. Seward into trouble."

He did not answer. He took a step back from the ladder and motioned Mr. Seward toward it with exaggerated courtesy. The young lieutenant scrambled down, then waited at the bottom while Evangeline descended, steadying her as she climbed from the last rung.

She straightened her skirts and looked back up at the deck. Austin had walked away.

"Captain Blackwell."

He was speaking to Lornham at the wheel, his back to her once more.

"I am no longer on your deck, Captain. You can at least answer my question."

He turned. He strode carefully to the edge of the deck, then planted his fists on the rail. "I have a ship to sail, Miss Clemens. Mr. Seward can see to your needs."

"I have asked him this already, and he could not help me."

Seward began making frantic signals to her.

"If he cannot answer, then I cannot either."

"I know you want to throw me into the sea, Captain, and you may when I've finished, but this is very important."

Austin shot Seward a glance, then turned back to her with slow deliberation. "Very well, Miss Clemens. What is it?"

She took a deep breath. Seward covered his eyes.

134

"You took my book of devotions from me. May I have it back?"

He looked at her for a long time. She could not read his eyes, but his black gaze held her and pinned her.

"No," he said abruptly, and turned away.

After midnight, Evangeline made her way across the dark deck to fetch her book from Austin's cabin.

Seward had taken her below that afternoon and tried to soothe her temper, but she remained furious. Such a simple thing she asked, and Austin would not grant it because he was pigheaded and liked his power. He seemed to have forgotten leaning to kiss her, running his large hand along the curve of her side, caressing her with his mouth. He'd forgotten that his eyes went dark, his voice raw when he called her his siren.

She scurried across the deck, keeping to the shadows. She knew Austin would not be in his cabin, because she'd heard him tell Osborn in the ward room that he would stand an extra watch tonight. Even so, she expected at any moment that he'd see her, swoop down upon her, and throw her back into her cabin. That is, if he didn't lock her in the brig and order Mr. Seward to toss her a bread crust once in a while, for which she'd have to fight the rats.

She made it to the stair without any such incident. The ship was quiet but for the wind in the rigging and the slap of the waves against the hull. The sea was calm, the moon high, the sails casting sharp shadows on the deck.

Evangeline crept down the stairs on silent feet. At the end of the passage lay the captain's cabin door. She remembered how she'd stood in this very corridor the day of the mutiny, and peered at the brass-hinged door, thinking it a formidable and frightening barrier.

It looked the same now. Lantern light touched its polished wooden panels and the shined doorlatch. The door was austere and unwelcoming.

When she'd stood here weeks ago, the body of young seaman Davis had lay slumped in the passage, dead. Tonight the passage was empty. Albright, the sailor now assigned to guard the cabin, was at the moment in the forecastle for the nightly card and dice games. She'd seen him go. Lord Rudolph had gone there also, with Mr. Seward in tow, both thinking Evangeline had gone to bed.

She would quickly search the cabin, take her book of devotions, and leave. Five minutes' work at most. Likely, he'd never notice it had gone.

She pushed open the door and went inside. The cabin was empty, neat and silent, but for the creak of the ship's timbers. The windows across the stern showed only the black of the nighttime sea, panels of glass that looked into nothingness.

She quietly closed the door. A quick look around confirmed Evangeline's belief that Captain Blackwell kept his quarters exceptionally tidy. The bunk under the eaves was unrumpled and the desk had been cleared of charts and papers.

When she'd washed herself in this cabin the day she'd escaped Havana, the captain had pulled her clothes from a cabinet above her head. Likely he'd secured all of her things in it. She went to the chair behind the desk and tugged the heavy piece of furniture across the room. She climbed on it, facing the row of identical, polished wood cabinets.

That was the right one before her, she was sure of it. She traced the keyhole below the latch with her fingers. Certain it would be locked, she grasped the handle and tugged.

The cabinet opened easily, revealing a shelf of coats, neatly folded; below them rested an equally tidy row of shirts. His clothes. She touched a coat, the wool smooth and warm. She had the strongest urge to crawl into the little cabinet and curl up around the coats like a cat, resting in his warmth and his scent.

She withdrew her hand, gave a little sigh, and closed the door. She moved the chair over and opened a smaller cabinet to the right. Here she found his pistol, hanging in a holster fastened to the door, plus the powder, balls, and cleaning tools, all snug in tight compartments so the movement of the ship wouldn't clatter them about.

She found her valise and her small box in the cupboard next to that one, with her red-covered book of devotions wedged between box and bag.

She drew out the book. It rested comfortably in her hand, familiar, a link to the life she'd left behind. Since childhood, she'd had the habit of reading the book every night. The verses had soothed her to sleep in the empty nights following her father's death, had comforted her when she'd realized that her mother's new husband disliked her, had received her tears the day Harley had betrayed her.

Much of herself lay inside this book of Bible verses. She opened it at random and scanned a page. So much had happened since she'd last read these words. She'd had adventure and peril and terror, and she'd tasted desire with a man who looked upon her as no more than a nuisance.

She hugged the book to her chest and climbed down from her perch. She slid the chair back to the desk, positioning it exactly as she'd found it. Mission accomplished.

A step sounded in the passage outside. Evangeline started, and the book slipped from her grasp. She grabbed it frantically, catching it between her palms inches above the floor.

Albright or Captain Blackwell? It could not be the captain. The watch ended at two, and Captain stickler-for-the-rules Blackwell would never leave a watch early.

Albright liked her, perhaps she could think of some plausible story to tell him so he'd let her dash back to her cabin without reporting her to the captain.

Even if it were the captain, she could brazen it out. He had no reason to deny her the comfort of her book.

Or she could hide under the desk.

The footsteps paused outside the door. She scrambled to the desk, dropped to her hands and knees, and crawled into the space beneath it. The door opened. Evangeline tucked her skirts under her, trying to still her breathing. The footsteps stopped, then the door clicked closed. Silence.

Evangeline buried her face in her knees and waited. Perhaps he'd only come in to retrieve something, and he'd fetch it and go.

Or, he might want to spread his charts across the desk, drag out the chair and sit down. Her heart hammered, and she stuffed her fist into her mouth.

If he'd returned to retire, she'd have to stay here until he settled into bed and slept. She'd wait until she heard him snore, then climb out and go. But she would probably stumble and wake him, and there he'd be, in bed, sitting up and glaring at her, the covers sliding from his bare torso . . .

His tread, measured and even, came unerringly to the desk, and around it. The chair scraped back. A pair of boots stopped in front of her. Above them, kid breeches molded to well-muscled thighs.

She looked up to a coat hanging unbuttoned, to a hand closed around a crumpled neckcloth, to a shirt and waistcoat unfastened, to a hard and unforgiving face.

"I knew I should have locked you in," he said.

Chapter Thirteen

Evangeline stared at him, and he stared back with eyes like glittering onyx.

"Did you find what you were looking for, Miss Clemens?"

"Yes."

Silently, he held out his hand.

Evangeline untwisted her arm from around her knees and lifted the heavy book toward him. He gave the book a cold stare, then his gaze slid back to her, his eyes as hard as if she'd admitted to entering to steal all his gold.

He took the book from her. "Come out of there."

Evangeline scrambled from under the desk and got to her feet, shaking out her skirt. "It's *my* book."

"It is."

His shirt gaped open at the throat, giving her a

140

glimpse of a hard, muscled chest and black curls of hair.

She swallowed. "I want it back."

"I will return it to you when we reach Boston."

"Good heavens, why? It's only my book of devotions. I like to read it before I go to sleep. It soothes me."

"Why have you not complained of this before?"

"Because I could not get near you before. You walk to the other side of the ship whenever you see me."

"Do you know why I do?"

"No, I don't. I think it's very rude."

"Because every time I am near you I either want to ravish you or throw you overboard."

Her heart beat faster. "Which do you want to do now?"

"I haven't decided. It is a difficult choice."

"I could simply take my book and go back to my cabin and we could forget all about it."

His eyes glinted. "Where is Seward? Why didn't he stop you?"

"He thinks I am in bed."

"I see I'll have to assign an attendant to you twenty-four hours a day."

"You are being most unfair."

His brows slammed together. "Captaining a ship isn't about being fair, Evangeline. It's about discipline and routines and getting an entire crew and cargo across the sea without losing anyone to violence or disease." He looked at the book in his hand, and all the fire suddenly left his eyes. "God, I hate it so much."

The deadness in his voice was unbearable. "No. You love it."

"I used to love it. Those days are gone."

"But you must love it. To rise in the morning and see the sun upon the water, to watch the fish playing in the waves, to wonder what exotic place you'll sail to next, and if the women there will have tattoos or be able bend their bodies into fantastic shapes—"

"What the devil are you talking about?"

"Lord Rudolph says ladies in Siam can bend their hands back like that." She took hold of her fingers and pulled them backward until they were at a right angle to her wrist.

"I stay in the harbors. I don't watch court dancers."

"I'd love to see them. I'd love to see even the harbors."

"Well, I am tired of them."

"You cannot be. I would never grow tired of such things. Not if I saw them with you."

He went silent. For the first time in days he looked at her, really *at* her, as if he could see all the way to the other side of her. She wished she were anywhere but under that black, scrutinizing stare.

"You are a dangerous woman, Evangeline. You say things I want to hear, and make me want to believe every word."

"I don't lie, Captain. Miss Pyne always stressed the importance of honesty."

"Ah, yes, the oracle Miss Pyne." He stopped. "Why did you come to my cabin, tonight?"

"You already know that. To find my book of devotions."

"This is the first time you've looked for it?"

"Yes."

"I will pretend to believe you."

"It is the truth. I tried to ask you, but you refused. Unreasonably, I think."

"So you decided to take it by stealth? Believing I wouldn't miss it?"

"Why on earth should you miss it? It is my book."

"Because I am potently aware of everything that has anything to do with you. I would know the instant something of yours had gone. I certainly will not allow you possession of a large, heavy book that can be turned into a formidable weapon."

"A weapon? Bible verses can't hurt anyone."

"They can if you hit someone over the head with them."

"I would never do that."

A muscle moved in his jaw. "You have a beguiling innocence, siren. It almost makes me want to put myself completely in your power."

"So, you will let me have my book?"

"I said almost."

He went to the cabinets and returned the book to the one she'd removed it from. He pulled a key from his waistcoat pocket, inserted it into the lock and turned it.

Evangeline blew out her breath. "If don't have my book, what on earth will soothe me to sleep?"

His gaze darkened. "I will see to that."

He moved to his bunk. He pulled back the blanket. A linen sheet was tucked neatly under it. He pulled back the sheet. Her heart sped.

He beckoned. "Come here."

Jennifer Ashley

Woodenly, she moved to him. Her throat felt like she'd swallowed parchment.

He reached under the mattress and drew out a small book and held it out to her. "This is my own book of devotions. I'll lend it to you to soothe you to sleep until we reach Boston. It's small enough that I don't think you can hurt anyone with it."

He laid the brown-covered volume in her hand. The heat from his own hand had warmed it. No doubt he was used to reading it while reclining in his bunk. In a nightshirt. Unlaced to show the dark curve of chest, dusted with black curls.

"I will call Seward to escort you to your cabin."

Evangeline jerked her gaze back to his face. "I can go myself. He does not need to be my nursemaid all of the time."

"When you claim you will return to your cabin, I am not inclined to believe you."

"I will. Where else am I to go?"

"I can think of a good number of places in which you could find more trouble. But know this, Evangeline. If you are anywhere but in your cabin five minutes from now, I will definitely throw you overboard."

She bit her lip. "I would drown before you could turn the boat around to fetch me. It would be murder."

"Yes."

She met his eyes. "You try to make me afraid of you. But I am not."

"No?"

"No. I am not. But I will return to my cabin, since you want that so much." She paused. "Before I go, will you kiss me good night?"

Silence lengthened and filled the room. His eyes, pools of midnight, fixed on her for a long time.

"No," he said softly.

His word struck like chill water on a dying fire.

But her feet refused to let her run away. She would stand firm, showing him she was neither afraid nor defeated.

Slowly she reached up and drew her finger down the parted placket of his shirt. His pulse beat in his throat and the smooth hollow over his chest was damp with perspiration. She traced the contours of his hard muscle, her fingers exploring the fascination of him. Black curls wound around her fingertip. "You try to be so formidable," she whispered. "You hide so much inside, never letting anyone see."

He remained stone-still. She raised her face to his, but he did not respond, so she kissed his chin, sandpaper rough beneath her lips.

"Good night, Captain," she whispered.

He said nothing. She withdrew her hand, reluctantly letting her fingers slide from the intriguing map of his body. She turned away, clutching the small book to her chest.

He opened the door for her. She refused to look up as she hurried past him, for fear she'd go all foolish and beg for another kiss.

He didn't offer one. He held the door firmly, and just as firmly closed it behind her.

Austin watched Evangeline scurry to the stairs that led to the passenger cabins, moonlight glinting on the lenses of her spectacles. His heartbeat hadn't quite returned to normal, and the chill wind did little to cool his burning blood. Her soft plea for his kiss echoed through his wildest dreams.

His longing had responded with yes, yes, yes! Take her, now, on the bunk, on the floor, it scarcely mattered. Have her, drown in her, use her to erase your fears and your sorrows. Why the hell not?

She had him trapped. She'd be his ruin, his downfall. He knew that, and yet, it had taken all his strength and the clenching of every muscle he possessed to say that one word. *No*.

And then she'd touched him, caressed him, broke him, knowing she had won, no matter what he did or said.

He should have stayed at his post and let her have the damned book.

She hesitated at the top of the stairs, and Austin pulled out his watch. She'd taken three minutes to get this far, and she was rapidly closing on four. A few seconds longer, and he would have to drag her to her cabin, to chastise her, to punish her, to show her who was master of this ship.

She disappeared. He clicked his watch shut, disappointment streaking through him.

The little fool thought it perfectly all right to run about a ship by herself. She had no sense at all of her own danger, from the ship, from his men, from Austin himself. A lone woman aboard a merchant ship faced constant peril, even when the captain did not have designs on her lush little body.

Which was why he'd called Lornham to take his post when he saw her tiptoeing toward his cabin in the dark.

He'd waited long enough to catch her in the act of whatever it was she'd gone to do, then casually entered, as if he'd come to retire.

He still didn't know if she'd come only for the book or if her purpose had been more sinister. He'd found her hiding under the desk, not rifling through it. But he'd know next time. By giving her his own book of devotions, he took away the excuse to come looking for hers. The next time he caught her searching his cabin, she'd have to come up with another story.

He scanned the deck. Where the devil was Albright? She should never have been able to enter his cabin in the first place. He would have to find a second sharp lad to put on the door so his cabin would be guarded around the clock.

He started for the forecastle. All men not on duty would be playing the nightly game of cards and dice, which, for some reason, they thought the captain knew nothing about.

The attack came from out of the blackest shadows of the mainmast. Something struck the back of his knees, and he fell hard, breaking his fall with his hands. His palms smarted as they dug into the rough wood of the deck.

He rolled to his back and caught his tackler with a fast kick. The attacker grunted and faded back into the shadows. Austin dove after him. He contacted with a tough, wiry body that fought him like a madman. They grappled together, rolling on the hard deck, splinters cutting him. Blows rained down on his face, and he blocked them, trying to get an opening to punch back.

A knife gleamed in a shaft of moonlight and the

blade came down, silent and deadly. Austin rolled out of the way and came to his feet in a crouch, arms spread.

The assailant attacked. Austin sidestepped and reached for the knife. The man slipped by, coming around for another wild attack. His face was shrouded in shadow, his hair covered, like the fighting men he'd seen in the East. He was too short to be Wittington, but he might be any number of the crew, including Osborn or Seward.

The man jumped him, sending them both to the deck. He struck with the knife, again and again, swift, silent blows. One sliced Austin's coat to his shoulder, and a brief bright pain touched him.

"Captain!"

Seward's startled voice sang out, and then the young man was there. He grabbed the assailant under the arms and hauled him up. They both disappeared into the shadows.

"He has a knife," Austin panted, his voice choked.

Seward's grunt told him the lad had discovered that. Austin ran after them, but he could see nothing. The moonlight illuminated the huge sails, but left this part of the deck in blackness.

Hurried footsteps sounded behind him, and Lornham's voice asked what was going on. Austin sensed a movement in the dark and grabbed, managing a purchase on the attacker's coat. He hauled him back and snaked his arm around the man's windpipe.

"Sir," Seward croaked. "It's me."

Austin cursed. He released the lieutenant who straightened up and rubbed his throat.

"Where did he go?"

"I don't know. I had hold of him, but he slithered away. I got his knife."

He held it up. Austin took it and went back into the light.

Lornham stopped by his elbow. "Sir? What happened?"

"Someone just tried to kill the captain," Seward announced.

"What? Who?"

"I don't know," Austin said. The knife was ordinary, not a souvenir he could easily match to its owner, but an eating knife that anyone could have gotten in the galley.

"None of the prisoners were missing when I checked earlier, sir," Lornham said. "All accounted for."

"It wasn't a prisoner. He was too crafty to be one of Foster's men, and it wasn't mutiny he had on his mind."

Seward stared. "Bloody hell, sir."

"You spend too much time with that damned Englishman. You sound just like him. Lornham, get back to your post. Seward, you're with me."

"Yes, sir."

Lornham saluted and moved off, giving him a doubtful look. Seward fell into step with Austin as he continued his journey to the forecastle.

A fixed ladder led belowdecks in the bow of the ship. The forecastle was a large open area where the petty officers and the men slept. The senior non-coms had their bunks between small partitions, which gave them a modicum of privacy, but the rest of the men strung hammocks from the beams.

Jennifer Ashley

Some of the hammocks were occupied, but most of the crew gathered in the open space of the floor. Some stood, some crouched, some leaned, hands on knees, to follow the progress of the complicated card and dice game going on there. Wittington crouched among them, calling out bets in his upperclass Englishman's drawl.

Someone saw him.

"The captain!"

Cards and dice fell to the floor. Boots and bare feet slapped on the boards as the men scrambled upright or dropped from hammocks to come to stiff attention. Murmurs died to whispers, which died to silence.

The men watched him out of the corners of their eyes, some in annoyance. This was their sanctum. The captain had no business coming here.

Wittington rose slowly to his feet, his cards still in his hand. "To what do we owe this pleasure, Captain?"

Seward stepped forward before Austin could stop him. "Someone just tried to murder Captain Blackwell. If any of you know anything at all, come forward, now."

No one moved.

"Good lord," Wittington said. "Are you all right? There's blood on your coat."

Austin shook his head. "Barely nicked me. I want to know who went up on deck from here in the last half hour, and who came back down just now. Tell me. It's important.

No one spoke. Seward moved back to him and whispered. "Maybe you should tell them to stand at ease."

Austin reined in his temper. "This is not an inspection. I need to find this man. Start chattering."

"Trouble is, Captain," Wittington said, "we've all been intent on our game. I have eyes only for the cards and the dice when my money is at stake. I for one have no idea who went in and out."

"Anyone else?"

Wittington swept his gaze over the room and gave them a short nod. As if he were their leader, they relaxed a fraction, and began to answer.

But most were no more help than Lord Rudolph. They had been focused on the game and paid no attention to what anyone else did. Some had gone out to the head, some had gone above to take the air when their hand was out, some had gone on duty, or come off it. A few had seen Wittington depart and return in the last half hour, but half a dozen sailors and Mr. Seward had gone in and out, as well.

Austin gave up. The assailant could easily have fled here and blended in with no one the wiser. He asked that anyone who remembered any additional details or knew anything that might prove helpful to seek out Mr. Seward or himself and report.

The men exchanged glances, uneasy. Austin pretended not to notice.

"Albright. I want you back on guard at my cabin door. You're losing anyway if those are your dice on the floor. The rest of you—" He glanced at Wittington's cards, gave the man a skeptical look, and shook his head. "As you were."

He led the way up the ladder with Seward behind. As they reached the top, he heard Wittington drawl a hearty curse.

Chapter Fourteen

Back on the dark foredeck, Austin turned on his first lieutenant. "What were you doing on deck?"

Seward jumped. "Sir?"

"You left the game for a stroll. Why?"

"I had to use the head, sir. When I finished, I heard the noise and found you fighting for your life. Why didn't you call for help?"

Austin thought back to the struggle that had seemed to stretch for a long time, but in reality had lasted only a few minutes. "I don't know. I was too busy trying to stay alive. Do you think you'd recognize the man again?"

"I don't know, sir."

"Damn."

Austin's blood burned, his reflexes straining to fight again. He wanted a clean end, not this uncertainty.

Whoever it was had gotten away and would wait to strike again. An itch sprang up between his shoulder blades, and he resisted the urge to look behind him.

The fight, coming on top of his frustrated desire for Evangeline, tautened his body like a violin string. He needed release.

"You should assign a bodyguard, sir," Seward was saying.

"How do I know that the man I choose to guard me isn't the one trying to kill me?"

"You have a point, sir."

"No, I will have to—"

Something moved behind a pile of sheets, a deeper darkness among the shadows. Adrenaline poured through him. He didn't care if the man had another knife; the attacker was going to answer questions *now*.

He rushed into the darkness and grabbed, closing his arms around a strong, writhing body that tried to shove an elbow into his ribs.

He dragged the assailant out into the light, hauled him to his feet, and spun him around. Moonlight glinted off crooked spectacles and golden-brown hair.

He let out his breath, disappointment swamping him. "Dammit, Evangeline."

She flinched, and he realized how hard he dug his fingers into her shoulders. He let go. "What the hell are you doing out here?"

Her breath came rapidly. "I heard fighting. I grew worried."

"So you decided to investigate? By yourself?"

"I was worried about you. When I reached the deck, a man ran right by me. I tried to grab him, but—"

153

"Sir, she's hurt."

Austin seized her hand and held it up to the moonlight. A dark red gash streaked her palm.

"You tried to grab a man with a knife?"

"I didn't know he had a knife. I'd only heard the fighting at that point. I would have called for help when I spotted you, but I saw Mr. Seward, and I knew you'd be all right."

Seward wrapped his white handkerchief around her hand.

"You should have gone back down," Austin growled. "It wasn't safe."

"I couldn't leave while you were in danger. I might have had to go for more help. I decided to hide until I knew you were not seriously injured."

"Did you get a good look at the man who attacked me?"

"I couldn't see his face. Don't you know who it was?"

"Where did he go?"

"Over there," she gestured vaguely in the direction of the forecastle.

Damn. "And you decided to hide here behind a pile of ropes for the rest of the night?"

"Only until I saw you come up from below again. I wanted to make sure you were all right." She touched his shoulder. "You're hurt."

Austin's built-up tensions erupted in a sudden frenzy. Standing still was no longer bearable. He bent and lifted his little siren, tossing her over his shoulder.

"What are you doing? Put me down!"

A sudden joy kicked through him. He'd wanted to do this for a long, long time. He took his palm and planted it right in the middle of her sweet, round backside.

She squealed.

"I told you, Evangeline. The next time, you were going overboard."

"You cannot. Mr. Seward, help me!"

"Sir, wait—"

"Shut up, Seward."

He carried her to the rail. The ship rose and fell beneath his feet, the sea foam pale in the moonlight. He slid her from his shoulder, and holding her fast, set her rump on the rail.

She clutched the lapels of his coat. "You will not dare toss me overboard."

"Why not? You disobeyed me."

"It will look bad for you."

"Why should I care about that?"

"Because you are an honorable man with an excellent reputation as a captain."

He lowered his face to hers. "I was looking for a promise of obedience, not an appeal to my character."

She shut her eyes tight. "I can't promise obedience."

"Why the devil not?"

"You might be wrong."

He looked at her for a long time. The sea wind floated tendrils of her silken hair over his hand.

She opened one eye, then the other.

"Overboard it is," he said, and gently shoved her backward.

She squealed and threw her arms around his neck. He caught her in a hard embrace and dragged her from the rail. He lifted her face to his and kissed her.

155

He poured all of his anger, his fear, his frustration into that kiss. He pressed his thumbs to the corners of her mouth to force her to open to him. A moan erupted from her throat, and he answered in kind.

His arousal ached. He could lay her back on the ropes, here on the open deck, and lift her skirt and have her.

He felt Seward's stare on the back of his neck. Dammit, the man could at least avert his eyes. But Seward was protective of Evangeline. Austin could not overlook the fact that Evangeline herself could have been his attacker. He doubted it, but his assailant had been small-limbed, and she could have cut her hand when Seward took the knife from her.

When she'd asked him to kiss her good night in his cabin, he'd nearly dragged her back to the bunk and fallen upon her. Every muscle in his body had fought against his command to stand still. Once he gave into his siren, she'd have him. She'd crook her finger, and he'd dance attendance and give her everything she wanted—the documents, his career, himself.

So much safer to stay on deck with Seward to chaperon.

He cradled her head in his hands and let her hair trickle through his fingers. The small, hard points of her breasts rubbed against him through his thin shirt, and she lifted her hips to his in unconscious surrender.

"My siren." He nibbled kisses along her jaw and the outline of her ear.

"Austin," she whispered. "Please do not throw me overboard."

156

He lifted his head, sliding his hands to cup her face. "You promise obedience, then?"

"No."

He touched her forehead with his. "What am I going to do with you, siren?"

"I don't know."

He gazed into her diamond eyes, and lost himself. And in that moment, he suddenly knew what he had to do. The answer came to him as if someone had stood next to him and whispered it into his ear.

"Go back to your cabin, Evangeline."

"Yes. I think that's best."

"Or you can stay out here all night and kiss me."

"I'd like that."

"Yes." He skimmed her lips. "You would like me begging for your kisses in the moonlight, wouldn't you? Weaving your siren's web around me. But we would have to make Mr. Seward stand guard."

Her breath touched him. "That would be unfair to poor Mr. Seward."

"This is my ship. He does what I command."

"But it would be unkind."

He brushed her lips once more, drawing her heat to warm him for his night alone. "If you are so concerned for Mr. Seward, you must go back to your cabin. And stay there this time."

She nodded, her eyes half-closed, her lips parted. His need screamed at him. Seward could turn his back. It wouldn't take long.

He straightened and slid his arm around her waist. She leaned into him, as if her body did not want to give up its place against him.

He made himself guide her across the deck, around the ropes and canvas until they reached the place where Seward waited, a worried look on his face.

"You did not see that, Seward."

" 'Course not, sir."

He unwound his arm from her waist, feeling suddenly ten degrees cooler. "Take Miss Clemens below. I want someone with her any time she leaves her cabin from now on, even when she's answering the call of nature. Understand?"

"Understood, sir."

"Austin—"

He forced the unrelenting captain within him to resurface. "If you do not like the arrangement, you can remain in your cabin until we dock in Boston. I want Seward or Albright or that damned Wittington with you at all times. Or you stay confined." He put his finger on her open lips. "No argument. Now, go to bed." He smiled faintly. "Sweet dreams, Miss Clemens. Seward."

He turned his back on Seward's "Sir" and strode toward the stern. His adrenaline still raged through him; kissing Evangeline hadn't assuaged it. If anything, her kisses had made his wanting worse.

"Good night, Austin."

Her siren's voice floated to him, promising him all the delights that waited under her spinster's gown. His arousal throbbed.

"Bloody hell."

He climbed back to the command deck and took over the watch post from Lornham, who beat a hasty retreat. Clouds were blotting out the stars to the north. Thank God, it looked like rain.

* * *

"Are you feeling better, my rescuer?"

Lord Rudolph climbed to where Evangeline stood in the bow, watching the setting sun. She lifted her bandaged hand in greeting.

"I heal quickly. And the ship's surgeon was so gentle."

He stopped beside her, the dying sun lighting his yellow hair. "Excellent. May I watch the sunset with you?"

She nodded her assent and they turned to face the colorful sky.

"It's quite a spectacle, is it not?" he said after a moment. "I will miss these sunsets once on shore, though I admit I am a bit tired of shipboard life."

Evangeline held the rail as she gazed at the sun disappearing into the sea. She could not imagine how anyone could grow tired of this life. "They are beautiful. I've never seen the like. Watch what happens when the last of it disappears. Any moment now."

She held her breath, waiting for the final streak of beauty that would take them into the night.

Lord Rudolph shaded his eyes. The disk of the sun slipped farther down, and the sea swallowed it. For a moment, the red orb was too bright to look at, reflected by the shimmering sea, then it slid below the horizon and winked out.

As it did, the sky flushed a brilliant green, the azure and gold melting before the emerald.

The breathtaking scene held for one shimmering, verdant moment of beauty. Then the sky darkened, the green glow vanished, and white stars appeared solidly above them.

Evangeline let out her breath. "Is it not splendid?"

"It is, my rescuer. I have seen sunsets at sea, but I never noticed one quite like that."

She pulled her jacket closer against the cooling wind. "Each one has a beauty all its own. We never have such sunsets in England."

"And yet we're so sentimental about good old England, aren't we?" He rested his arms on the rail and sighed. "I will be glad to see her shores again, and London's foggy lanes. I've been away too long."

"But you seem to so enjoy your travels. You tell wonderful stories."

"I do enjoy them, but I intend to cease. My pater's getting elderly, though he does not like to be reminded. Time for this wandering son to return home and learn the business of the estate."

"You sound like Captain Blackwell."

He slanted a smile. "Do I? Does he want to rest, as I do?"

She nodded. "After this voyage, he'll remain in Boston and work there. I think he'll miss the sea, though. I cannot imagine him happily sitting behind a desk the rest of his life."

"Where he cannot make some sailor's life a misery? Neither can I."

She looked at him in surprise. "The captain is a very kind man. His crewmen aren't miserable."

Lord Rudolph held up his hand. "Please. I admire Captain Blackwell and sense he's a man of intelligence, but do not spin me fables of his kindness. He is ruthless, and will do what he must for what he wants or what he perceives is right."

"He might be ruthless, but he is also kind."

He chuckled. "I vow, you're smitten with him."

Her face heated. "Indeed not."

"Your maidenly blush belies your protest. No, no, sheath your claws, kitten, I did not come here to tease you. I came to ask what you intended to do once you reach Boston."

She took a firmer grip on the rail. "I have a cousin there. She will—"

"I know, she has found a position for you as a governess. The captain told me." He shook his head. "Give up the idea, Evangeline. A woman like you deserves better than to wait on some merchant's brats. I have been meaning to ask you this for some time, but I wanted to give you a chance to rest first." He faced her. "I'd like you to return to England with me."

Evangeline's lips parted, and a sudden longing welled up inside her, fierce and sharp. To return with Lord Rudolph would not carry the disgrace she'd face if Austin sent her back. Traveling as the guest of a peer's son would be much different than being shipped home as a nuisance. Tendrils of hope shot to her very fingertips. "Return—? No, it is impossible. There is nothing for me in England."

"You do not have to go back to your mother and stepfather. They all but tossed you out, like jewels on the family dungheap. Come with me to London, to stay with my family. My mother would love you."

She blanched. "Your mother? The marchioness of Blandesmere? Why would she interest herself in the likes of me?"

The wind carried his hair into his face, and he

brushed it impatiently aside. "In the first place, because you would bring her wandering son home to her. Second, you are perfectly adorable. She has lamented that I have no sisters since I can remember, as if this is somehow a failing of *my* character. She will rub her hands with glee at the chance to matchmake for you. She's quite a matchmaker, God knows." A note of bitterness entered his voice.

"Matchmaker?" Evangeline squeaked.

"Good lord, yes. She'd find you a husband that would put dear Harley to shame. You could trample him beneath your slippers, if you deemed him worthy of even that."

Anna Adams had said something similar. But what Lord Rudolph offered was so different than what Anna had promised. A good marriage would bring her wealth and respect for the rest of her life. And he offered it offhand, as if such gentlemen were strewn about waiting to be plucked up.

"A husband who values you," he went on. "One whose estates and fortune would keep you in silks the rest of your life. Who knows? My mother might find you a peer. Even a marquess." He flashed a grin.

Evangeline did not feel like smiling back. The ship swayed, and her seasickness suddenly returned.

She had reconciled herself to the thought that she would never see England again. Never see the green hills of the Cotswolds, nor its misty lanes, its sheep-strewn meadows, its quiet villages. She had turned her back, and that was that.

But the Wittington family was a powerful one. Her stepbrother's gossip and her mother's magazines had told her that. Lord Rudolph did not boast idly that his mother easily could find an eligible gentlemen for her. The marchioness presided over the best circles, knew everyone, appeared in every society paper. If she did not quail at her son dragging home plain Miss Clemens and laying her at her feet, Evangeline would no doubt be in very good hands.

The world opened new possibilities. She shivered.

"But I am ruined. Captain Blackwell said that. I have run about unescorted on frigates and broken into prisons. No gentleman will want a disgraced wife."

"You leave that to me. I'll spin a tale that makes you the golden heroine. Gentlemen will fall all over themselves to propose to you."

She clutched the rail. He had the power to do it, to wipe her free of stain and dare anyone to talk. He was the son of a marquess, who was lower in rank only to a duke. Just the thought of that kind of power made her dizzy.

"It would be horribly scandalous for us to travel together," she said weakly.

He waved that aside. "We will hire a companion for you in Boston. And I will persuade Captain Blackwell to release your stepbrother. He is only guilty of foolishness. We will all journey together."

She turned to the sliver of horizon still visible. Ahead, to the west, lay America. They would be there in a few days' time. She would leave behind the heady chill of the sea wind, the glee of the waves rising and falling under the ship, the glorious singing of the wind in the rigging. She would leave behind the ship's captain, a man who loved the freedom of the sea. A man who had kissed her with passion, as if she were a great beauty rather than a plain spinster with spectacles. She felt hollow.

"I don't know."

"Think on it. There is nothing for you in America; only a servant's life. You can be mistress of a great house, with servants of your own. I want this for you. What better reward could I give my rescuer?"

He caught her hand and lifted it to his lips. She barely felt the caress.

"Lord Rudolph—"

He grinned at her. "I'd be honored if you called me Rudy. As my intimates do."

Intimates. Evangeline glanced at his handsome face, his roguish smile. Many a maiden could swoon over this gentleman. She imagined him in the ballrooms of London, dressed in kid breeches and embroidered frock coat, his hair sleek gold beneath the candlelight. She imagined many young ladies vying for his attentions.

"Why haven't you married, Lord Rudolph? I mean, Rudy. Certainly you are a most eligible match."

His grin died. He released her hand and leaned on the rail again, staring out into the growing darkness. "Now that is a long story. I will tell it to you someday."

"I would be most interested. It is odd that no lady has yet ensnared you. You and Captain Blackwell are of an age, yet he had a wife who has been gone these five years now, Mr. Seward said."

"We are of very different circumstance." His voice

sounded distant, portraying no interest in Captain Blackwell.

He turned to her suddenly, his blue eye glittering in the darkness. "Evangeline. Marry me."

Chapter Fifteen

Evangeline gaped. The ship pitched and she nearly lost her balance. "What did you say?"

His hand whitened on the rail. "I said marry me, you silly girl."

"*Marry* you?"

"Don't say it as though it repelled you. Dammit, Evangeline. Blackwell has designs on you. You are not safe from him. I've heard tell that he's kissed you. More than once."

Her face heated. A wave of spray scattered icy droplets on her scalding cheeks. "He may have."

His lip curled. "Unwise of you to let him, my dear. Though I suppose to a young woman he is dashing. We can marry quietly in Boston, then take a ship to England. *Fait accompli*."

"Why on earth should you want to marry *me*?"

"Why not?"

"Because I am, as you called me, a silly girl, and not very pretty at that. And I have no connections or money to speak of. You will one day be a marquess. You must not throw yourself away on me."

"Who put it into your head that you are not pretty? It wasn't the captain was it? I'll run him through."

She stared in amazement. "Good heavens, no. He—he said—" She flushed. "He's said many things, but he never called me ugly."

"He is a blackguard. But I am not. The marriage can be in name only if you like. I offer it to save you from his attentions and to give you what you deserve."

She put her hand on his shoulder and gently smoothed his black sleeve. "You offer it for other reasons, too. I don't know what they are, but when you asked me, you were thinking of something else. As if you'd suddenly thought of a clever idea. And marrying me was part of it."

His jaw hardened. "I would never use you in so base a fashion, Evangeline."

"Perhaps I wrong you. But you've confounded me. I don't have an answer for you—not even about going back with you to England. Give me time to think."

"Of course, my dear, take all the time you like. We don't land for another few days."

A few days. To decide the rest of her life.

She turned and walked away from him. Lord Rudolph didn't follow. Above her, the sails billowed, full and white in the growing darkness. Three sailors pulled a line, hand over hand, adjusting a topsail to the changing wind.

Evangeline watched, her troubled thoughts slipping and sliding where she could not catch them. She made herself focus on the fascinating mechanics of the *Aurora*. She'd always thought ships kept their sails square to a tailwind, and couldn't imagine what happened to them when the wind didn't blow in the right direction. But the three-masted vessel was a marvel of engineering. The sailors could change the angle of the sails to take advantage of almost all winds, even those perpendicular to the ship. A simple adjustment of the rudder, and they ran straight where they wanted to go. Or they did the little zigzag through the water that Mr. Seward called tacking.

She watched the sailors wind up the line and tie it fast. They took themselves off to another task, laughing among themselves. From far forward the glow of the galley winked, the cook preparing food for the men and officers.

When Evangeline turned back to the rail, Lord Rudolph had gone. She drew a breath of cold sea air. Marry him. Good heavens. Had he gone mad?

She had a vision of herself, gowned in silk and decked in jewels, receiving guests at a Mayfair mansion while her dashing, blond husband stood next to her. Of Harley, dismayed when he saw her, of her own stepbrother apologizing for the slights he'd made her in the past.

Spray stung her face, and the dream vanished. It was difficult to be a regal lord's wife with flyaway hair and spectacles.

But he offered her salvation. Whether she went back to England as his wife or his guest, she could begin her

— Join the Historical Romance Book Club —
and GET 4 FREE* BOOKS NOW!

A $23.96 Value!

Yes! I want to subscribe to the Historical Romance Book Club.

Please send me my **4 FREE* BOOKS.** I have enclosed $2.00 for shipping/handling. Each month I'll receive the four newest Historical Romance selections to preview for 10 days. If I decide to keep them, I will pay the Special Members Only discounted price of just $4.24 each, a total of $16.96, plus $2.00 shipping/handling ($23.55 US in Canada). This is a **SAVINGS OF AT LEAST $5.00** off the bookstore price. There is no minimum number of books I must buy, and I may cancel the program at any time. In any case, the **4 FREE* BOOKS** are mine to keep.

*In Canada, add $5.00 shipping/handling per order for the first shipment. For all future shipments to Canada, the cost of membership is $23.55 US, which includes shipping and handling. (All payments must be made in US dollars.)

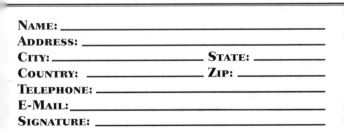

NAME: _____

ADDRESS: _____

CITY: _____ **STATE:** _____

COUNTRY: _____ **ZIP:** _____

TELEPHONE: _____

E-MAIL: _____

SIGNATURE: _____

life all over again. No matter that she'd helped in a mutiny, or broken into a prison, or run away to an English frigate. No matter that she'd begun as a plain spinster, whose one suitor had betrayed her. No matter that her parents had considered her an inconvenient weight on their shoulders.

He could give her a new life. She had but to take it.

Farther to stern, Captain Blackwell emerged from the stairs to his cabin. He stopped and spoke to Mr. Osborn, nodding at something the lieutenant said. Mr. Osborn saluted and moved on, and the captain climbed the ladder to the command deck above.

Evangeline moved to the shadow of the mast, not wanting him to see her and toss her below or berate Mr. Seward for leaving her unescorted. He did not seem to notice her. He turned his face to the stars, studying the sharp pricks of white light. His bare head gleamed in the moonlight, his hair dark and sleek. He looked down again and made a motion to one of his officers. The officer's voice raised as he shouted an order. Several sailors jumped up and unwound another line.

He laid his hands on the rail, one knee bent as he stared out over the dark waters. He belonged here. Tall and immovable, he faced the sea, his home.

For a long time he watched the sea, then he turned from the rail and looked unerringly at Evangeline.

She froze. Their gazes locked across the deck, his dark eyes held her in place as easily as if he stood next to her.

He descended the ladder and headed toward the mainmast. Sailors scurried out of his way. He stopped a few feet before her, his hands behind his back, his hard face sharp with shadow.

"Miss Clemens."

"Hello, Captain."

"I must ask the obvious question. Why aren't you below?"

"I was watching the sunset. The air is so pleasant, isn't it? I thought I'd stay above."

"You are hindering my men in their duties."

One sailor glanced up, his mouth open in surprise. The captain shot him a look, and the sailor suddenly became very absorbed in tying off a line.

"I was going to take a stroll. Before retiring."

He held out his hand. "Stroll with me."

She took his hand, closing her eyes briefly as his warm, calloused fingers folded over hers. Lord Rudolph had behaved as if Austin had forced his attentions upon her. She'd found it too difficult to explain that she'd thrown herself at the captain, begging for his kisses, his touch, his caress. With his hard hand on hers, she realized why she begged for him so. She simply could not help herself.

They moved forward of the mainmast, directly to the short ladder that led to the officer's and passenger cabins.

She pulled back. "I thought we were taking a walk."

"We are. We are walking to your cabin."

"Why? So you can lock me in?"

"No. I want to speak with you."

"We cannot speak while walking about the deck?"

"No."

She gave up. The quiet of the ward room filled her

ears as they left the wind behind. Lornham lingered at the table, a wine glass in one hand and a thick book in the other.

"Mr. Lornham."

He jumped, nearly spilling his wine, and scrambled to his feet. "Sir?"

"Where is Wittington?"

"Lord Rudolph, sir? He's uh—yes, I saw him. I think he went to the forecastle."

"For the nightly card game. Why don't you join him?"

Lornham shook his head. "I don't play, sir."

"But you might place a wager, all the same."

"I don't game at all, sir. Gambling's a crippling vice."

Austin fixed him with a gaze. Lornham flushed. "But I might uh—take a turn about the deck. Fine weather."

Without waiting for Austin's dismissal, he saluted hastily, tucked his book under his arm, and hurried up the stairs.

Austin watched him go. Then he opened the door of Evangeline's tiny cabin and gestured her inside.

She scurried in. The narrow confines of the cabin emphasized the tossing of the ship. The floor heaved, then dropped, and she clutched the wooden post that kept the bunk in place. Austin rested his hand lightly on the doorframe, never losing his balance, drat the man.

"Well, here I am, Captain. Out of the way of your men. Only, I cannot fathom why you sent away Lieutenant Lornham. I was hardly in *his* way."

"I wanted to talk to you privately."

He took a step inside the rocking cabin. Evangeline took a step back. She met the curved wall of the hull.

His gaze flicked from her face and moved down her body. She tightened her hold on the post, and a splinter worked its way into her finger.

"My marriage was a disaster," he said.

Evangeline let go of the post and sucked her finger. "Your wife died, I know. Mr. Seward told me. I'm sorry."

"The marriage failed before that. I obtained a separation from her."

"Oh." A separation meant they had been married in name only. It meant he had paid her an allowance and lived apart from her. Although separation carried nowhere near the stigma of divorce, it was shocking all the same.

"She hated my life and everything that went with it. Hated me, too. I tried—" He broke off, staring at the doorframe where his fingers rested.

"It must have hurt you dreadfully," she said softly. "You must have loved her."

He went on, as if he hadn't heard her. "This time, things will be different. I will not sail any more, but live out my life in Boston. My wife will see me every day, same as a banker's wife or a lawyer's wife sees her husband. My days will be routine; my habits clockwork. My wife will sit down to supper every evening with me, rise with me in the morning, retire with me at night. She will spend no long months alone, wondering if the ship has gone down and the sea has swallowed me. We will walk on the Common on Sundays and attend balls on Saturdays and visit the vicar."

"Will you?"

"Yes, we will."

Her mouth went dry. "We—"

"No woman likes a wandering husband. I will stay at home and walk to work every morning, while you buy frocks and furniture and whatever else it is wives get up to during the day. You will see to the domestic staff and keep the fires stirred, and I will pay for it all. That is the usual arrangement, isn't it?"

"Austin."

He broke off. "What?"

"Please tell me what the devil you are talking about."

"I am asking you to marry me. And watch your tongue. You curse like a sailor."

She thumped back against the bulkhead. "Marry *you?*"

"Yes. Marry *me*. Is it so repugnant?"

She opened and closed her mouth, trying to find the air that had deserted her lungs. "I am—dazed, that is all. Why do you want to marry me?"

His voice turned rough. "Siren. Can you ask me that?"

She shivered all the way to her toes. The splinter pricked her, and she popped her finger in her mouth again. "You cannot marry me." She spoke around her finger. "You are already married. To the sea."

His scowl returned. "What?"

"You have but one mistress, and her name is *Aurora*."

"What are you talking about? I will give up the *Aurora*, marry you, and settle down."

"You do not look happy about it."

"I do not—Good God, Evangeline, what has that to do with it? And why the devil are you sucking your finger?"

"I have a sliver."

"A sliver."

"From the post." She pointed at it.

He came to her and dragged her hand from her mouth. "Let me see."

She winced as he folded her fingers back. "It's only a tiny one."

"That doesn't matter. It may fester."

He raised her hand to the light, then isolated the offended finger. His bulk rested warm against her, his thigh pressing her hip as he gently pried at the sliver.

She studied the sweep of his dark lashes as he focused on his task. His hair burned red under the lantern light, like polished mahogany. One long lock of it, escaping its binding, straggled down his neck.

"There." He eased out the tiny bit of wood and dropped it. He raised the hurt finger to his lips.

"Thank you."

He moved his kiss to her next finger. Ever so gently, he sucked the tip of it.

Evangeline swallowed. "I have no sliver in that one."

His dark gaze swept up to regard her. He moved to the next finger, again caressing with his mouth.

A feeling almost like panic welled up inside her. "Why are you doing that?"

He sucked the tip of her smallest finger. "So you will ask me to kiss you."

"You do not mind it when I ask you to kiss me?"

"No."

"I—I supposed you thought me silly, or forward, or unwomanly, or—"

"Evangeline. Ask me to kiss you."

She drew a hoarse breath. "Captain Blackwell, will you—"

"Call me Austin."

"Austin. Will you kiss me?"

He leaned down, and smoothed her hair from her face. "Indeed, I will. If you promise to become my wife."

Chapter Sixteen

The ship pitched suddenly. Evangeline lost her balance. She stumbled backward, hitting her knee against the bunk. "Ouch!"

Austin caught her in his steady arms. "Take care, Evangeline."

"I am sorry. I am not as used to ships as you are."

"Why are you apologizing? An ocean swell is not your fault."

"Perhaps I should say I am not used to kissing in small cabins on board ship."

"Neither am I."

"Then perhaps we should give up the enterprise."

"Not likely, my siren."

He lifted her, his strength startling. He cradled her to him and turned with her, almost as if they danced, and rested her back against the doorframe.

"Austin, I—"

"Hush."

His mouth came down on hers. She met it hungrily, letting her confusion and astonishment die in a rush of warmth. His lips opened hers, and he sought her, his body pressing her against the ridged doorframe. She cupped his shoulders, her fingers sinking into his coat. She welcomed him, melting for the now familiar fire of his tongue.

She hooked one leg around him, drawing her booted foot up his thigh. Never mind that she was wanton. Never mind that Miss Pyne would swoon. His hard arousal wedged against her heat, fanning the flames already inside her. She shifted a little, rubbing against him.

Passion scalded her. She moved her hands to his hair, smoothing it under her palm, drawing it from its queue so she could bury her fingers in it.

He made a noise in his throat and lifted his lips a fraction from hers. "Siren. Damn you. Blessed siren."

He touched the hooks of her bodice, parted them, while his lips came against hers again. Cool air touched bare skin, and then his hand, warm and large, slid beneath the fabric.

She arched back, wanting her breasts in his hands, wanting her secret places to twine with his, wanting his body to take hers. She locked him to her with her wanton foot, and played her hands through his beautiful, beautiful hair.

A step sounded in the ward room.

Evangeline jumped, and would have screamed, except that Austin was still kissing her. She jerked her hands from his hair, unwound the foot that disgraced her, and squirmed away from his mouth.

He stared at her, his dark brows like thunder. "Dammit, Evangeline."

"I would call you out," Lord Rudolph's mild tones sounded behind him. "But I do not know how to steer this barge. Once we reach port, however—"

Austin turned. He took in Lord Rudolph, his stance, his scowl, then very carefully removed his hand from Evangeline's bosom. He lowered her gently to the floor.

"It is a ship. Not a barge."

"I do not care what the devil you call it. Dear God, to find you pawing her, you blackguard, you bastard—"

Evangeline hastened to him. "Lord Rudolph. I mean, Rudy, he didn't—I mean, I asked him to kiss me."

Austin swung around. *"Rudy?"*

She clasped her hands. "Austin."

"Austin?" Lord Rudolph quivered.

"I did ask him to kiss me, Lord Rudolph. I am afraid I am quite wanton."

"You are not wanton," Austin and Lord Rudolph said at the same time.

"This is not the first time I've asked him to kiss me. On the occasion of our first meeting, I tried to seduce him, even though I did so for fear of my life and his. I have never been wanton until now, but it seems that I have become so. What I mean is, if you do not want to marry me, Lord Rudolph, I will understand."

Austin glared. *"Marry you?"*

"Yes, Captain," Lord Rudolph snarled. "The girl you were fondling is my future wife."

"The woman I was kissing is *my* future wife."

"No, indeed. I asked her to marry me not an hour ago."

"I asked her to marry me not ten minutes ago."

Both men turned to Evangeline.

She wished the floor would open so she could fall to the deck below and spend the rest of the voyage huddled behind the cargo. She looked at Austin. "I would have told you. But then I had the sliver—"

Lord Rudolph started. "You had the *what?*"

She held up her forefinger. "A sliver. Of wood. In my finger."

"Are you trying to wrap both your hands in bandages? But we are wandering from the point. I arrived here to find the captain forcing his attentions on you."

"He wasn't forcing—"

"Yes, I was," Austin broke in. "I would have forced more attentions on her, if you had remained at your card game."

"Do not boast to me of your filthy intentions. I will marry her and put her out of reach of men like you forever."

"*You* will not come within ten feet of her. I will marry her and keep her from lying Englishmen such as yourself."

They faced each other, shoulders squared.

"You go too far, Captain."

"Not far enough, Wittington. Tell her who you really are and why you were roaming the Caribbean. Or maybe I'll have you spend the rest of the voyage in the brig."

Lord Rudolph took a step closer to him. "So you can ravish her in peace? I will not allow it."

Austin took another step. "I determine what is allowed and not allowed on my ship."

"It's the captain's privilege to ravish the women? You *are* a bastard—"

"Stop it, both of you!"

Both men broke off with a start. Evangeline pushed between them and placed one hand on each gentlemen's chest. A girlhood friend had once told her of two rival gentleman who had fought for her hand. She'd laughed and said how delightful it was. Evangeline didn't find it delightful at all. She felt sick.

"I have not said I will marry either of you! I did ask Captain Blackwell to kiss me, and I do not know why he says otherwise. I think you are both horrible, and I would be well rid of the pair of you!"

They both stared at her in astonishment.

Biting back a sob, Evangeline pushed away from them and ran from the passage. She scurried across the wardroom, scarcely able to breathe, then charged up the stairs to the welcome air of the deck.

Lieutenant Lornham, who chose that moment to return from his walk, ran straight into her. His weathered face blurred before her tear-filled eyes. He stared at her, stared down the stairs to the ward room, stared at her again, then turned his back and walked swiftly away.

Wittington's hand landed on Austin's shoulder. "Let her go. She needs to be alone."

Austin longed to ball his fist and punch Lord Rudolph in his remaining good eye. He wanted to dash up the stairs after Evangeline and shake her until she promised to marry him and him alone. But he forced his temper to cool. The one thing he had learned during his disastrous marriage and his equally disastrous affairs was how to read the signs when women wanted to be run after, and when they did not.

He turned back to Wittington. "You asked her to marry you. What claim do you have upon her?"

"She is an Englishwoman. And she's done me a good turn. She deserves a reward, as I told you. What claim have you?"

"My claim is that I—" He hesitated. "I have need of a wife. She would do well with me."

"She would do better with me."

"That is a matter of opinion. Her opinion. It is her choice."

"I can give her wealth, prestige, respect, a title. What can you give her? The pay packet of a used-up captain."

"I have a fine house in Boston and plenty of money. She would be well-respected as my wife."

"I can make her the marchioness of Blandesmere."

"There is nothing wrong with her becoming Mrs. Blackwell."

Except that his first wife had hated it. Evangeline might, too. Lord Rudolph held higher cards than he, and the man knew it. What woman would not prefer to marry into the peerage? She was English. No doubt she'd want English money and an English name. Perhaps the pair of them would run about the world and spy together.

His muscles tensed. Imagining her anywhere near Wittington made him boil with rage. He'd be damned if he let her go that easily.

Wittington was still arguing. "Her brother might have a thing or two to say about it."

"He is her stepbrother, she is of age, and forced marriages are a thing of the past." He squared his shoulders. "I am going up to make certain she is all right."

Lord Rudolph didn't try to stop him this time. Austin swarmed up the ladder, his blood pounding, his temper at the breaking point. It had taken him two days since the moment he'd realized that he needed to marry Evangeline to work out how to propose to her. In the night he'd thought of speeches, which, when he wrote them down in the light of day looked foolish and insipid. And when he'd finally blurted out—all wrong—that he wanted to marry her, he'd discovered Wittington had gotten in before him by half an hour.

He'd have to explain to her why marrying him was the best solution to their problem. She did not want to go back to England; he didn't want her going anywhere with Wittington. Her governess plan would no longer work, and like Wittington, he did not want to see her in such servitude. Nor did he want to hand her to a magistrate for her innumerable crimes. Whether she was guilty or not, he could not give over his siren to be hanged or imprisoned.

Ergo, he must marry her. It was the only way.

As he gained the windswept deck, he heard Wittington following. He bit back curse words and scanned the deck for Evangeline.

She appeared to be fine. She was standing at the forward rail with Lieutenant Seward, speaking to him rapidly and earnestly. He held her hands in his, and made the occasional nod, as if soothing her.

Lord Rudolph halted behind Austin. "You know, Blackwell, we are two virile fellows, not unattractive to the female sex. Why then, does the woman of our dreams flee us for a chap like your Lieutenant Seward?"

Austin ground his teeth. As he watched, Seward reached out and brushed a tear from Evangeline's cheek.

He growled at Wittington and stomped away to find some distasteful and back-breaking task he could give to Mr. Seward.

Two days out of port, the weather changed. A bank of leaden clouds rolled in, the sea rose, and squalls of rain spated down on the sailors who hunkered in their coats and tucked their raw hands under their arms for warmth.

While not a full-blown storm, the weather slowed their progress to a crawl while they battled prevailing winds. Austin bent his back with his men to trim sails and roll canvas. Rain beat on his bare head and trickled irritatingly down his spine. His crew wore the grim looks of men trying not to crack under impatience and strain. They were so close to home, and yet the sea pushed them back.

Both Evangeline and Lord Rudolph stayed below, out of the weather. Austin seethed. He had half a mind to order Lord Rudolph to lend his aristocratic hands to help. They needed every man. Seward had stood more than one double watch, and the young man was near to exhaustion. Austin imagined Lord Rudolph sitting snugly with Evangeline in the ward room, drinking tea and persuading her to return to England with him, maybe inspiring her to ask *him* for a kiss.

Damn, and damn, and damn. He needed to get her safely married to him so he could let his passions free and keep that blasted Englishman away from her. He threw back his head and let the rain hit his face full force. It cooled his scalding cheeks, but did little to quash his ardor. Never in his life had a woman prevailed over a rainstorm.

Toward the end of the first day, the sun made a brief appearance, slanting through a tear in the clouds. An eerie yellow light bathed them all, turning the men's faces a sickly color. Then the ray winked out, and darkness closed in.

Austin ordered lanterns lit.

"You should turn in, sir," Osborn called to him. "It's been a double watch for you, hasn't it? Weather's lightened a little."

"It may turn worse."

Osborn shook his head. "If it does, I'll wake you, sir."

Austin nodded. His lieutenant spoke wisely, even if he was loathe to agree. A well-rested captain thought better than an exhausted one.

He told Osborn to take over and for Lornham to help him, then left the command deck. He trudged wearily to the stairs that would take him to his cabin. Damn weather. Well, it would all be over soon. He'd sail into Boston, turn over his cargo and the dangerous papers and go home. Forever.

He paused in the passage. Albright was absent again. The lad did tend to slip away to relieve himself, or to have a quick nip of grog with the men or play a hand of cards. Or maybe he'd reasoned that no one would try to enter the cabin in this weather. Everyone was either on deck working or asleep.

Still, Austin's pulse quickened. He remembered the heart-stopping evening when he'd opened the door to find Evangeline sitting under his desk with her thick book of devotions in her hands. She'd returned it readily enough, but not before his heart had lodged itself in his throat. Every time he convinced himself of her innocence, she'd shake his faith again.

He tamped down on his irritation and opened the door.

He stopped. He waited until the searcher turned his head, and saw him.

"Albright," he said quietly. "I'll restrain myself from killing you as long as you tell me who sent you."

185

Chapter Seventeen

Albright's face turned putty gray.

He had not found the letter. He held a locked wooden box, in which Austin kept papers relating to the cargo and mail he delivered from port to port.

"Who do you work for, Albright? Speak up lad. Or would a flogging loosen your tongue?"

Austin rarely sentenced the lash, and then never to excess, preferring to have his sailors whole and well rather than maimed or dead. But in his fury he made the threat, and it wouldn't hurt to put the fear of God into the boy.

Albright's face screwed up. "Traitor! We'll see justice done, and men like you will die a traitor's death."

"Fine words, lad. I could argue that you are the traitor."

"You would say that. You don't know what loyalty

186

and honor mean. You broke from England because it was inconvenient to you, because you could make more money separated from the old country. You dragged us all with you for your convenience."

"You were a child during the war, Albright. You have no idea why we fought. Men died to be free of a crown that bled us dry and took everything we had, even our dignity, even our hearts. They will not give that up again."

"The new country will never hold. Everyone knows it. England will retake it, and the traitors will pay."

"You bandy those words as if you know what they mean. Who sent you, boy?"

"I will never tell you!"

He hurled the box at Austin. Austin brought up his arm and deflected it, but in that instant, Albright sprinted for the door. Austin clamped down on his shoulder, spinning him around. Albright aimed a punch at Austin's face. He sidestepped, caught the boy's fist and twisted Albright's arm behind his back.

Austin had good strength. But Albright was young and enraged and he fought like a wild thing. Austin only wanted to knock some sense into him and wrest from him the name of his employer. But Albright was trying to kill him, just as he'd tried to kill him a week ago on the dark deck.

The boy wrenched himself from Austin's grasp and dashed through the door and down the passage. He'd gained the first step when Austin grabbed him around the waist and pulled him back. Albright swung, a knife in his hand. Austin ducked, avoiding the blow. His hold loosened, and Albright shoved him away and charged up the stairs.

Austin scrambled after him. Albright sprinted across the deck, shoving aside bewildered sailors as he ran.

Austin pounded after him. The rain bit his face. The lanterns threw eerie circles of light into the wet and mist. Through it, Albright ran. He gained the forward bow, leapt up on the rail, and hurled himself over the side.

Austin swore. A splash sounded far below.

A shout went up. "Man overboard!"

Seward screamed over the wind. "Turn! Throw him a line!"

Sailors scrambled to obey. Austin ignored them. Albright would die before they could turn the ship to find him, before they could throw ropes to his struggling body.

He stripped off his coat. He vaulted to the top of the rail, raised his arms and dove into blackness and the waiting sea.

Before he hit the water, he heard Evangeline scream.

Evangeline rushed to the rail. She slammed into it, the sturdy wood bruising her abdomen. From far below, she heard a splash.

"Austin!" she screamed.

A strong arm caught her about the waist. "Bloody hell, Evangeline, you'll go over."

"Help him!" She strained to catch sight of him, pulling against Lord Rudolph's arm. The ship lurched and turned and lurched again. Rain stung her face, mixing with her tears.

Seward bellowed orders like a sea dog with twenty years under his belt. Men scurried to obey him. Evangeline leaned over the rail as far as she could, but saw nothing but the dark, roiling water. No head broke the surface, no man floated there.

Lord Rudolph's voice sounded in her ear. "They will find him. They are lowering the boats."

Her voice caught on sobs. "It will take too long."

"Evangeline, damn you, don't you dare jump in, too."

She clutched the rail until it gouged her hands. Far below, ropes flung by the sailors bobbed on the surface. A rowboat slowly winched downward, lanterns hanging on its sides.

And then she saw him. The ship had turned, and he surfaced far to starboard, out of reach of the ropes. He was only visible because he'd emerged in a patch of sea foam made luminous by the chance ray of a lantern.

"There!" she screamed.

Seward bellowed. "Hard to starboard. Get that boat in the water, now!"

The rowboat hit the waves and rocked. Two men crawled rapidly down to it and began to row furiously toward where Evangeline pointed.

Far below, Austin swam through the water, arms propelling him away from the ship. Then a great wave washed over him, and he was gone.

Albright, damn you boy, where are you? Austin surfaced again, blowing hard, his lungs aching. It was madness to try to find him in this murk. He could have swum anywhere, or been sucked down by the water, his body tossed far away.

Austin dove. He reached out blindly, hoping God and his luck would aid him. When he broke the surface again, he dimly heard the commotion onboard. They were trying to reach him. The water was ice cold, already numbing his limbs. What madness had possessed him to dive in after the boy?

Because he knew the efforts of his men would never reach Albright in time. Because Albright had decided death under the waves preferable to betraying whoever had sent him.

Damn, damn, damn. Austin stroked through the black water, groping for a body, for flailing limbs, for anything to seize. He came up for breath. A wave swamped him. The sea pulled him under before he was ready, and water surged into his mouth. He fought back toward the sweet rain-drenched air. Another wave carried him sideways, but at last, his head broke the surface. He coughed and flailed, and felt something kick him.

Austin grabbed and found his hands full of coat. He gulped air, and went under. He tightened his hold on the coat and tried to drag Albright's head above the waves.

The young man was still alive. And strong. He fought, pummelling and twisting. Austin hung on grimly, kicking hard to reach the surface. Albright suddenly flung his arm around Austin's neck and dragged him down.

They fell together. The sea closed overhead, black and final, blotting out light and noise and air. Albright fought like a mad thing. Austin was trying to save him;

Albright sought their deaths. His arm tightened around Austin's throat, pulling him down, farther down, away from the precious surface.

Austin's lungs burned, compressing, begging for air. He knew at any moment, he would no longer be able to control the desperate gasp for breath, and with that uncontrolled gulp for air, he would die.

He brought his elbow up hard and hit Albright in the groin. The lad doubled over, his grip loosening. Austin kicked for the surface. He was breaking the water, opening his mouth for air, when Albright's arm clamped tight on his neck again and pulled him back down.

Green and black water smashed against him. His lungs felt like fire, his legs weak, numb. Albright held on. They sunk, away from air, away from life.

Austin had faced death before. In his long career, the sea had nearly claimed him a dozen times. A dozen times, he'd fought his way back to life, defeating uncaring death to survive another day.

Those other times, he had recognized that his death would not matter. He would die, but the world would continue. Once, just after his separation from his wife, he'd fallen from the yardarm into roiling seas. He'd not fought very hard then. A lieutenant had pulled him out of the drink at the last moment, and Austin remembered wondering whether the young man had done him a favor.

This time was different. This time, Austin did not want to die. This time he had something to live for, a reason to fight for life.

A spinster with spectacles. A gray-eyed, soft-skinned

woman he desired. She'd given him a tantalizing glimpse of the joy of herself, and he wanted more. The sea, and Albright, and the irritating Lord Rudolph would not keep him from her.

Austin. Her flute-like voice seemed to wrap around him, touching his flesh with warmth. *Austin.*

His cold limbs relaxed, reaching for that warmth. He felt himself open his arms for her, draw her to him, bend his head to touch her lips.

She smiled at him, her mouth wide, her arms wrapping around him. She stroked him and kissed him, and Austin closed his eyes. Yes, I want this, my siren. I want you.

Austin. Come to me.

He reached for her, opening his mouth. Her warmth poured in.

Albright's fingers, heavy and lifeless, dragged across his throat.

The shock jerked his eyes open. He realized that he'd stopped struggling, that he dangled among the waves, letting the numbness envelope him. Albright hung on him, his body a dead weight.

Austin clamped his arm around Albright's neck and clawed for the surface. He broke it within seconds, the rain-studded wind flowing over him, freezing him. He opened his mouth and air poured into his lungs like cold sand. He coughed, fighting to tread water and to drag Albright up with him.

His heart pounded furiously, pumping blood, drawing air. He'd come so close to sleeping forever in the seductive drift of the ocean. He welcomed the sting of rain on his face, the cramp in his arm that held Albright's head above the surface, because all of it meant he was alive.

The gunwale of a rowboat nearly knocked him in the head. He put his hand up, deflecting it. The boat swerved and three anxious faces peered over the side.

With all his strength, Austin flung Albright up toward them. The men caught him and dragged his limp body on board. Austin reached for the gunwale, but his fingers were too numb to find purchase on the slippery side.

Three pairs of hands caught his arms and pulled him upward. He rolled over the side and landed at the bottom of the rowboat, which was blessedly solid.

"Well done," he rasped at them.

His voice caught, hoarse and unintelligible. He coughed and spat. The sailors grabbed oars, and rowed hard for the ship.

When Austin climbed over the rail and back onto the deck, Evangeline's knees went slack with relief. Only Lord Rudolph's grip kept her from falling entirely.

His dark hair was plastered to his head, his clothes were dark with water, and blood trickled down his cheek. But he stood upright, face flushed, scowl in place.

Two sailors dumped Albright unceremoniously in front of him. The young man groaned, still alive, barely conscious.

Austin flopped him over with his boot. "Get him dried out, and put him in the brig."

His voice grated, raw and harsh, his low baritone ruined by the sea.

Osborn looked at him in surprise. "On what charge, sir?"

"Theft. And nearly getting me killed. Twice."

"Yes, sir."

Osborn and a sailor each grabbed Albright's arms and legs and hauled him away.

Austin glowered at the officers and sailors around him. They moved back, a semicircle forming with him at the apex.

"Well?" He swept them with his gaze. "Anyone else? Step up now. Anyone else want to try his hand at mutiny, theft, kidnapping—"

He swung to the right, and the line of men shifted back. "This ship is two steps from hell. Seward!"

"Sir?" The young lieutenant took one tiny step forward.

"Take note, Mr. Seward. Fifty lashes to *any* man who steps out of line for any reason. Understood?"

Seward cleared his throat. "Yes, sir."

"Including that damned Englishman. Am I clear?"

Seward's gaze shifted to Lord Rudolph, whose hand tightened on Evangeline's shoulder. "Yes, sir."

Austin's turned to the left, and a ripple of uneasiness spread to that side of the arc. "Get back to work on this travesty of a ship. I want it so clean the ropes shine. We sail into Boston harbor with all flags flying and all brasses polished. I don't want one damned thing out of place, one duty undone. And if any of you goes anywhere near my cabin without permission, you will enter Boston hanging from a yardarm. Is that understood?"

White faces peered anxiously at him, eyes blinking against the rain.

"I *said*, is that understood?"

As one, the sailors and officers snapped to attention. "Yes, sir!"

Austin turned on his heel and marched toward the stern. The men parted for him.

Seward was the first to break the spell. He called to the cabin boy. "Get him some hot coffee and blankets, and someone get down there and make sure he gets himself dry. Do not let that man catch pneumonia. *I* don't want command of this blasted ship!"

The men broke up then, hurrying to duties. Two rushed off with Cyril.

Evangeline's heart was ready to burst. He *wouldn't* take care of himself, the idiot. He'd gone overboard and almost died, and now he would take sick and waste away to break her heart. And he hadn't even looked at her, hadn't even come to reassure her that he was all right.

She shook off Lord Rudolph's hand and dashed for the stern. Her thoughts tumbled, incoherent, and tears streaked down her cheeks.

"Evangeline, wait."

She heard the Lord Rudolph's command, ignored it. She ran across the rain-soaked deck and plummeted down the stairs. The door to Austin's cabin was open. She heard his voice, torn by the salt water, and the voices of the men who'd come to help him. She burst inside.

He stood in the middle of the cabin, stripped to the waist, water gleaming on his flesh. His boots lay next to him and puddles formed around his bare feet. The cabin boy was advancing on him with a blanket.

Evangeline flew at him and flung her arms hard around his waist.

Austin, off-balance, took a step back. Evangeline went with him. She heard his voice rumble inside his chest, but couldn't make out what he said.

The wool of a blanket scratched her hands. Someone had tossed it around his shoulders.

"Your coffee, sir," Seward said behind her. "Cook laced it with brandy. Drink up."

"Leave it. Are we back on course?"

"Yes, sir. Storm's slacking off, too. Is everything—er, all right?"

"Yes." His large hands rested on Evangeline's back. "I will be fine." He paused. "That was well done, Mr. Seward."

Seward stammered. "Thank you, sir. Doing my duty, sir."

"Yes, all right. Get back up there. They need you."

"Yes, sir. Cyril, you're with me, lad."

Evangeline heard Cyril's light footsteps hasten out of the cabin. Seward followed, and the door closed.

Evangeline, with her face buried in the muscles of Austin's chest, had no idea if they had been left alone. She didn't care. Her hands clamped into his back, as if she'd never let him go. The damp curls of his chest tickled her cheek, and she heard his heart pound, steady and slow, under her ear.

His fingers furrowed in her hair, and he tilted her head back. "Everything is all right now, Evangeline."

His handsome face, his dark eyes, blurred before her. "I thought you gone forever."

He rested his cheek against her hair. "I am safe and sound."

"And so cold." His flesh under her hands was icy to the touch, and still damp. "You need to get warm."

She yanked the blanket closed over his bare chest and reached for the coffee. The bitter aroma rose with the steam, heating the tears on her face. Her hands shook, nearly spilling the liquid. Austin rescued the cup, and drank, closing his eyes as the steam touched his skin.

She babbled on. "You must get out of those wet clothes, or you'll catch your death. Hurry. I'll send Cyril back to you."

She started for the door.

"Evangeline, don't go."

She turned. He set the cup and saucer on the desk. "I don't want you to go. Not yet."

"But you must be tended to."

His face was gray, drawn, as if he'd aged ten years in the last five minutes. "When you walk away from me, I can feel the water closing over me, dragging me down. Stay with me. I don't want to feel that."

The desperation in his voice caught at her heart. "But you must get dry. I must let you undress."

"No bother about that."

He drew the blanket all the way around him, covering himself from neck to ankles. His hands moved beneath it.

He was undressing right in front of her.

Her instincts told her to turn around and close her eyes, but that was ridiculous. The blanket covered him completely; she could see nothing.

197

His breeches landed on the board floor with a wet splat, followed by his lawn underbreeches. Evangeline stared at the crumpled pieces of fabric, her face scorching. He stood naked before her. Well, under the blanket, anyway.

He lifted his broad hand and crooked a finger at her.

"Come here, Evangeline."

Her mouth went dry.

"Do not blush, my siren. I remember you walking into my cabin once upon a time and brazenly unbuttoning your bodice."

"That was different."

"Ah, yes. You were taking part in a mutiny. All is explained." His smile turned wicked. "I was ready to let the ship go to hell for a chance to sample your delights. I feel the same way now."

"You would never abandon your ship."

"I might for you, siren. Now come here."

Fire danced in his dark eyes. His broad hands clutched the edges of the blanket, holding it closed, but his gaze stoked fires inside her. Her blood warmed, her pulse quickened. Everything inside her begged, *go to him!*

Slowly, she took a step toward him, and another. Miss Pyne would gasp in shock; Evangeline should turn and flee, ignore his plea, ignore the desperate look in his eyes to save her virtue.

Miss Pyne belonged to another world.

Evangeline ran the last two steps. His smile scalded her, then he opened his arms and gathered her to him.

Chapter Eighteen

Her hair was so warm under his hands. Austin ran his fingers through its softness. He leaned down and rested his cheek against her head. The waves had almost taken him from her. Taken him before he could hold her, touch her, bury himself inside of her.

Your siren song let me live. Now let me feel alive.

He opened the blanket. Evangeline instantly averted her eyes, then, as if she couldn't help herself, her gaze swiveled to him again.

Her face flamed from neck to forehead. He chuckled. Innocent, and yet so sensual. Still holding the blanket, he wrapped his arms around her and drew her close, closing the blanket around them both.

Hesitantly Evangeline raised her arms and circled them around his waist. Her warm, warm hands rested on his back, unmoving, unsure. He gathered her close, kissing her fragrant hair. Her clothed body pressed all along his nakedness. The soft cotton of her bodice, stiffened with boning, caressed his skin; the flowing cotton skirt twining his bare legs. The lift of her breasts pressed his ribs, and her heart thumped and pattered against his body. She rested her head on his chest, her hot breath warming his skin.

"Evangeline," he murmured into her hair. "You smell so delightful."

Her hands moved, igniting fires all through him. "You are still cold. Your skin is icy."

"Warm me then, my siren."

Her palms held heat as she brushed them against his flesh. Her movements were slow, uncertain, shy. She slid her hands up his broad back, pausing at the muscles at his shoulder blades. Her brows furrowed, as if she concentrated, and her fingers played the muscles, stroking and skimming each one.

He leaned his forehead against hers. "That feels lovely, my siren." He closed his eyes.

And black water rushed over him, drowning him, pulling him away from the beautiful creature in his arms. His lungs went tight, he couldn't get enough air, his heart pumped crazily.

He gasped aloud and opened his eyes.

"Are you all right?"

Evangeline looked up at him, brow puckered in concern. Austin's muscles had gone rigid and he'd stood straight up, unlocking her embrace.

He forced his breathing to slow, his hands to unclench. "Yes." His voice was hoarse, all wrong. He reached for Evangeline, gathered her to him, clinging to her now where before he'd held her lightly. "Yes, I'll be all right. Keep me from drowning, Evangeline."

She did not answer, but her hands slid around his waist again. Austin lay his cheek on her shoulder and forced his eyes to remain open. He studied the white curve of her neck, the fine hairs at the nape, the silken lock that had fallen down her back. He smelled the perfume of her, soap and sea air. He rubbed his cheek on the stiff cotton of her bodice, tracing the stripes of the fabric down over her straight spine, her curve of hip, down her luscious legs to the floor.

She was real. The floorboards were solid under his feet, she was warm in his arms. Gently, he drew one hand to the small of her back, pulling her closer still. Her thigh pressed through her skirts against his throbbing arousal, speeding his pulse yet again.

Her lips brushed his wet hair. "You should sleep," she whispered.

He shook his head against her shoulder. "No. When I close my eyes I see the water. It takes me. I cannot sleep. I will dream of it."

She turned her head so that her lips hovered so close, oh so close, to his. The cold of her spectacles brushed his forehead. "You should rest anyway. Lie down. You're shivering."

Shivering with need, perhaps. His blood had turned molten inside his veins. He raised his head and brushed a lock of hair from her forehead. "Stay with me."

She gave him a worried look, but nodded.

Austin carefully removed her spectacles and set them on the desk behind her. He leaned down and brushed his lips over her furrowed brow, smoothing the lines away. Then he took her hand and led her to the bunk.

Evangeline's legs shook, but she walked beside him to the bunk tucked under the eaves. He leaned down to strip the bedding back. The blanket slid from his arm to bare his shoulder and most of his back.

She let her gaze run along his muscles as they rippled smoothly beneath his skin. Such strength he had. And yet, when he'd commanded her to stay with him, his voice had shaken.

Austin folded the blankets back and plumped the pillows, making a nest to receive his large body. He glanced up at her, sideways under his long lashes, his lips curving. "I should be plenty warm with the extra blankets. And you."

Evangeline's heart missed a beat. "The—the bunk is too narrow."

He sat down. The blanket slithered down to pool in his lap. "For us to lie side by side, yes."

She saw the bruises then across his shoulders and back, the angry red marks on his arms as if someone— Albright—had clawed and fought him. When he flicked his gaze to her again, she read desire in its dark depths, but she read fear there, too, raw and primal.

She reached down and brushed her hand over the blackening bruise on his shoulder. He flinched, as if that slightest touch caused him pain.

"You should have these dressed."

"Later." He caught her wrist, his fingers biting. "Just now I need salve for my heart. My skin will wait."

He brought her hand to his lips and kissed her palm. Heat trickled through her.

"What do you want me to do?" Her lips could barely move.

He slanted her a lazy smile. He reached up and touched a hook of her bodice. "Remove this."

The heat flared, streaking through her limbs, stabbing at her loins. Miss Pyne was going to be quite ashamed of her.

Evangeline unfastened the top hook, then moved to the next one, and the next. Her fingers, which had shaken so the first night she'd come in to seduce him, remained strangely firm and steady.

She pulled the placket open and slid the garment from her arms, baring them to the heated air of the cabin. Carefully she unpinned the bodice from the top of the skirt, and let the drab cloth fall to the floor.

The boning in the bodice had acted as her stays, and now her breasts spilled loosely behind her chemise. Austin's dark eyes flicked to them, his strong lips parting.

She untied the tapes that held her skirt closed. The skirt slithered to the floor, the dull gray cloth lying meekly on the boards. She felt as if she were throwing off the cocoon of her stifling, drab, spinster's life, emerging from a shell to spread her wings.

Into the arms of a man who watched her with eyes of fire.

She sent her underskirt to the floor after the overskirt, then untied the ribbons that held her chemise closed.

Austin's chest rose and fell sharply as the chemise fell away from her body, baring it to him. The points of her breasts tightened, heat swirling there and staying.

"My siren," he rasped. His gaze traveled down her body, pausing at the join of her legs, trailing down her thighs to her calves and her feet, still in her little boots. "You leave me powerless in the face of your beauty."

She resisted the urge to cover herself with her hands. "I—I am not beautiful. I am too thin, for one thing."

"Who has told you so? I will call him out."

Her teeth chattered. "Most people have. Most of my life."

"They wronged you."

He lifted his large hand and rested it on her abdomen. Evangeline closed her eyes. All of her life, she'd dreamed of a gentleman who would look at her and find her pleasing. As her girlhood had slipped to womanhood, she'd given up the childish fantasy, realizing that a willowy body, straggling hair, and spectacles would never draw the attention of a man.

She'd never dreamt that a man so handsome, with dark eyes and a rare, but wicked smile, would look upon her and call her beautiful.

He cupped her waist and drew her to him. She opened her eyes. The scar on his cheekbone stood out, angry and white, an old wound from she knew not where. She leaned down and did what she'd longed to since the night she'd come to his cabin at Anna Adams's order; she traced the scar with her tongue.

He tugged her down, and she landed on his lap. The blanket across his thighs prickled her backside.

"Shall I take off my boots?" she gasped.

His lips curved into a half-smile. "That may be wise."

He held her hips while she leaned over, unlaced her

boots and tugged them from her feet. She flexed her toes. A marvelous feeling of freedom swept through her. Except for her cotton stockings she was naked, and a man held her on his lap, and she had not one morsel of embarrassment. Instead, exhilaration filled her, frightening and glorious at the same time.

He laid down, swinging his legs up on the bunk and maneuvering her to sit beside him.

She leaned over him. Several locks of her hair escaped their pins and tumbled forward to brush his face. He smoothed them back, giving her his warm smile.

"What are we going to do?" she whispered.

He chuckled, his chest rumbling. "You are going to lie with me and warm me, my siren."

Evangeline peered doubtfully at the bunk. Austin filled it from side to side, his broad shoulders touching the slope of the wooden wall. "There is no room."

"We will make room. Lie down."

She lowered herself on top of him, moving her legs to overlap his. The blanket still formed a barrier between her hips and his. She was grateful for that blanket, because she thought she would have burst into flame otherwise. Bad enough that his hard chest pressed her breasts, that the curls of hair tickled her skin. He wrapped his legs around hers, muscles playing as he enclosed her in his embrace.

He arranged the blankets over her backside, enclosing them in a warm, snug cocoon. The lantern light touched his face, shadows playing along his cheekbones. It glistened on the moisture of his damp hair and eyelashes.

She lay her head on his chest. Beneath her ear, she heard the slow, steady beat of his heart.

"Warm. You are so warm."

His lips brushed her hair, and his hands, calloused and hard, moved across her back under the blanket. "When I think of a man and wife sharing a bed, I think of this." He grinned. "I think of other things, too, but I always imagine this sharing of warmth, of comfort. A real marriage will have that."

He had asked her to marry him. She had not given him an answer. She wondered if he'd ever shared warmth and comfort with his wife.

His voice lowered to a murmur. "Evangeline, I always get it wrong. With you, I want to make no mistakes. A perfect marriage. Do you suppose such a thing exists?"

The vibrations deep in his chest soothed her. The ship rocked slowly in the swells, the storm spent. Evangeline closed her eyes.

"A fine house, lovely frocks, a carriage at your beck and call."

His hands moved up and down her spine. Slow, warm, comforting. She'd been so frightened when she'd looked into the sea and lost sight of him.

The noose that had tightened around her heart loosened and flowed away.

"A husband who returns home every night at seven o'clock precisely." His voice drifted to a whisper. "Returns to his wife like clockwork. Everything tidy and taken care of. Would you like that, my siren?"

"Mmm."

Her mind felt like rich, thick cream. His words penetrated, but the meaning slithered away and was lost.

His hands, hard from the bite of the sea, smoothed away every fear, every worry. His encircling arms kept her safe from all harm, from all dangers. At this moment in time, she believed it with all her heart.

"Evangeline," he whispered.

Evangeline's limbs loosened, and she drifted into sleep.

Austin did not sleep. Death still hovered too near; the brush of its wings had touched him too closely. Holding Evangeline in his arms, the scent of her surrounding him, soothed him somewhat, but the terror of the depths still haunted him.

The feeling would leave him, he knew. He'd brushed death many times in his career, more often than he cared to, both as a merchant captain and as a lieutenant in the Continental Navy. Part of life at sea was constant danger.

Tomorrow he'd rejoice that he'd evaded death once more; tonight he would hold Evangeline and draw solace from her presence.

He listened to her deep, even breathing, enjoying the heat of her breath on his skin. Her soft breasts pressed his chest, her long legs fitted between his as if she'd been made to lie against him. Her hair was silken beneath his palms; the candlelight reflected on the smooth wave of it.

When they married, he would hold her like this every night. He would come home to her, as he told her, on the stroke of seven, and he'd hold her and drink her in. The joy of that would compensate for the end of his life as he knew it.

No more secrets. No more errand-boy. Austin Blackwell would pass the intrigues onto the man his mentor chose. Austin would sit behind a desk, give orders, write things in ledgers, and return home every evening to sit by the fire with his wife and talk of mundane and dull things.

His wife, who might be an English agent.

Austin was past caring about that. She would stop her agenting when she married him, the price she'd pay for her secrets to remain secret, to prevent him giving her over to his mentor.

He would make it worth her while.

The night wound on. Evangeline slept, her body relaxed. Above him he heard the tramp-tramp of feet, the bells ringing each hour of the watch. Occasionally, Mr. Seward's voice rose to give an order. In the cabin, the candle in the lantern burned low, stretching the shadows, until it winked out altogether.

Dawn would come soon, signaling time to return to his duties. His respite in the arms of his siren would end.

When the fourth hour of the watch rang, Austin gently eased himself from under Evangeline's limp weight. He slid from the bunk and got to his feet, pleased that his legs did not tremble. His muscles ached from fighting the sea and Albright, and his scraped and bruised shoulders throbbed. But warmth had filled him, driving out the deadly cold, and his limbs, though stiff, were not brutally sore.

He crossed the gently rolling cabin and relit the lantern. He opened a cabinet and withdrew a shirt and breeches. He pulled these on, then tugged on a dry pair of boots.

"Austin?"

Evangeline had raised herself on her elbow. She regarded him sleepily. Her shining hair spilled over her shoulders, covering the blanket that hid her breasts.

"What time is it?"

"Still the wee small hours. Go back to sleep."

She sat up farther, looking worried. "Where are you going?"

He gave her a crooked smile as he crossed to the cabin door. "I took in so much water from the sea, I must give some back. Sleep, my siren."

Her brow still puckered, but obediently she lay back down. Her eyes shone in the shadows; she would lie wakeful whether he liked it or not.

Austin opened the door and went out.

On deck, the air was bracing, but holding nowhere near the power of the gusts of the storm. The last watch of the night was usually quiet, with the sailors speaking in subdued, rather tired voices.

Austin tramped all the way forward. No one was using the head at the moment, for which he was grateful. From the head, he had an unobstructed view of the prow and the white waves that rushed back from it. The windows of his cabin gave him a view of where he'd been, but here, all was new. Though he knew the ship headed for Boston Harbor, still something tugged at him as he gazed at the dark horizon, where the stars, brilliant and thick, marched down to meet the water. There was a sweet happiness in it, and a constant power. Lives and ships would come and go, but the stars and the sea would always be forever.

Austin gave up his water, then turned back toward

the stern. As he passed the foremast, Seward stopped on an errand to somewhere and saluted him.

Austin returned the salute. He studied the young man's chapped face in the lantern-light. Seward had changed from the very young, somewhat bewildered puppy Austin had taken on board at the beginning of the voyage. Somewhere along the way, Seward's back had straightened, his shoulders had squared, and his tone of voice had changed from a hesitant murmur to a full-throated bellow. He had met danger head-on and learned and grown.

"Well done tonight, Mr. Seward. Your actions more than likely saved my life and young Albright's. I will recommend you for permanent promotion when we reach shore."

Seward still went shy under praise. He looked as if he wished to shuffle his feet and hang his head, but he raised his hand in another stiff salute. "Thank you, sir. Truly, sir."

"No need to be effusive. Carry on."

"Aye, sir."

After another salute, Seward turned smartly and jogged off in pursuit of his duties, his step buoyant.

Austin nearly made it to the stern without further interruption. But as he neared the stairs that led to his cabin, Lord Rudolph stepped from the shadows of the mizzen mast, his one eye glinting.

"Where is Evangeline?"

Austin stopped. "She is asleep."

"You have ruined her, then."

He restrained himself from kicking the man. "She will become my wife as soon as we reach shore."

"She will throw herself away on you. She could have so much, as my wife."

"She will have plenty as my wife. I am not a poor man."

"She deserves adulation."

"I will take care of her."

Lord Rudolph's brows lowered. "And I would not?"

"You would until you grew tired of her. Until the novelty wore off. I am not distracted by every woman who looks my way. In fact, it will be a relief to not have to worry about them any more."

"Good God, and you say we English have cold blood. Listen to yourself. The girl needs affection. She's starved for it. I doubt she's ever had a morsel of it. Certainly not from that fellow who calls himself her brother."

Annoyance bit him, but Austin clenched his jaw against it. "I will give her everything she needs."

"Except affection."

"You cannot tell me you love her."

"And you do? You love nothing but your control over everything and everyone. You love being captain of your ship, whether that ship is the *Aurora* or a house in Boston. You will stifle the girl."

"She has made her choice."

"Yes, I suppose she has." He glanced down the stairs to the lit passage that led to Austin's cabin. "You made certain she chose you, didn't you?"

"Are you implying that I threw myself overboard to send Evangeline into my arms?"

Lord Rudolph shot him a look of disdain. "I am certain you would have if you had thought of it. Good night, Captain."

He strode away into the darkness. Austin watched him go. The man possessed all the arrogance and self-assuredness of Englishmen who believed they should have power over all—politically, economically, socially. He'd known such men before the war, sons of aristocrats who came to the colonies and took what they wanted, then left for England with their pockets full and ruined men in their wake. Aristocratic sons had been army commanders, billeting their men haphazardly in American homes. The soldiers had destroyed crops, stolen cattle, taken women, then had laughed when called to pay.

Austin and men like him had made sure they paid.

Austin suspected that, during the War of Independence, Wittington had strongly supported England in keeping the colonies to heel.

And probably still did. A Wittington reposed on the list in Austin's cabin. And Lord Rudolph had never satisfactorily explained his presence anywhere outside of England. He should be in London, strutting about in the first stare of fashion and visiting his fashionable mistress, not gallivanting about the seas. Second sons wandered the earth; first sons like Lord Rudolph stayed home and ensured the succession.

Austin waited until the man was a good distance toward the forecastle before he finally turned his back and descended the stairs.

Evangeline waited for him behind that door, in his bed. His pulse quickened and his arousal stirred. Wittington had called him cold and told him he'd give Evangeline no affection. Wittington was a fool.

He pushed open the cabin door and went inside.

Chapter Nineteen

Evangeline turned her face to the wall as Austin opened the door.

Every word of his conversation with Lord Rudolph had carried down the stairs to her, and every word had torn her heart.

She had never assumed he loved her. Austin Blackwell, the handsome, powerful ship's captain, would not fall head over heels in love with an English spinster with spectacles.

She'd hung on every word of the conversation, willing Austin to explain to Lord Rudolph that he truly did care. But every time Lord Rudolph accused Austin of not having affection for her, Austin did not deny it.

Why hadn't it been Lord Rudolph who gave the cold, matter-of-fact answers and Austin who hotly retorted that he could give her affection? Why was the world so

213

backward? She should love Lord Rudolph, an Englishman, a wealthy and titled gentleman who would take her back to England where she belonged. Why did she instead fall for the colonial with his strange, flat accent and dark eyes, who bellowed orders people scrambled to obey?

He would expect her to obey him. He already did.

"Evangeline."

And when his low voice caressed her, she knew she'd follow any order he gave.

"Are you asleep?"

"No."

He approached, his tread heavy and slow. She tucked the blanket under her chin and closed her eyes.

His hand on her hair was cool. Chill clung to his clothes, and the smell of the sea. "You may return to your cabin if you wish."

She could not leave him now, and he knew it. His cabin was warm; the decks above, cold. Her bed was narrow and empty; his, full with his presence.

"I would like to stay here."

He leaned down and skimmed his lips across her temple. His breath played on her skin, sending trembling warmth through her body.

"If you stay, I want to make love to you. I want to love you with my hands, and with my mouth, and with my body. Will you let me?"

Let him? As if she could resist.

She rolled over onto her back. His face hung above hers, his loosened hair spilling forward to touch her cheek. She smelled brandy and coffee and cold wind and salt water.

She did not trust herself to speak. Instead, she raised her head and kissed his lips.

He groaned. His dark lashes swept down to shield his eyes as he slid his tongue into her mouth. The warm, velvet strokes of his kiss loosened her limbs, sending heat surging through her.

Would it be worth it to stay with him forever, if he'd only make her feel like this?

He pried the blanket from her fists, drawing it down her body, draping it over her legs. He slid his large hand behind her neck, pressing her mouth harder to his. His lips sought and caressed her, his tongue flicked through her mouth like flame.

Yes, it might, just might, be worth it.

He made a raw noise in his throat. He slid his hand between them, his calloused palm rough on the tender skin of her bosom. He cupped her breast, gently cradling it in his fingers. The sensitive nub just fit between his thumb and forefinger. He tugged it.

She almost swooned with delight.

His hand drifted, warm, to her belly, then to her hip. His eyes were half-closed, heavy with passion. His touch had warmed, and his hand lay heavy on her thigh, his fingers tracing a pattern on the sensitive skin there.

"We will marry as soon as we reach port," he murmured.

"Will we?" Her voice squeaked.

"We will. I will arrange it."

"You arrange everything."

He lifted his gaze to her, fire glinting in the depths of his eyes. "I excel at it."

He moved his fingers down her thigh, fingertips brushing lightly. Heat followed them, fire slithering through her veins.

"Where will we marry? In a church?"

"In the parish church near my house. You will like it." His touch floated to her knee, sliding behind it, tracing warmth there. "Are you Catholic?"

She exhaled. "No. Church of England."

"Excellent. Father Baldwin is a transplanted English vicar. As long as we avoid discussing politics, all will be well."

Heat filled her. To speak calmly of vicars while he touched her naked body . . .

"Why should we avoid discussing politics?" She gasped as he drew his thumbnail along the crease behind her knee.

"Because he is an awful bore on the subject. He came to America because of corruption in the English church."

He skimmed his fingers up her thigh again, drawing ever nearer to the hot, throbbing place that was damp with need.

"But corruption is found everywhere," he whispered into her ear.

"Is it?"

"It is."

His voice went flat. He brushed his finger over the curls at the join of her thighs.

Evangeline gasped. Her body bucked, rising to meet him.

A little smile tugged the corner of his mouth. "You like this?"

216

"Oh, yes. Do you?"

His chuckle sounded warm in the dark cabin. "I do." He stroked gently up to her belly again. "I have touched the finest of silks. In China, I have handled silk like the smoothest fall of water. But none can compare to this."

He brushed over the swell of her breast.

"Surely not."

"Mmm?"

"You must be exaggerating. My skin cannot feel like the finest of silks."

"I assure you, it can."

She reached up and parted the placket of his linen shirt. He wore nothing beneath it but himself. His smile widened as she dipped her hand inside to his warm body.

She traced the hollow of his throat, then slid her fingers down his smooth skin to his chest. Ridges of muscle rose and fell beneath her touch, hard, yet supple. He went motionless, as a man might who did not want to startle a small bird.

"Your skin feels . . ." She paused, trying to form the right words. "Like satin. I like touching it."

"I like you touching it."

She moved her hand farther down, her questing fingers opening the shirt. She flattened her hand, drawing her palm over the rock-hard muscle under his shoulder, down to his—

"Heavens, I did not know that men had . . ."

"We do." His voice sounded strange.

She raised her head to look at the pale nipple resting among the dark hair on his chest. She pulled his shirt open to his navel, studying all of his chest at once.

"Evangeline." It was almost a groan. "How I ever thought you were anything less than pure innocence, I cannot imagine."

She raised her head. His hair hung forward, shadowing his face. His lips parted with his uneven breathing.

"Why did you think I was less than innocent?"

"Because you strolled in here the first night and started unbuttoning your bodice under my nose."

"Miss Adams told me to do that. She said it would gain your attention."

"Hell yes, it gained my attention. You were provocative and enchanting, and obviously did not mind showing me all your delights. I was ready to take your virtue then and there, God help me."

"You were?"

"And did you scream and swoon or strike me? No, you came into my arms and let me touch you, just as you are doing now."

She traced the nub of his male nipple. It tightened and gathered, just as her own did when he touched her. She wondered if he felt the hot tightness inside, as she did. She leaned forward and brushed it with her tongue.

He groaned. "Stop that, my siren. You will undo me."

"Undo you?" She drew back, tracing the muscles of his abdomen. "Your shirt is undone, anyway."

He gripped her wrist and forced her hand from him. "Let me do this my way, siren."

He leaned forward, his loose hair falling to tease her belly, and licked the crevice between her breasts.

She gasped, truly knowing what fire was.

His tongue moved over her skin, and stroked across her nipple. Scorching heat tightened beneath his mouth, and she gave a little cry and fell back onto the bunk.

He followed her down. *With my hands, and my mouth, and my body,* he'd said. He nipped the soft skin of her breast and drew the nub between his teeth.

Oh, she must be wicked, indeed, or she would not like this. She arched up, wanting to fill his mouth, wanting his hunger.

"Oh, my. *Austin.*"

He skimmed his lips to the side of her breast. "Yes? Did you want to say something?"

"I—I wish I could go to China."

He raised his head. His eyes glinted like black fire. "Do you? And what would you do there?"

"I don't know. Whatever you told me, I expect."

He ran his tongue over her belly. "I would be there with you, would I?"

She drew in a ragged breath as his tongue snaked lower. "If we are to be married, it is doubtful I will run off to China without you, is it not?"

He looked up at her, his eyes traveling the length of her body. "When I marry you," he said fiercely. "I will not let you out of my sight."

"But—"

His voice went hard. "But what?"

"That would be rather impractical, would it not? I mean, if you wanted to take ship again, you would not be there to watch me. Unless you took me with you?" She slanted him a glance, hope in her heart.

219

Jennifer Ashley

"Certainly not. One voyage with you, siren, is enough to drive any man insane."

He lowered his head again. His breath burned on the small circle of hair at the join of her legs. No, she couldn't bear it. Her heart beat swiftly, and her breathing was ragged, hurting her lungs.

He licked her.

She cried out, then clapped her hand over her mouth. He couldn't mean to go on. He could not. His touch inflamed her, and he was handsome as sin, and she was so wicked . . .

He did go on. He moved lower still, his tongue rubbing the nub of her need. She gripped the sheet beneath her, twisting it in her hands. Little sobs escaped her, whimpers dying into the silence of the cabin.

Blessedly, cursedly, he stopped.

"Siren, you want me."

"Do I?" she whispered.

He sat back on his heels. "Your body does. As much as mine wants yours."

He drew his shirt off over his head. The lantern light traced the muscles rippling through his shoulders, shadows sharp on his body as the sinews moved beneath his skin.

He was beautiful. His hair burned red in the light and fell to brush his shoulders. His dark gaze held hers, mesmerizing her, as his hand went to the buttons at his waist.

She ought to look away. Miss Pyne would have looked away.

Miss Pyne faded back to the depths of her memory.

The buttons popped open, one by one. He wore

220

nothing beneath the breeches, either. The arousal she'd felt pressing her back and bare buttocks when they'd slept together now stood out full and hard and much larger than she could have imagined.

Crisp, dark hair, circled it. She wanted very much to touch the tip with her finger, to explore the long shaft. She shivered and clutched the sheet.

He chuckled. He seemed to be very amused about something. She could always swoon, of course. Prove that she was not fast and wicked. Of course, if she swooned, she might miss something interesting.

He tossed his breeches aside and returned to the bunk. He reached down and casually stripped the blanket from the bed. Cool air touched Evangeline's toes, and she curled them.

He cupped her cheek. "You are beautiful."

Evangeline swallowed. "You are the only one who has ever said so."

"Then I am the only one not blind." He leaned closer, his breath touching her skin. She tilted her head back, hungry for his kiss. But he did not kiss her. He pushed her down into the bunk, his large body curving over hers. His knee nudged her thighs apart. She tried to make room for him on the bunk, but her hip ground against the boards of the hull.

"It will be a tight fit."

"Mmm. I hope so."

He lowered himself down to her, bracing his weight on his hands. His warmth covered her, igniting her. Excitement crawled up and down her limbs, curious and nervous.

Jennifer Ashley

He slanted a kiss across her mouth, his lips bruising. "Evangeline. My siren."

She slid her arm around his waist. The gentleness of his earlier caresses evaporated. His mouth took hers greedily, hungrily, his lips grinding into hers.

She could not breathe. She drove her fingertips into the hard muscles of his back, opening her mouth for him. Blackness swam before her eyes, and his warmth enveloped her, his body on hers removing any awareness of herself. Dimly she felt the blunt tip of him press her entrance, which had gone hot and slick.

He was so big; how could he ever hope to fit?

His mouth left hers, and she dragged in a breath.

"I will try not to hurt you." His voice was raw, and his arms trembled. He smelled of desire and untamed longing.

"Please."

He made a hungry noise. Then the hardness of him pressed her, opening her, stretching her. She gasped aloud, sensations pouring over her, trickling up and down her nerves. She turned her head and squeezed her eyes shut.

His words tumbled out in a rush. "Evangeline, if I go any farther, I will not be able to stop."

She did not know whether she wanted him to stop. She opened her mouth to discuss it with him. What came out was, "Please, Austin."

He exhaled. In one swift movement, he sheathed himself in her fully.

She cried out. Tears leaked from the corners of her eyes. She felt as if she were being torn in two; she wanted the moment to go on forever.

222

"Hush. Don't cry."

She wanted to tell him that her tears were not tears of pain, but of joy. Of the pleasure of holding him in her safe harbor, of being completely his for this moment.

She could only make a sound of need.

He lifted her hips, sliding himself even deeper. The ship rolled suddenly, pitching upward on a swell, sending her into him. He came down as the ship boomed into the wave, and began a rhythm with his hips.

Evangeline's heart soared with the ship, flying into the wind, the night, the stars. Pleasure laced her, beginning where they were joined and sweeping her whole self.

Small cries of joy escaped her lips. Her nails sank into his back, her legs parted, wanting more and more of him. He groaned her name, his voice torn, his hungry need filling her. The friction where they joined was unbearable, but so good, so right, so hot. His fingers hurt her. But she hurt from the inside out, a hurt she could not escape, a hurt that was more pleasure than pain, and she sobbed with need of it.

The ship crashed down, and mingled with the hollow noise, Austin cried her name. She answered. He tumbled her hair, kissing her face, her lips, her throat. His hot seed filled her, streaked a jolt of longing and love through her body.

She fell back, limp and spent. He licked the hollow of her throat, swirled his tongue over the shell of her ear; his teeth found purchase in the curve of her shoulder. He breathed in great, shuddering sighs, and whispered *siren* over and over.

She was well and truly ruined now. She pressed a kiss to his hard shoulder, then wrapped her arms around him and buried her face in his neck.

When Evangeline awoke, she was alone. Sunshine flooded through the stern windows and warmed the cabin. The blanket, tucked around her, wrapped her in a snug cocoon.

Evangeline freed her arms, stretched, and yawned. The ship rocked gently from side to side, the huge swells of the night before gone.

She yawned again, waiting for shame and remorse to overtake her. She'd shared a bed with Austin. She was wicked and lust-filled.

She hugged her knees to her chest and smothered a giggle. She liked being wicked, and she liked the way he had been wicked with her.

Before she'd fallen asleep, they'd lain together, limp and lethargic for a long time, neither speaking. Then he'd touched her again, his skillful fingers bringing her to glorious readiness before he'd slid inside her once more and driven her to a mad frenzy.

She didn't remember much after that.

She had a vague memory of him rising, laying the blanket over her, and pressing a kiss to her forehead, gentle as a mother's touch. No doubt he had returned to his duties. They would be in port soon, and he must have much to do. And then, he and Evangeline would be married.

A qualm stole through her exuberance. Austin would marry her and take her to his home, and not once had he seemed happy about his choice.

Evangeline threw back the covers and slid from the bed. She looked down at her naked body and blushed. She had felt no shyness snuggling with him and letting him touch her, but in the clear light of day, her face heated at the memories. A dark red mark showed on her shoulder where his mouth had bruised it.

She found her gown, chemise, and underskirts hanging neatly from pegs near the bed. Her small boots had been placed carefully before them. She hoped Austin had done the tidying up himself and had not admitted someone else, like Cyril, while she lay, unclothed, in his bed.

She pulled on her chemise and moved to the washstand. The cool water stung her hands and face, nudging her back to reality. Of course Austin had not sounded happy about marrying her. His first marriage had ended in sorrow, and he had no reason to suppose his second would not as well. In addition, Austin was about to give up what he loved most dearly—his life at sea.

If only she could convince him not to. She bit her lip as she dried her face and smoothed her hair, remembering the stubborn glint in the back of his eyes. He would not be easy to convince.

Evangeline pulled on her gown. She found, on the other side of the desk, her valise packed with her things. Austin must have removed everything from the cabinet for her. He certainly liked to arrange things.

She fished out a pair of clean stockings and pulled them on, then took up a comb and ribbons and returned to the washstand and mirror to brush out her hair and complete her toilette.

The captain's cabin offered better accommodation for dressing her hair than her own narrow cabin, and she was able to pin up the shining masses of her braids to her satisfaction. When she finished, she turned to the covered silver tray on the desk and lifted the lid. The warm smell of bacon and bread wafted out at her, and her stomach growled. Making love certainly gave one an appetite.

After she finished her breakfast, she sat back in Austin's desk chair, wondering what to do next. She could go out on deck for fresh air—the morning certainly looked lovely. But she blushed at the thought. Everyone on board must know she'd spent the night here, including Lord Rudolph. She didn't think she could face anyone, yet.

Idly she opened a drawer of the desk. Inside lay her red-covered book of devotions. She smiled a little and took up the familiar, heavy book. She opened it to a random page, smoothing the sheets covered with the well-known words, and began to read.

But the words failed to appease her, as they usually did. She had seen too much violence, too much evil, in the past few weeks, that she doubted she would ever be content again.

Miss Pyne had once said that a woman should not travel, but should be happy with her place at home. Evangeline had thought this advice dull and unimaginative. Now she saw the wisdom in it. Ever since the awful day when Harley had betrayed her, her life had turned upside down. If Harley had been true and noble, she would be spending peaceful days at home in the Cotswolds. She never would have discovered the joy of sailing on a ship, or the terror of a mutiny, or the desire stirred by a dark-eyed man's touch.

She flipped pages, looking for the psalm that always quieted her mind, the twenty-third, her favorite. She began to read the words she knew by heart, her lips moving in silence.

She turned the page to continue. She frowned, and stopped.

She had only turned one page, but two had flipped over. The paper between her fingers was thick and stiff, and she realized what had happened. Two pages, probably dampened with sea air, had stuck together. She picked at them with her thumbnail, but they had been glued fast. She grimaced. She hated to tear her beloved book, especially the page with her favorite psalm.

She laid the book down flat and held the page up straight. She ran her finger all the way around the edge. There was no break in the seam.

She let the page fall, and opened another drawer. The inside was as neat and tidy as the rest of the cabin. Everything lay in little compartments, built to keep things from sliding around with the roll of the ship. Snug in their slots were sheets of paper, quills for pens, an ink pot, blotting paper, a sander, sealing wax, and a small paper knife, the kind used for cutting open books.

Evangeline drew the knife from its place. The blade gleamed, polished and oiled, fixed in a plain black handle. She pushed the drawer closed and stared thoughtfully at her book.

She lifted the page again, tilting her head to examine it. She steadied the knife and carefully nicked the paper. If she drew it just inside the edge of the page, she might be able to loosen it from the other without marring the book.

The blade was sharp. Slowly, she slid the knifepoint along her page, leaving a razor-thin cut in its wake. She drew the blade all the way around, cutting slowly, not wanting to tear the paper. When the knifepoint rested against the binding again, opposite her starting point, she laid the knife down. It slid down the desk, responding to the roll of the ship. Evangeline absently stilled it. She pulled open the two pages.

Three thin sheets, folded, lay nestled between them. Evangeline stared at them for a moment, then she slowly took them up. The dry papers rustled as she unfolded them and smoothed them across the desk.

The handwriting was precisely slanted and unfamiliar. Neither she nor her stepbrother nor anyone in her family had penned these sheets. What they were doing in her book was a mystery.

She lifted each one in turn, skimming the contents. The pages appeared to be nothing more than a list of names, which had not been written in any order.

P. K. Chesterfield, Concord, Massachusetts
Adolphus Mannering, Philadelphia, Pennsylvania
George Wittington, Boston, Massachusetts
C. Sheridan Bartlett, Wilmington, Delaware . . .

Evangeline sat back, lips pursed. Why on earth had Austin hidden a list of names in her book of devotions? The task had been skillfully done, so that only someone determined to read the book page by page would have found it. If anyone searching for the list had shaken the book by its spine, nothing would have fallen out. The pages had been so closely sealed, even flipping through probably would not have revealed the discrepancy.

She remembered the night she'd come to this cabin to fetch the book, thinking to soothe herself to sleep. He'd deftly forestalled her and taken the book from her. At the time, she'd only found his actions high-handed and irritating, but now she understood. He did not want her to find these papers. Did not want anyone to find them.

He had glared at her that night, fire in his black eyes that had seared her to the bone. He'd meant to frighten her, but he'd only inflamed her. She had begged shamelessly for his kisses, just as she begged for them every time she went near the man.

Her skin tingled, as if he bent his hot glare on her now. She raised her head.

Austin stood in the doorway, his hand on the doorhandle. He gazed at her, then at the papers in her hand, his eyes holding chill hostility.

Chapter Twenty

He closed the door. Silence blossomed in the room, building and rising until it pressed on Evangeline's flesh.

He had dressed fully in captain's regalia: collar and stock, blue coat with his captains' bars on his shoulders, leather gloves, high, shined boots. A far cry from the beautiful man in only his skin who had leaned into her in the night and taken her mouth in hungry kisses.

His sleek hair was damp with spray, but the ribbon that held it in its queue was tied neatly. He crossed the room in slow, deliberate strides.

Her throat went dry as desert dust. When he reached her, he leaned down and pried the papers from her numb fingers. With deliberate care, he folded the pages and slid them inside his coat.

"What do they mean?"

He regarded her with eyes as hard as steel. "They mean danger."

"I don't understand."

"You read them." He did not ask it.

"It is only a list of names."

He watched her, his gaze still, like a cat watching a mousehole.

She wet her lips. "Mr. George Wittington. Is he the cousin of Lord Rudolph Wittington? Our Lord Rudolph?"

"I do not know."

"Have you asked him?"

"No." He leaned his fists on the desk. "And neither will you. You will not speak one name you found on that list to anyone, will not mention one word of it."

"Why?" The word was a thin squeak.

"Because I ask it of you."

He turned away.

"Austin."

Austin halted, every line of his back tense. He turned back. Under that black and smoldering gaze, Evangeline's nerve quivered. "If you are to command me not to do something, I at least want to know why."

His face stilled. "You will do it because I ask you, as the man who will become your husband."

"But you are not my husband yet."

He grasped her jaw. His hand trembled, holding in his fierce strength. "This is not a matter for a test of wills. Knowledge of these papers is dangerous, no matter what the names mean or do not mean to you. Vow to me that you will speak of them to no one."

She had never seen this look in his eyes. No tenderness, no hunger, no teasing, not even anger resided there. He gazed at her in deadly earnest, and she sensed that he did not ask her idly.

"I promise."

His fingers slid away. "We will marry as soon as we reach port."

"We will?"

"Yes. You are marrying me, not that dissipate Englishman."

On this topic, however, she could be good and defiant. "I do not find him dissipate. He is quite a gentleman. Always courteous and deferential."

His jaw hardened. "You will marry me, Evangeline."

"Yes."

His expression became if anything, harder. "I am pleased you agree."

"Well, I must, mustn't I? I am a ruined woman, now."

His eyes flickered, a sardonic light entering them. "You are ruined only if you do not marry me."

"As I said."

He looked at her for a long moment, his chest rising with a heavy breath. After a time, he held his hand, rock-steady, out to her. "Come with me."

"Where are we going?" She quailed at facing the rest of the crew, and Mr. Seward, and Lord Rudolph.

"To the brig."

She cringed back. "No, Austin, I promise I will not say a word about the list. You may lock me in my cabin if you wish, and feed me hard tack and water. Only, do not throw me in a cage, please."

"What the devil are you babbling about?"

"I do not want to be locked in the brig."

He held out his hand again. "I am not going to lock you in there. We're going to see Albright."

She sucked in her breath. "Oh. Why is Mr. Albright in the brig, anyway? Is it a crime to jump overboard?"

"No." His brow puckered. "A cage?"

"That is what you have in brigs, is it not? Cages and men groaning and jailors tossing crusts of bread and laughing when you do not catch them . . ."

His mouth twitched. "You read too many novels. Come along."

She came around the desk and took his hand. She felt his hard, calloused palm under his glove. He was like his hand: tough, roughened by years at sea and hardships she could scarcely fathom. This man would become her husband, the man who would guide her, lead her, command her.

She could not decide if this worried her or excited her.

He opened the door and she gathered her skirts and stepped out before him.

"Traitorous bastard," Albright said. "Mother-loving traitorous . . ." He clenched his manacled hands, and his words turned foul. Evangeline whitened.

Austin grabbed Albright by the shirt and yanked the young man off the floor. "None of that before the lady. Answer my question. Who sent you?"

"Go to hell."

"I have. And back again. It no longer frightens me."

Albright's pale lids dropped over his eyes.

The young man seemed to have recovered from his near drowning. Dry now, his strength was evident in his

Jennifer Ashley

clenched fists and the cords that stood out on his neck.

Austin had ordered Albright interned separately from the other mutineers. The lad sat in a corner made by the bulkhead and shielded from the rest of the hull by crates of cargo. His manacled hands were chained to the wall, but the chain was long enough for him to lie down and to reach the chamber pot provided for him in the opposite corner. Deep straw lined the floor, and the men had provided him with a blanket.

"How old are you, Albright?"

Albright looked at him sideways. "Sixteen."

"Then you were just a lad during the war. You don't remember it."

"I remember my father going and not coming home."

Evangeline made a sound in her throat. Her lashes glistened with tears.

"So you resent the ones who did come home?"

"It was a stupid cause that took my father. If the bloody arrogant gentlemen in Philadelphia hadn't decided to go to war, we'd all be living peaceably. As Englishmen."

"We are living peaceably. At last. Do you want your bloody arrogance to start it all again?" Austin lowered Albright to his feet, but kept his face thrust at the young man's. "I watched men die beside me as cannon shot ripped through them. I watched them drown, I watched them burn. I damn well never want to see that again. If the gentlemen in Philadelphia wanted to fight for a glorious cause, I see that as no different from what you want. You want the ideal so much, you cannot imagine the reality."

He straightened. "Men dying, more young lads like

yourself whose fathers go and do not come back. That's what I will prevent, Albright. Tell me who sent you."

Albright wet his lips. "Never."

"Torture is not pretty, lad. I've seen it done. But it loosens the tongue remarkably."

The boy's eyes widened slightly, but he pressed his lips together.

Austin shrugged. "Think on it. I will speak to you later. Miss Clemens."

He gestured for her to follow him back around the crates.

After a moment, he realized he did not hear Evangeline's careful footsteps behind him. He swung around. Dear God.

She had stepped up to Albright and now laid her hand on his shoulder. "It will be all right. Captain Blackwell is a kind man—underneath it all."

Albright stared at her. Austin's heart stopped, waiting for the young man to grab her, to take her hostage, to ransom her safety for his release.

But Albright simply watched her. Evangeline patted his arm, then turned and trotted to Austin.

Austin caught her by the arm and dragged her from the hold. They emerged into bright morning. The clean, bracing breeze raced across the deck, buffeting Evangeline's skirts and his coat. Soft tendrils of her hair escaped her severe braid and floated in the sunshine, like gauzy strands of gold silk.

"That was a dangerous thing to do, Evangeline. I did not take you down there to mother him."

"Why did you take me down there, then?"

He drew her aside, to the rail, out of the way of the

sailors dashing about to prepare the ship for their arrival in Boston. He kept his voice low.

"I wanted to show you the danger of that list. Albright would kill you to take that information back to whomever sent him. He almost killed me for it, twice."

"He was the one who attacked you with the knife?"

"Yes. For those names. To him, words like *traitor* and *loyalist* are black and white, glorious words to die for. I just saw the dying. I never want to see it again."

He swept his gaze beyond the bow to the horizon, where a low, dark land could just be seen. He raised his arm and pointed. "Look there. That is the Cape. North of that will be your new home."

Evangeline shaded her eyes. "So near."

"I will convey you to my house as soon as we land. We will be married when I finish the business of the voyage."

"No."

The wind whistled through the rigging, moaning through lines drawn taut. In the stern, Lieutenant Osborn shouted orders to sailors who swarmed to make the ship ready to put to shore.

"No?"

"I have been thinking, Austin. There are many reasons why I do not need to become your wife."

Something tightened inside him. "There are two very good reasons you are going to."

She peered up at him like a lawyer waiting, condescendingly, for the other to make his case. "What are they?"

"The first is last night. You shared my bed. I might have given you a child."

236

She shook her head. "I have heard it does not always occur on one—um, on the first occasion."

"I have been at sea most of my life, Evangeline. I've known and had charge of dozens of young sailors and lietenants, and I know it happens more often than not. I have presided over many a hasty wedding."

Red burned her cheekbones. "Well, I am six-and-twenty, not an eighteen-year-old girl. It may be that I am past my prime."

"I do not intend to take the risk."

She looked unconvinced. "What is the second reason?"

"If I do not marry you, I can't keep an eye on you. You know too much, and you won't be safe alone."

"Which is entirely the wrong reason to marry someone."

"The wrong reason? To keep you safe?"

"A man—or a woman—should not marry where there is no caring."

He let his gaze linger on her lips until a faint blush stained her cheeks. "Do you think last night meant no caring?"

The flush blossomed. "Last night was—base lust."

"On your part, or mine?"

"On both parts. You were overly happy that you had rescued Mr. Albright and that you hadn't drowned. You needed to release your exuberance. That is why you wanted me."

"I admit that I was celebrating life."

"You see? That is no reason to marry someone."

"I think it every reason to marry someone."

"Sweet faith, but you are stubborn."

"Stubborn in the face of nonsense."

She put her hands on her hips. "I will not marry you, Captain Blackwell."

"You seek to become my paramour instead?"

Her jaw dropped. "What? Good heavens, of course not. How could you think that?"

"When a woman spends a night of passion with a man and then refuses to become his wife, he can only think she wishes an illicit liaison."

Evangeline glanced hastily around her. "Lower your voice, Austin, for heaven's sake."

"Evangeline, I forbid you to refuse to marry me."

"On what authority do you forbid me? You are not my father, or my brother, nor any kin to me."

"On the authority of the man who is to be your husband."

"Now *you* are talking nonsense."

A shout went up from the command deck. Two sailors began to run up the flags that would tell the harbor master who they were: what ship, from what company, from what state.

"There is no more time for discussion. Come."

He took her hand and towed her astern, back toward the stairs that led to his cabin. She trotted beside him, shooting him dark looks.

He led her down the stair and all but pushed her into his cabin. She jerked out of his grasp once inside and swung around.

"A forced marriage is no marriage, Austin."

He rested his hand on the doorhandle. "It will not be a forced marriage. You will be a most willing bride."

"I will never willingly drag you into misery."

"Into misery? What are you talking about?"

"Oh, Austin, you will be wretched with me. You will miss your ship and the sea and your men, and you will want to leave as soon as you are settled."

Austin drew a long breath. "I have explained. I am tired of this life. I want to stay on shore and rest."

"Your first wife made you wretched. As will I."

A vision rose in Austin's mind, the vision of a very young dark-haired lady who had stood next to him at a wedding ceremony ten years before. He had been very young as well, pleased that he'd found such a pretty wife. She'd been terrified of him on her wedding night. Austin had tried to gentle himself for her, to make her feel the pleasure he did, but he had never been able to. She had simply refused to let him.

His mind strayed then to Evangeline in his arms in his narrow bunk, to her unfeigned response, to her lips lifting for his kiss, her body rocking up to beg for his. His hands remembered the delight of her, his loins hungered for her again.

"The failure of my first marriage was my fault. My wife wanted a conventional husband, and I left her for my duties at sea. When I stay home as other gentlemen do, neither of us will be miserable."

She shook her head, her eyes large. "Do you not see, Austin? You left her at home because you felt strangled by her, trapped by the conventions of everyday life. That is why you escaped to the sea. And why you've never entangled yourself with another woman since."

She was wrong. He had entangled himself again and again. And each time he had fled.

But perhaps she was right. Each time that he'd found

239

himself landbound, perhaps sixty days would pass before he grew restless and the walls of the city began to hem him in. Then his mistresses' demands for his time, his attention, his gifts, would begin to pall and then to irritate and then madden. And so he'd seek an assignment out to sea, where he could feel the clean wind on his face and smell the sharp ocean, where he could put the stink of the city, the closeness of the walls, the cloying grasp of his mistresses far behind him.

Austin firmed his jaw. Not this time. This time he would have Evangeline by his side during the long summer days and the long winter nights. He would not want to leave. Whatever grief the city threw him would be soothed away in her arms. . . .

Would it not?

Or perhaps I am not a man who can make a woman a steadfast and comfortable husband. Not even a woman as beautiful, as desirable, as funny, as charming, as innocent, as enchanting as Evangeline.

He gave her a long look, his jaw refusing to unclench. Then he backed out of the cabin and closed the door. He pulled a brass key from his pocket, fitted it in the lock and turned it.

He was halfway up the stairs when her scream of outrage reached him. His jaw relaxed enough to allow him to emit a chuckle.

"Let me out!"

Evangeline banged her palms against the door. The slap echoed through the cabin. "Austin, let me out of here at once."

She put her ear to the keyhole. She heard the creak-

240

ing of the ship, the billow of the sails in the wind, the hollow boom of the waves on the hull. She heard men shouting, sailors singing a chant as they heaved on ropes to move the sails. But no one hastened down the stairs to help her, no one called out.

She turned around and leaned against the door, folding her arms and grinding her teeth.

The man's stubbornness would ruin him. Could he not see he needed freedom, unhampered by her or anyone, to decide whether he remained on land or at sea? The flash in his eyes had told her that what she'd spoken had hit home. He had fled the encumbrance of a wife, and no doubt he'd do it again.

What she ought to do was accept Lord Rudolph's offer to return her to England—not as his wife, which would be a ridiculous *mésalliance,* but what he'd offered at first, as a friend.

Both men must be dazed by the sea air. As soon as they reached Boston and Austin and Lord Rudolph saw other women their odd fascination with Evangeline would end. The best thing for it was for Evangeline to disappear, to beg her cousin to help her travel to another colony, perhaps even to change her name.

Evangeline Clemens could cease to exist, and she could start anew. She'd read of many people who had gone to the former colonies to start a new life, to bury a past. Many of them had been criminals, true, but the romance of it appealed to her.

And then perhaps, once day, she'd return to Boston and seek out Captain Austin Blackwell, an old widower, and they could laugh over old times.

The ship rocked, jerking her back to reality. She

could hardly run off to another colony when she was locked in this cabin, on a boat taking her into Boston. She clenched her jaw and muttered a few choice words about Austin Blackwell under her breath.

Sunshine flooded the room from the stern windows, sun that glittered hard upon the sea. The beauty of it slid through her, calming her temper. Perhaps he had an extra key hidden in the room. It would not do her much good, because she was still on the ship he commanded, but she did not intend to sit complacently until he came back for her. She crossed to the desk, sat down in his chair, and began opening drawers. None held any keys.

She did find the miniature of a young woman with black curls. She had pink cheeks, black eyes, a pert nose, and a round chin. The miniature bore no date.

Evangeline held the picture in the palm of her hand. She must be his wife. This was the woman he'd legally separated himself from; the woman he'd pursued the sea to escape. And yet, he still kept her portrait.

She set the miniature back in the drawer and slid it closed. She leaned her elbows on the desk and her head in her hands. The man would drive her mad.

The sun slid westward and the shadows lengthened as the ship made its slow way into Boston Harbor. A thorough search of the cabin had not turned up any keys, and Evangeline had resigned herself to being a prisoner until Austin chose to send for her.

She napped a little on his bunk, trying to put out of her mind the warm embrace they'd shared there the night before. She rose and returned to the windows, but because they faced astern, they only gave her a view of open sea.

She knew they neared a harbor, however, because more ships soon became visible, large schooners weighted down with cargo, narrow packets bound for who-knew-where. The different nationalities of the boats fascinated her. She noticed the flags of England, France, the Netherlands, Italy, Spain, and some she did not know. All had crossed the waters to ply trade with the brash new American nation, which was ready to embrace business with the world.

She seated herself in the captain's chair and observed the busy port out of the window, marvelling at the practiced way the boats slid through the water, never colliding. Men climbed the riggings like spiders, balancing with habit of long practice to obey the captain's orders. She could hear Mr. Seward and Mr. Osborn shouting similar orders above, and knew that the *Aurora*, too, joined the dance of ships.

A long while later, the ship turned, and she at last beheld what she assumed was Boston. A long, low bank lay huddled against the water, with scatterings of dwellings clumped here and there against the green of slopes and trees. With the westering sun on it, the scene looked quite idyllic. High clouds streaked the sky, stained pink and gold and orange.

So much space. America was a vast land; no one had actually explored all of its interior. Liverpool had crowded one corner of England; her tiny hamlet in Gloucestershire had been surrounded by similar tiny hamlets. Here the coast seemed to go on forever, the man-made buildings small and uncertain against the backdrop of the untamed wilderness.

Apprehension touched her, but laced with it came curiosity and wonder. She longed to see this strange, new place, to travel under the huge sky, to discover all that the new nation had to offer.

She moved to lean against the sill, watching out the window until the sky darkened, and the *Aurora* turned again. Ships' lanterns winked on, floating on the darkness, and the lights of the harbor shone forth, snuggled together between patches of darkness. Overhead the sky blossomed stars, thick and spiraling, thin clouds snaking through them.

Still Austin did not fetch her. She heard much commotion above, but no one came down the stairs.

When the clean sea breeze gave way to the stench of the harbor, Evangeline returned to sit on the bunk. She rehearsed her speech to Austin—that is, the speech she would make if he ever came back and did not leave her here to rot. She would make him see that the best thing would be for her to go to her cousin, or back to England with Lord Rudolph, and he should think no more about her.

When the watch bell struck the first watch of the night, the tossing of the ship ceased and they glided into the harbor. Evangeline sprang from the bunk, too impatient to sit. She returned to the window, staring at the ships without, many of them floating by within arms' reach.

By the second bell, the ship moved only at a crawl. Slowly, slowly, the *Aurora* slid past a long dock, and finally, after weeks and weeks at sea, she came to a stop.

The noise above multiplied. Shouts rang into the night, sharp thuds sounded on the deck above, whistles blew, bells sounded. Commotion she could not see thronged the ship, locking it to land, to civilization.

She sat by the window for a long time; she did not know for how long. But it was very late when the muffled sound of booted feet at last came to her from the other side of the door.

Evangeline rose and scuttled to it, putting her eye to the keyhole. She could not see in the darkness who came, but whoever it was moved stealthily.

"Austin?" she whispered.

"It's me, miss."

He spoke softly, so she answered in a hiss. "Mr. Seward. He's locked me in."

"I have a key, miss."

Evangeline stepped back from the door. The key clanged in the lock, too loud, she thought, then turned. The door swung open.

"Mr. Seward, I am so pleased to see you. Where is the captain?"

"Meeting with the harbor master—"

"Excellent. You must help me, Mr. Seward. Will you—"

"I have a carriage waiting. Best gather your things."

"Yes, certainly."

Evangeline snatched up her valise and mantel, and tucked her book of devotions under her arm. Mr. Seward motioned her to follow. He had a lantern, but kept it dark, allowing only one beam of light to touch the floor. Evangeline followed the beam, relieved to be free of her cabin prison.

Seward led her above and quietly made his way across the deck to the lowered gangplank. The ship clamored with activity below as cargo holds were opened and men paraded back and forth with boxes and bales on their backs. Mr. Osborn stood among them, watching, directing. Captain Blackwell was nowhere in sight.

A pang smote her. She would never see him again. Her last view of him would be the haunted look in his eyes just before he slammed the door of the cabin. The look that meant he'd just realized another marriage would be a mistake.

Just as well he knew it. Evangeline took firmer hold of her valise and swallowed the lump in her throat. In time, he would forget her. And she would forget him. Their lives would take them apart. It was meant to be.

"This way, miss," Mr. Seward whispered. He took her arm, and led her down the gangplank.

Chapter Twenty-one

A dark carriage awaited them at the end of the dock. Square, sleek, and polished, the carriage gleamed in the coachlights that adorned it. A pair of fine gray horses waited in the traces, and a coachman in dark livery took up the reins as they approached.

Mr. Seward assisted her into the carriage, then he climbed in as well and settled on the seat opposite her. Evangeline sat back, breathing hard, trying to banish the core of pain in her heart. But she trembled with excitement. A new world lay at her feet, waiting for her to explore it, with or without Austin Blackwell.

The door slammed, the coachman cracked his whip, and the carriage lurched forward. Its wheels rumbled on the cobble and brick street, but the vehicle, well-slung, jarred Evangeline little.

Mr. Seward had tucked her valise under the seat.

Evangeline hugged her book of devotions to her chest, the hard edges of it pressing her breasts.

She cleared her throat. "I did not see Lord Rudolph, as we went. Is he still aboard? I wish I had dared stop to search for him."

Seward shook his head, looking surprised. "He was the first to disembark. Was waiting when the gangplank lowered."

Apprehension twinged her. "He was?"

"I believe he was in a hurry to find his English friends. And he thought Captain Blackwell would be happy to see him depart."

"Very likely. But—"

He could not have been very sincere, then, when he asked her to marry him and to accompany him back to England. He should have remained, ready to sweep her away from Austin the moment she appeared. That he'd simply gone puzzled her. And hurt.

"But what?"

She looked back at Seward's affable face. "Nothing. I would have liked to see him before he went, that's all."

She sat back, depression settling over her. Men were unfathomable.

The carriage swung into another street and began to climb. She hung onto the strap above her as the conveyance lurched from side to side.

Wherever Mr. Seward had obtained the coach, it certainly was luxurious, even more luxurious than Squire Dobbins's coach back home. The squire had been quite proud of it and had given rides to the neighbors he deemed high-born enough to grace it. But this coach far surpassed it. It had plush squabs, satin-lined walls, and a firebox on the floor that glowed with warmth.

"Where are we going?" she asked after a time. "My cousin lives in Queen Street. You can take me there."

"We are going to Beacon Street, to Captain Blackwell's house."

She stilled. "To Captain Blackwell's house?"

"Yes. This is his carriage. He told me to escort you to his home."

"He told you."

"An order, he said. I was to stay with you and keep you from harm."

The misty regret she'd conjured vanished in an instant. She ground her teeth. "He is the most insufferable, arrogant male creature I have ever known. Stop the carriage and let me out at once."

Seward's eyes widened. "No, indeed. He told me to keep you safe, and I will. I can not leave you here in the middle of the Boston waterfront."

"You were in it with him all along. And I thought you were my friend."

"I don't understand. Why would you not want to go to Captain Blackwell's home? You are going to marry him. He asked me to stand up with him." His round face beamed pride.

"Because he is forcing me into this marriage. I do not wish it."

He looked troubled. "I thought you loved him."

Evangeline opened her mouth to retort, then subsided and sank back into the cushions. She was not sure what she felt. Her emotions tumbled one over the other and confused her. Whatever she felt, she could not find the words to explain it to the affable Mr. Seward.

She contemplated flinging herself from the carriage and taking her chances on the street, but with an inward sigh, she dismissed the idea. She would no doubt simply injure herself, and she had no idea where she was. Charging headlong into a Spanish prison had seemed less intimidating than finding her way alone at night in this dark and busy city. Perhaps once at Austin's house, she could ascertain where her cousin's house lay, and then plan her escape.

The carriage climbed and wound through narrow streets lined with lighted dwellings hidden behind tall trees. Some of the houses had a stretch of garden in the front and an iron gate separating them from the street. The coach pulled to a halt in front of just such a one. Both its neighbors showed lights in the upper floors, but what Evangeline could only assume was Austin's house appeared dark and cheerless.

A lad who'd perched on the back of the carriage jumped down and ran toward the house, cupping the flame of a lighted taper in his hand. He unscrewed the chimneys of the lights that flanked the front door, and lit the wicks inside. The lamps warmed and glowed.

Mr. Seward descended and handed Evangeline down. Her boots touched the hard brick of the path and a qualm stole over her. She sensed that once she walked up this path, she would never leave again. Her life would end here, all tangled up with Austin's desires and her own confused emotions.

His red brick house loomed over her, as austere and forbidding as he was. The lanterns shone on a painted, black-panelled door and a polished brass knocker. Mr. Seward fumbled in his pockets and produced a slim key, which he fitted in the keyhole.

An upper window of the house next door opened and a woman in a white mobcap thrust her head out. The cap's ribbons fluttered in the breeze like flags of surrender.

"Captain Blackwell is not at home," she called. "He is expected any day."

Mr. Seward took a step back and lifted his bicorne hat. "We've just come from his ship. This young lady is to be Captain Blackwell's wife."

The woman's mouth popped open. The mobcap disappeared inside. "Did you hear that Mr. Milhouse? Our captain is getting married." She thrust her head out again. "I am coming straight down."

Evangeline imagined the woman plummeting directly to the ground in her haste, but the cap disappeared again, and window slammed shut.

Mr. Seward opened the door. The lad with the taper entered first, moving about to light candles left in readiness.

Evangeline found herself in a white-paneled foyer with a floor of polished marble. A staircase rose along one side of this hall, sweeping in a straight line to the floors above. Double-paneled doors on either side of the hall stood closed.

The house oppressed her, chill and unwelcoming. She pressed her lips together and stood in the middle of it, daring it to overwhelm her.

A rustling sounded at the door, and the woman from the next house bustled in. She came to Evangeline and

Jennifer Ashley

seized her hands in her warm, plump ones. "Oh, my dear. I am Mrs. Milhouse. We've been Captain Blackwell's neighbors for years and years and years. I am so pleased he is marrying again. God bless you, child."

After the ship docked, Austin worked all through the night, all the next day, and well into that night. He met with the harbor master, the shipping company's representative, the merchant whose cargo he delivered, his officers. He'd argued with the merchant, who was inclined to believe his stores damaged, until Austin had to personally open a few crates and show him that his French brandy was well intact.

The harbor master's assistant had later oiled aboard, expecting his usual bribe, only to swallow hard and depart when he saw that the ship's captain was Austin Blackwell.

Lord Rudolph had departed without a word and without honoring Austin's request that he state where he would be staying while in Boston. Austin had his cabin boy follow the man discreetly, but Cyril had come scampering back within the hour to announce he'd lost the Englishman's trail. Austin cursed, but wasn't terribly surprised. He would inform a few people in town of Lord Rudolph's presence. He had little doubt he'd find the man again when he wanted to.

He handed over the mutineers to the magistrates. Many of them were cowed, afraid. He handed Albright over, as well. He'd spent many hours with the lad, but neither hard questioning, nor threats had produced the name of the man who'd sent him to murder Austin and steal the papers. Albright gave him a look of hatred as

252

he was led away in chains. Austin merely turned his back. He wasn't finished with Albright yet. He'd wrest his secrets from him any way he could.

He then had the great joy of marching Evangeline's stepbrother off his ship, purchasing him a ticket on a packet returning to England, and personally loading him aboard.

The one person he did not see in all that time was his mentor, even though they'd made plans to meet shortly after the *Aurora* docked. Austin had the papers well hidden, but he would feel better after he'd talked to Captain Gainesborough. He wanted to ask the man several pointed questions, and end this business with the documents.

Late the second night, he finally quit the ship and headed for home. His coachman brought the carriage as summoned and loaded Austin's locker on the top. Austin carried his personal papers in their box inside with him, and the coach rolled through the dark streets toward Beacon Hill.

He wondered how Evangeline had settled in. He'd sent her off with Seward to keep her both from prying eyes and from danger. His butler and housekeeper, always kept informed of his schedule, had had instructions to open and warm the house and replenish supplies so that Austin could return to a comfortable house rather than a cold one.

His pulse quickened as he descended the carriage and made his way up the brick walk to his front door. They would have put Evangeline in the front spare bedroom, the most elegant in the house. She would be there now, her head pillowed on her arm, her lovely golden hair spilling over the sheets.

His blood heated. He opened the door to a lit foyer, and took up one of the candles to light his way. He ascended the stairs, bidding his footman to leave the locker downstairs. Plenty of time to unpack later.

He should let her sleep, he thought as he neared the door of the front spare bedroom. There was still much to do to prepare for the upcoming wedding. She'd been through so much on the voyage; she deserved the rest.

But he so wanted to see her. All through the day and night and through the irritating business of landing the ship and unloading it, he'd thought of her. He craved her so much he could taste it. For too many years to count, he'd not felt the utter peace he'd finally discovered while lying in her arms in his cabin. She'd filled the empty places in his heart, filled them until they overflowed and he was happy to drown in her.

He put his hand on the doorhandle and softly pushed his way into the room. The window stood open a crack, and a sliver of cool air brushed him. His candle flame danced in the draft, sending a sputtering of warm wax over his thumb.

Over the soft breeze sounded a loud, masculine snore.

Austin stopped dead. The bed's curtains were drawn, obscuring his view of who lay there. The snore came again, long and drawn out and full of little snorts. He strode across the room, blood pounding, and ripped the curtain back.

Sprawled under the blankets on his back, one arm outflung, lay Lieutenant Seward.

He raised the candle. A drop of wax dropped on the young man's nightshirt.

"Seward."

The young man jumped, then blinked. He dug the heel of his hand into his eyes, saw Austin, and jumped again.

"Sir." He sat up and tried to salute.

"Where is Miss Clemens?"

Seward glanced around, as if expecting to find her under the pillow.

He'd damned well better not.

"Next door, sir. With Mrs. Milhouse."

Austin relaxed. "Ah. I forgot about my busybody neighbor."

"She said it would be more seemly if Miss Clemens stayed with her until the wedding."

Austin swallowed disappointment. He'd wanted to make love to Evangeline, then marry her and make love to her some more. He'd wanted to glide in here, strip to his skin, slip under the covers with her, and kiss her awake.

Thank God Seward snored.

"It's all right, there's no harm done."

Seward visibly relaxed. "Yes, sir."

Austin dropped the curtain. "Go back to sleep. And when you get up in the morning, lad, go on home to your family. They'll want to see you."

Longing, then fear, then longing again chased their way across Seward's face. "Yes, sir."

"Right. Good night."

" 'Night, sir."

Austin left him to it, trying to stifle his disappointment, and made his way down the hall to his own cold and dark bedroom.

He paused a long moment in the doorway, studying the tester bed that stood in the middle of the room, its brocade hangings heavy and oppressive. He'd spent much of his first marriage in that bed. Alone.

Evangeline slept somewhere on the other side of the wallpapered wall the headboard rested against. So close, yet miles might have separated them. He needed her. He needed her with fierce intensity, needed her to soothe the darkness inside him. He needed to tell his fears to her and then to bury his face in the curve of her neck and seek her comfort.

And he needed to do it now, because right now he had so many fears.

He gave his elegant bed a glare of loathing. Then he turned and left the room and spent the night in one of the spare beds in the back of the house.

In the morning, Austin received a letter from Captain Gainesborough. His mentor had made a short journey to Cambridge, which was why he had not been at the docks. He had returned now, and requested that Austin call on him at nine that evening.

Austin breakfasted, dressed, and strode around the iron railings that separated his house from his neighbors'. Their doorknocker fit, cold and heavy, in his hand, and thudded hollowly against the door when he thumped it.

His collar itched. He thrust his hat awkwardly under his arm and smoothed the misty raindrops from his hair.

His right boot felt too tight, and he suddenly wondered if he'd buttoned his waistcoat right.

The door was wrenched open, and the innocent face of the Milhouse's footman peered out at him. The young man looked puzzled when Austin gave his name, but turned and led Austin toward the back of the house.

Two ladies sat in the back parlor, where a fire in the hearth danced merrily, pushing back the gloom. One lady, wearing a fantastically trimmed mobcap, sprang to her feet.

"Dear Captain." Mrs. Milhouse advanced, hands outstretched. "Welcome home. We are so pleased to see you again."

Austin took her hands, and dropped his hat. The footman discreetly retrieved it and drifted from the room.

"And to bring a bride with you. How romantic. She has been telling me of your harrowing adventures."

Oh, good lord. Austin squeezed Mrs. Milhouse's hands and released them. He could imagine what kinds of things Evangeline had been telling her.

The other woman in the room rose to her feet, but remained standing by the camelback sofa. Austin turned to her, and stopped.

He beheld a vision. Evangeline wore a dress of rich gray-blue, which gathered a little above her waist and fell in a full sweep of skirt to the carpet. A fichu hugged her shoulders and crossed over her breasts, then tucked into the gown's sash. A small cap, floating with lace, adorned her hair. Ringlets, burnished like gold, escaped and wisped to her shoulders. Behind her spectacles, her gray eyes shone like polished diamonds.

Austin paused for several full heartbeats, drinking her in. Yes, she held beauty. Whether dressed in formal loveliness, or rushing about in a torn chemise and too-large coat, or twined in the sheets of his bunk, she held beauty. His breath hurt him.

"Well," Mrs. Milhouse said brightly. "I must see what Mr. Milhouse is up to this morning. He likes me near when he writes his letters. Pray, excuse me."

Austin murmured, "Of course," and made her a slight bow. Evangeline said nothing at all. Her gray gaze fixed on Austin, and her hands curled into fists.

Mrs. Milhouse beamed a smile on them both, exited the drawing room, and pulled the door nearly closed behind her.

"You are well?" Austin said into the pool of silence.

Evangeline played with a fold in her gown. "Mrs. Milhouse has been quite kind."

He felt the strain in the air between them, as if a curtain of sticky molasses had dropped. "I am sorry to have deserted you. I had many duties, and I thought you would be more comfortable away from the ship."

"And so you sent poor Mr. Seward to be my watchdog."

The curtain crumpled and fell.

"You could not come alone. And I want you protected until this business is at an end."

"Do you mean the—" She jiggled her hand as if rattling papers. "Or our wedding?"

"Both."

"I see. I'm surprised you did not give Mr. Seward orders to lock me in my room of nights."

Austin said nothing. He studied the painted cornice that covered the ceiling joints.

Evangeline flushed. "Oh, so you did."

"I will do whatever it takes to protect you, Evangeline."

"Or keep me prisoner."

"Whichever you prefer."

She folded her arms. "Austin, please stop this foolishness. You do not want to marry me."

"Yes, I do."

"You only wish to keep me close to you so I will not tell anyone about—" She jiggled imaginary papers again. "You know."

"They will soon be in the hands of the highest officials and we will both be safe from harm."

She took a step toward him and lowered her voice. "What does it all mean, Austin? Who are those people?"

Austin's skin prickled. The scent of her filled him, driving away trivial worries like the potential fall of his new nation. "I will tell you when it is safe for you to know."

"I could simply go away. Perhaps if I traveled to one of the far-off colonies, way to the south, maybe, where no one has heard of me, I will be safe there."

Let her go? Ludicrous. He'd lost her once, and he'd hated every minute of her absence.

"They are not colonies any more."

She made an expansive gesture. "Whatever you call them now. No one would know me in the Carolinas."

"You do not know that. We are a small country, in terms of people. Everyone seems to know everyone else's business. Gossip travels, even as far as the Carolinas."

She planted her fists on her hips. "Austin Blackwell, give me one logical reason why you should marry me."

A smile tugged his mouth. He reached out and

caught a loose tendril of her hair. "Logic has nothing to do with it. You need looking after."

"So I heard you tell Lord Rudolph."

Ah, so she'd heard that conversation on the deck that night. Annoyance prickled him. He'd only been trying to make Lord Rudolph shut up and go away. Women so enjoyed misinterpreting things.

"So I did."

Her eyes sparked dangerously. "I heard you say that other women would leave you alone now, and you would be relieved. Do so many women pursue you?"

"A captain's wife has a certain—prestige."

"Then why do you not marry someone who wishes to become a captain's wife?"

Austin's throat went tight. He released her lock of hair and slid his hand behind her neck. "Because I do not want a woman like that."

Her eyelids fluttered, and her blush deepened. Their breaths mingled. Hers smelled of sweet tea.

"You make a mistake," she said. "You are giving up what you love because you think you ought to."

Austin shook his head. He kneaded her soft neck, loosening the cap. "I have run away for too long. I ran away from my wife, from my—" He stopped. "From my life. I want to stand still, now."

"You will grow to resent me."

He brushed his mouth over the corner of her lips. "Resent the woman who has awakened me? You underestimate me, my sparrow."

She breathed faster. Austin kissed her lower lip. She closed her eyes and gave a little sigh, her limbs loosening—surrendering to him once more.

Chapter Twenty-two

Her lips warmed him. Soft, pliant, tasting a little of sugar. Austin drew the lower one into his mouth, suckling gently. He closed his eyes. She would be his soon. His wife. As soon as formalities were taken care of.

His to kiss, to touch, to lie beside every night. His arousal stirred.

She slid her hands to his shoulders, fingers sinking into his coat. Her head tilted back, and her breath touched him, feather soft.

His arousal lifted and swelled. He ran his tongue over the seam of her lips, then delved inside, opening her mouth to his. Her tongue moved in response; he'd taught her to kiss, and she'd learned her lessons well.

He released her lips, and she whimpered.

"Do you want me, my sweet?" he asked softly.

"Yes."

Triumph laced him, but burning, untasted desire drowned it.

He loosened the fichu from her sash, pushing it back to bare her shoulders. He kissed her creamy flesh, tasting the salt of her skin. Her breasts rose quickly over the low decollatage, and his hand came up to meet them.

A low moan escaped her throat. Her fingers furrowed through his hair, and she arched her body to his, soft, pliant, wanting. Oh, yes, she was his. Even if she denied him with her words, her body begged for him.

He slid his strong arms around her, cradling her as they tumbled gently to the floor. The wool carpet prickled Austin's hands as he braced himself, lying against her, not crushing her with his full weight.

She gazed at him from behind crooked spectacles. "Austin, when you touch me I feel—" She shook her head against the carpet.

"You feel what?"

She lowered her gaze. "Wicked."

He chuckled. "Do you, my siren?"

"Yes."

Mine. Austin lowered his head and kissed the swell of her breasts. She drew her leg up, bending at the knee. He reached down and skimmed his hand over her ankle, up her slim calf, dragging the light skirt as he went. His fingers moved to her thigh, satin smooth.

"Oh, my." She bit her lip.

He pushed her skirt high, and slid his hand under its warmth, resting his palm on the swirl of curls it hid. Evangeline gasped, and her hips rocked.

She would be his wife soon. He could wait. It would not be long.

He moved his hand and she moved with it, seeking to press against him. The dampness of her arousal, the scent of her, poured over him. To hell with waiting.

He knelt back, pushing her skirts up to her abdomen. Her head lolled on the carpet, her cap loosening, coming free. She touched her tongue to her moistened lips, her gray eyes heavy with desire.

Austin unbuttoned the fastenings at his waistband, his fingers clumsy. Never, never, never had he wanted a woman as much as he wanted her. She did not even have to touch him. Simply entering a room with her in it had made him hard.

He readied himself, then knelt over her. He slid his hands beneath her buttocks and lifted her hips forward. She helped him, arching her body, reaching for him. He pressed his tip to the scorching hot place asking for him, then entered her to the base of him in one swift, silent stroke.

She cried out in delight, and he muffled it with his lips. She squeezed him, tight, oh so tight, but he was a perfect fit. He kissed her, opening her mouth, ravishing her with his. Mine, mine. Siren.

He realized he babbled the words as he kissed her. She cried out again, drunk with passion.

"Shh, my Evangeline." He kissed her skin, her lips. He slid into her so easily. It hurt him all the way down to his soul, and yet it was not pain but the erasing of pain. He opened his eyes and drank in the sight of her: her shining hair straggling on the carpet, her eyes glittering with tears, her lips swollen and parted. "You're so beautiful."

Her lips formed words, but she only whimpered and groaned. Her hips lifted against his, again and again, her little gasps following the rhythm.

With this act, she became his. His lover, his wife, his life. The loneliness that had filled him for ten years splintered and fled.

His control snapped. He forgot to be gentle. He drove into her, wanting her, needing her. He kissed her lips hard; his fingers left bruises in her flesh. He snaked his fingers through her hair, wrapping it around his hand, pulling her head back to kiss and nip her long, sensuous throat.

From a long way away, he heard his own cry of joy, as the world spun away and a wave of bliss drowned him. He gasped for breath, clawing for the surface, as he had the night he'd rescued Albright from the sea. He shook his head, trying to clear the fog, reaching for the control that drove his every waking moment.

He spilled his seed inside her, driving himself far into her, wanting this moment to stretch an eternity.

Her eyes flew open. She clutched him, pulling him to her in movements that pressed him into her over and over and over. And then she cried out, her voice sweet and filled with longing. Austin gathered her to him, his own climax ebbing, his breath shuddering.

He laid down on her, burying his head in the curve of her neck. She stroked his back, her movements languid, and her hot breath touched his forehead.

The room grew quiet. Austin's own labored breathing

broke the silence. Evangeline lay noiselessly beneath him.

He raised his head. Her eyes lay closed, her lashes against her cheek. Tears leaked from beneath her lids and slid silently down her face. A red mark laced her throat, and bruises showed dark on her white shoulders.

"I've hurt you," he whispered, anguished. "Evangeline, I am sorry."

She opened her eyes, met his gaze, and implored, "Austin, please do not give up your life for me. I could not bear it."

He brushed a lock of hair from her forehead, then laid down and rested his head on her breast. "I already have, my sparrow."

Evangeline traced patterns on the windowsill as she watched Austin Blackwell's front gate from Mrs. Milhouse's second story window. The sun set behind the houses to the west, lighting the sky brilliant pink and blue. After weeks of traveling under the huge open sky, Evangeline found the buildings stifling, the sunset disappointing.

All day long, people had been coming and going from Austin's house. All day long, Evangeline watched them, blushing at the memory of her wanton behavior.

If Mrs. Milhouse had guessed what she and Austin had done on her sitting room floor, she said nothing. She smiled a secret smile, though, whenever Evangeline nervously adjusted her fichu. She prayed that it covered the dull mark Austin had left on her throat, and hoped Mrs. Milhouse would ask no questions.

Austin had gone from her with a triumphant light in his eyes. Her shameful behavior seemed to please him. But of course, he wanted her to feel too ashamed to face her cousin, or anyone else, and so remain with him. As his wife.

She could no longer dismiss the possibility that she might have a child. Coupling once may produce nothing, but twice upped the odds. No doubt he'd thought of that too, damn the arrogant man. He wanted to marry her, so he would arrange for it to happen no matter what.

She sighed, ruffling the petals of the rose that reposed in the slim vase next to her. Austin had sent the rose, along with a host of instructions. They would marry the following morning. She would stay with Mrs. Milhouse until then, as he had much business to take care of that day.

Evangeline wrote to her cousin that morning, explaining that she'd at last arrived in Boston, and where she stayed. Mrs. Milhouse's servant had delivered it, but Evangeline had received no reply, and the servant had reported the family not at home. Evangeline felt her last hope crumble and fall away. Austin would get his way.

Throughout the day, when she could, Evangeline watched the comings and goings next door. The footman who had opened the house upon her arrival ran back and forth on many errands, his young frame unbowed. Mr. Seward departed early, then returned later that afternoon, his step buoyant.

Evangeline plucked a petal off the drooping rose and slid the smooth blossom through her fingers. The fragrance filled the air. She wished she had a friend she could confide in, could turn to for advice. Mr. Seward and Mrs. Milhouse both thought it a fine thing for her to marry Captain Blackwell. Mr. Milhouse, whom she'd met at breakfast, had grunted and said it was high time the man married again. No doubt her cousin, Beth, would believe the same thing. Why shouldn't a useless spinster rejoice at marrying a wealthy and handsome captain?

Because if she gave him her heart, he'd break it, and her loneliness would consume her. She would lie awake in their bed at night, alone, while he roamed the world to shake off the chains that bound him to the land.

A dark carriage, pulled by plumed horses, rolled to a stop before Austin's house. The carriage, low and sleek, spoke of wealth, as did the liveried footman who sprang to the ground and opened the door.

She recognized the figure who emerged. He had discarded the plain clothes one of the officers had lent him and was now dressed almost foppishly in embroidered frock coat, striped waistcoat, skin-tight kid breeches, and high, polished boots. He removed his tricorn hat, and the setting sun touched his gold-blond hair and the patch that covered his left eye.

Evangeline abandoned the window. She snatched up a light shawl and left the room, hurrying down the stairs. At the front door, the young footman sprang up from dozing on his bench, and wrenched the door open for her.

"Tell Mrs. Milhouse I have stepped next door," she panted. "I will return in a few minutes."

The footman nodded, scrubbing his eyes with the back of his hand.

Evangeline hastened down the brick walk. A breeze moved the green leaves that hung over the gate and the shrubs that wound through the iron fence. She stepped out of the Milhouses' gate and through Austin's. No footman reposed at his front door—she'd seen him speed away on another errand.

She opened the heavy door herself and emerged into the cool, marbled front hall. Voices spilled from the back of the house, Austin's and Lord Rudolph's. She pushed open the white double doors her and found herself in a music room. A pianoforte stood prominently before the window, and chairs, still covered with sheets, were grouped before it.

On the other side of the room, another set of double doors stood open. The setting sun filled that room with red light, staining the yellow tiles a faint orange. The voices came from there.

Evangeline hurried across the room and through the second set of doors. She found herself in a small drawing room. The furniture covers had been removed here. Gold damask chairs and a sofa had been placed in a square before a fireplace, which stood cold and empty for summer. Mr. Seward stood before this fireplace, his face hard. Austin and Lord Rudolph faced one another in the center of the room, Austin with brows lowered thunderously, Lord Rudolph regarding him with cool disdain.

Both men turned when Evangeline pattered into the room.

Lord Rudolph smiled. "Evangeline. My rescuer." He

came forward, reaching for her. She lifted her hands to his, and he kissed her fingers.

"Rudy, you never said goodbye," she accused. "Mr. Seward said you left the ship right away."

Lord Rudolph released her hands and looked abashed. "I had—business to attend to."

"He means he scurried away before anyone recognized him by ill chance," Austin said. "He's a spy."

Lord Rudolph stilled. "You presume."

"It is the only likely explanation for your presence in Havana and your reluctance to tell anyone your story. I doubt an important lord's first-born son would be traipsing about the world getting himself arrested in odd places simply for entertainment. But someone like you can so easily admit himself to high social circles and keep an eye on what other governments are doing. And it explains why you know so much about things you shouldn't."

Mr. Seward's look turned murderous. "An English spy? You should have let me kill him when I had the chance."

Lord Rudolph went white about the lips. "I came here to save your worthless neck, Blackwell, not to listen to abuse. Evangeline, your husband-to-be has got himself mixed up with dangerous intrigues. You deserve to know that."

He must mean the papers. She bit her lip.

Austin continued smoothly. "Which you would know nothing about if you were simply an English lord's dissipate son."

Lord Rudolph gave a nod. "Very well, you are right. I do, as a favor to his majesty, keep my eyes and ears open for things he might find—interesting. But my travels this time have nothing to do with your little mission. I discovered it entirely by accident, and I'm here to tell you to keep well out of it. For Evangeline's sake, if not for your own."

Evangeline took a step forward. "I wish you would be plainer. What danger is he in?"

Austin shot her a narrow look. "Nothing you need concern yourself with. Go back next door and wait until I send for you tomorrow."

She planted her hands on her hips. "I am going to be your wife, Austin. I want to know what kind of danger my husband will be in."

He raised a brow. "Ah, so now there is no more argument about the fact you will be my wife."

"You have taken the decision from my hands and you know it."

"Your knowledge is dangerous, Blackwell," Lord Rudolph said. "Everyone on that list is going to be out to make certain you never speak of it."

"You have seen it, then?"

Lord Rudolph shook his head. "I know of its existence. I do not know the details."

"I do," Evangeline broke in. "I've seen it."

Lord Rudolph's jaw dropped. "You let her see it, Blackwell? Are you mad?"

"*Let* is not exactly the word," Austin said. "But yes, she did see it."

"But I do not know what it means. It's something to do with the war, is it not?"

Lord Rudolph nodded. "It is a list of damn fools who

wish to pull the colonies back under English rule again."

Austin's gaze rested on him. "And you do not wish it?"

"No. It was a stupid war in the first place. England had not ruled the colonies in any practical way in decades. This piece of the empire was expensive and not worth keeping."

Mr. Seward scowled, his face reddening. Austin motioned him to silence. "What would you do with this list if you had it?"

"Destroy it."

There was a heartbeat of silence.

"Thus protecting the gentlemen on it?"

"They are only guilty of foolishness."

Austin shook his head. "They will spread their foolishness in other ways. They must be stopped."

Lord Rudolph subsided. "Either way, you endanger your life. And Evangeline's."

Austin's hands curled into fists. "After tonight, there will be no more danger. I have arranged everything." His voice went quiet. "Unless you came here to stop me."

"I came here to discover what you were doing playing with the kinds of secrets you do not know how to handle."

"Tonight will bring the end of that. Your concern is noted."

"Then at least put Evangeline under my protection until your transaction is finished."

Austin went still. "Under *your* protection?"

"I have a place she may stay until all is over. Safe and

sound. You will not have to worry about her."

Evangeline's pulse quickened. Lord Rudolph could take her to England, to give her over to his mother, as he had offered. Then Austin would not need to bother with her.

"Yes, Austin, I would feel safer with Lord Rudolph than at Mrs. Milhouse's, if there are enemies about."

Austin swung on her. The cold in his eyes sent her back a step. "I am not letting you out of my sight."

Lord Rudolph scowled. "Did you plan to take her with you tonight?"

"I will lock her in the cellar and set guards on the door if it will make you feel better."

"This is not your ship, captain. You can't throw her in the brig."

"The hell I can't."

"I will guard her," Mr. Seward said suddenly. "With my life."

Lord Rudolph looked him coolly up and down. "It *would* be with your life, lad. You do not know what you are up against. I will stay here with her, if you will not allow me to remove her from the danger."

Austin nodded once. "It may be as well to let you."

Evangeline blinked. He did not object to Lord Rudolph staying here with her? Then her anger mounted. He wanted Lord Rudolph as a guard, yes, but under his roof, under his control.

"Does my opinion matter for naught?" she broke in tartly.

All three gentlemen turned to her in surprise, as if they'd forgotten her presence. She made an exasperated noise. "If I am the one in danger, should I not be consulted?"

"Not in this instance, my dear," Austin said.

"You will be in more danger than I. No one knows I have read the papers but the three of you. They know you have had them with you during your voyage. What precautions will you take?"

His dark eyes flickered. "I have already taken them."

"I do not believe you."

"It is of no matter whether you believe me or not. It is you who dismiss danger. I believe the cellar is an excellent idea."

"Don't you dare lock me up, you—you tyrant."

"What better way to both keep you from harm, and ensure that you will attend your own wedding?"

Evangeline flushed. "You are determined to run headlong into this foolish marriage."

His eyes sparked, rage tethered. "Indeed, I am."

"Even if I do not wish it?"

"You do wish it. You are just being stubborn."

"Stubborn for your own good."

He took a step toward her. "I will not allow any female to tell me what is for my good."

"You tell me what is for mine."

"That is my right as a husband."

"You are not my husband!"

"Not until tomorrow, but we have lain together as husband and wife. The wedding is a mere formality."

Evangeline's face went scalding hot. *"Austin."*

Lord Rudolph scowled. Mr. Seward's mouth popped open.

"Let us have no more argument, Evangeline, or I truly

will lock you in the cellar." He turned away.

Evangeline strode across the room after him. "You arrogant beast! Miss Pyne warned us about gentlemen like you, men who force their attentions upon you, and then humiliate you—"

He swung around, his large body stopping Evangeline in her tracks. "Your Miss Pyne is a foolish spinster with no experience of gentlemen at all."

"Miss Pyne was my dear friend. My only friend."

She bit her lip as the truth of that remark struck her. In her entire lonely life, only her gentle instructor, a lady of middle years, had ever proved to be a friend. Now that lady was far, far away, and she would never approve or understand the choices Evangeline had made that had brought her to stand in Austin's back parlor arguing with him today.

His severe look softened. "You will have time to make plenty of friends in Boston.

"And you, sir, have no experience of women if you dismiss their friends so offhandedly."

"For God's sake, Evangeline, I was married and had three mistresses. Of course I know about women."

She stared, her heart beating hard. "You had—?" No gentleman ever spoke of his amorous intrigues to ladies, but Evangeline had simply assumed Austin had had none.

"Oh, hell." He stormed away from her, leaving anger in his wake.

Lord Rudolph said softly, "I should call you out for that, Blackwell."

"Duelling is for idiots." He turned back, his iron control at his command once more. "I beg your pardon,

Evangeline. I spoke in anger. Forget I mentioned it."

He'd had mistresses. Lovely ladies who'd shared his bed, who'd beckoned him with their long arms for his embrace, for his kisses. Miss Pyne had explained in an agonized whisper that most gentleman kept such women. Why should Austin not as well?

Hot tears pricked her eyes. She blinked them back, forcing her chin up.

"It is of no moment."

He stood silhouetted by the dying light in the window behind him. His broad shoulders were so strong. She'd clung to those shoulders in her passion, taking his strength to fortify her own. She could not, would not, give him the satisfaction believing her jealous of his former paramours.

Assuming they were *former* paramours.

A tinkling of glass sounded just beyond his left shoulder. Evangeline saw a pane of the French window crumple and shatter. As Austin swung around, a small black shape thunked on the carpet just at his feet.

Evangeline's breath stopped. It was an explosive, just like the kind she'd been forced to lay at the prison in Havana, small and round, spiked so that it would cling to wooden windows or doorframes when thrown. The lit fuse sparked merrily in the semi-darkness of Austin's drawing room.

Chapter Twenty-three

Evangeline screamed and sprinted toward Austin. He brought his boot heel down on the fuse, tearing it from the explosive and grinding the sparking flame out on the carpet. He shoved away the small explosive and it rattled and bounced to a far corner of the room.

He turned. "Evangeline, you do not run *toward* a lit bomb."

She halted, her breath coming in gasps. "But you could have—it could have—"

"What a pity it didn't."

The cold voice came from the French door, now standing open. In it, framed by the dwindling light, stood the curvaceous body of Anna Adams. She had a scarf wrapped around one side of her face and a pistol in her hand, which she pointed straight at Austin.

A man stepped through the door behind her. Tall and

hulking, he filled the doorframe. His bulk ran more to fat than to muscle, and he reeked of tar. His black beard was braided into two plaits and his hair hung in greasy locks over his shoulders. He carried a brace of pistols, both of them cocked, and his grin spoke of evil Evangeline could not comprehend.

"Get out or I send for the constable," Austin said levelly.

Anna smiled, half of it lost in the scarf. "No, captain. We are not leaving. I want all of you sitting down." She kept her pistol firmly trained on Austin. The man came around her, motioning with his guns at the others.

Lord Rudolph stood his ground, as did Mr. Seward. Austin swung around, keeping his body between Evangeline and the intruders.

"Sit down, I said."

No one obeyed.

The man moved swiftly. Thrusting one pistol into his belt, he swerved around Austin and grabbed Evangeline by the hair. His fetid smell washed her and pain shot through her scalp. She brought her hands up to fight him.

Austin's voice rang like a slap. "No. Sit down. Do as she says."

Lord Rudolph moved slowly to the sofa and sat. Mr. Seward, scowling, took the seat beside him. The large man dragged Evangeline to the chair opposite them. Tears sprang to her eyes and her limbs shook, but inside her anger brewed.

"It is pleasant to see you again, Miss Clemens. May I introduce Sebastian?"

Sebastian jerked her head back. It cracked on the top of the chair, jarring her teeth.

How could she have ever mistaken Lord Rudolph for this man? Lord Rudolph was refined. Sebastian was a brute, disgusting and vicious. He and Anna made a fine pair.

"I dragged him out of that prison after you so blundered." Anna cast a scornful glance at Lord Rudolph and his eyepatch. "I took Sebastian from that place. And paid with this." She snatched off her scarf.

Half of her face was creased and leathery, red skin crackling over cheekbone and jaw. Her eye was swollen shut, perhaps even gone. Only her lips had escaped the burning, but her smile twisted what had once been a beautiful face into a mockery. Evangeline gasped.

"This is your doing," Anna said to Austin. "And your slut's."

Austin held her gaze with his and spoke with calm fury. "If you hurt Evangeline, I will kill you."

"You will have nothing to say about it."

Silkily, Anna moved away from Austin to stand next to her pirate, who still had his fingers laced through Evangeline's hair.

Evangeline looked back up into the woman's face. The evil she'd sensed on the boat lay naked on her face; she did not bother to conceal it now. She pressed her pistol to Evangeline's cheek. "No one in this room will move until I give them leave, or Miss Spinster Clemens will die. You are still a spinster, aren't you, my dear? Or are you his lover now?"

Evangeline flushed. Anna laughed out loud. "You worked quickly, my dear." She looked up. "Ah, Mr. Seward. You here." She nudged Sebastian. "He is the one I told you about, my love."

Sebastian laughed, spraying his foul breath over Evangeline's face. "Is my lady not good enough for ye?" His voice was harsh, uneducated. Evangeline noticed he only spoke when Anna prompted him, as if he were well under the woman's thumb. "There's some merriment in this, I warrant." He lifted his pistol and pointed it at Seward. "Show your captain how much you admire him, boy."

Anna burst out laughing. "Rich, my love. Take the high-and-mighty captain down a peg or two."

Sebastian leered. "Swallow him down, lad."

Evangeline did not understand what they meant, but Seward stared at them in horror. She sensed the evil in them, the delight in playing with their captives. Lord Rudolph sat tense like stretched rope, his hands in kid gloves balled into fists. Only Austin stood, unmoving. He looked straight at Anna, his black gaze never wavering.

Sebastian shoved his pistol into Evangeline's temple. "Do it, boy."

"Mr. Seward," Austin said quietly. "Get up and come here."

"But, sir—"

"Now, Seward. That's an order."

Lord Rudolph looked away. Anna laughed. Sebastian caressed Evangeline's temple with the mouth of the pistol, its barrel cold and hard.

Mr. Seward, his face a study in misery, approached Austin, who remained at the other end of the sofa. Austin spoke quietly to him, words of reassurance, Evangeline thought. His gaze remained calm. Mr. Seward's back trembled.

She still didn't quite understand what was happening. Lord Rudolph kept his gaze firmly averted. Slowly, Mr. Seward sank to his knees in front of Austin.

And then she understood. Horror welled up inside her, stinging her eyes with tears. She flinched, but the cold, round opening of the gun dug into her flesh.

"No." Her sob echoed through the room.

Austin's gaze fixed on her, his face expressionless. "Evangeline," he said softly. "Duck."

And then Mr. Seward was rising, pulled up as if by some unseen force. He turned swiftly, a pistol in his rock-steady hands.

A roar filled the room and the stink of smoke. Evangeline threw herself forward, ripping her hair from Sebastian's grasp. She hit the floor with her shoulder, her breath whooshing out of her.

She heard Anna scream. Another pistol shot rang out. Evangeline scooted under the sofa, drawing her arms around her body. Sebastian's heavy boots were inches from her ear, and as she watched, a scarlet splatter appeared on them, then another, then another. The boots wavered, the red drops fell like rain. Then Sebastian pitched backward, his huge body crashing to the ground like a mighty oak. He caught a tea table along the way, taking it to the floor with him in an explosion of mahogany splinters.

Anna's shriek rent the air. "You killed him. You bastard. You killed him."

Dear lord, she'd shoot Seward, or Austin. Evangeline scrambled out from under the sofa and tackled Anna around the knees. Anna cried out, and went down.

She twisted from Evangeline's grip and crawled, head down, to her lover sprawled across the floor. His shirt was smeared with blood, a wet hole in his throat where Mr. Seward's shot had struck. His mouth was open, his eyes wide with confusion.

Anna gave a hoarse sob, and Evangeline's heart twisted. She must have loved the brute to have schemed and sacrificed so much for him.

"Miss Adams," she whispered.

Austin cursed. "Christ, his second pistol."

Lord Rudolph leapt over Evangeline, scrambling for the body. Anna reached it first. Her hand snaked out and yanked the unfired pistol from her lover's dead grasp. She swung around on her knees, holding the weapon in triumph.

Lord Rudolph halted, crouched, ready to spring. Evangeline sensed Austin and Mr. Seward behind her, tension sparking in the air. Anna smiled.

"Which of you?" she purred. She moved the pistol to Mr. Seward, then Austin as she spoke. "You, who killed my love? Or you, who told him to do it." She switched her aim to Lord Rudolph. "You, who this silly girl freed instead of my love, and cost me my beauty." Last, she trained the pistol on Evangeline. "Or you, my sweet, who have thwarted all my plans. You spoiled, selfish, willful girl. If you'd done as you were told, you'd still be in England, happily bearing a brat or two, instead of here, facing your death."

Evangeline wet her lips. "There, I would be living my death."

"Feeble simpleton. If you had helped me mutiny, you

Jennifer Ashley

could have had your captain crawling before you. Men like it when the woman holds the whip. Instead, he has you under his thumb." Her gaze flicked behind Evangeline. "Well, how do you like watching your lover die?"

She moved her attention back to Evangeline. But in the split second she had looked away, Lord Rudolph moved. He leapt at Anna, knocking her to her side.

Anna did not drop the pistol. She brought it up and around.

"No!" Evangeline screamed. She scrambled to her feet.

Anna smiled wildly. She pressed the barrel of the pistol to her own temple and pulled the trigger. Noise rolled through the room like an avalanche. Under Lord Rudolph, Anna Adams's body went limp.

Evangeline refused to return to Mrs. Milhouse, refused to take a calming drop of laudanum, refused to go to bed.

Austin watched her as she huddled on a divan in his library, her hands balled into fists on her lap. Mr. Seward had escorted her here after the violence and at least had convinced her to drink brandy. Austin regretted he hadn't had the chance to slip the laudanum into the glass.

Curious and frightened neighbors had converged on the house, then constables, then passersby. In the hours since Anna and her ill-fated lover had died, Austin had managed to have the bodies removed, the crowd disbursed, and his terrified footman calmed enough to round up people to help him clean the room. Austin ordered the blood-stained carpet taken away and burned. He did not want Evangeline ever setting eyes on that carpet again. Most of Anna's face had been ripped away by her shot. Evangeline had seen that, and she'd crawled away, white-faced and ill.

Now Evangeline sat still on the divan and stared at her slippers.

Lord Rudolph—*still here, damn him*—entered the room, seated himself next to her, and gently took her hand.

She said softly, "She must have loved him so very much."

Austin scowled. "For God's sake, Evangeline. She tried to kill you."

"I agree, do not waste your pity on her," Lord Rudolph said. "There was no good in that woman's heart."

"But what she did, right or wrong, she did for him. It makes me sad."

Austin still boiled with rage at Anna and her paramour for endangering Evangeline's life. "Perhaps when they broke in here, and started throwing explosives about, I should have asked them to tea." He pulled open the drawer of his desk and extracted a thin, flat oilskin packet. "I am going out."

Evangeline lifted her head. "Out?"

"What, now?" Lord Rudolph demanded.

He slid the packet inside his coat. "I'm already late."

Lord Rudolph's eyes narrowed. "You are delivering the documents."

Austin nodded. Lord Rudolph continued. "I should go with you."

"I want you and Seward to stay here with Evangeline.

283

She may return to Mrs. Milhouse's, but you must stay with her."

Lord Rudolph rose and strode to the desk. His aristocratic mouth pinched. "You're leaving her in *my* care?"

Austin regarded him steadily. "It is not that I particularly trust you, but you can protect her. And I trust Seward."

"Earlier you believed the danger negligible. And Anna and Sebastian are dead."

"Negligible after I've made my delivery. Until then, I want her protected."

Evangeline rose and advanced on them. "Will you both stop talking about me as if I'm not here?"

Warmth flooded him. His hand itched, wanting to reach to her, to smooth her hair back from her brow. "Evangeline, when you walk into a room, I always know." He flicked his gaze over her mussed hair, her bent spectacles, her full, ripe lips. "I will return as quickly as I can. Go back to Mrs. Milhouse if you feel safer there."

"I'd rather stay here."

"If you prefer."

"Austin, be careful."

The words hung between them. Austin longed to draw her into his arms, to kiss her, to hold her and lose himself in her. But Wittington hovered at his shoulder, frowning, and his appointment awaited.

He gave her a brief nod, turned, and left the room.

Wittington followed him out to the hall. Austin took up his hat and greatcoat and motioned his footman to follow. He'd take the servant, even though his mentor urged the appointment to be kept secret. His footman, while perhaps not an asset in a fight, could at least shout a warning if something went wrong.

Lord Rudolph stopped him as Austin started out the door. "I was wrong, Blackwell. You are besotted with her, aren't you?"

Austin gave him a measured stare. "Keep her safe."

His mouth twitched. "You poor sod." He clapped him on the shoulder with a firm hand. "I'll look after her. Don't worry."

Austin gave him a nod. It had fallen into place in the last hour just who his friends truly were. The knowledge hurt him at the same time it gladdened him.

He put on his hat and stepped out into the chill darkness of the night.

Captain Gainesborough's home welcomed him. Austin had come here so often that he knew the flaws in the house—the chip in the brick beside the front door, the wavy pane of glass in the palladian transom, the creak of the floorboard just inside the entrance—even more thoroughly than he knew the flaws in his own.

The scent of beeswax and hothouse flowers filled the hall. A runner in crisp green and blue ran the length of the passage, and a mural of a country scene filled one wall.

Austin left his hat and coat with Gainesborough's footman, and let himself into the recesses of the house. His own footman stayed behind.

He went unerringly through to the back of the house, to the library where he knew his mentor liked to spend his evenings. Gainesborough was there.

A silver-haired man with a sharp face, long nose, and gentle eyes, he rose from an armchair and extended his hand. "Austin."

Austin crossed to him. Captain Gainesborough shook his hand hard, then caught him in a strong embrace.

The captain released Austin and stepped back to look at him. "I worried when your ship was late."

"I had to make a slight detour."

The captain's brows raised slightly. He waited a moment, then shook his head and gestured to a chair. "Sit down, my boy. Would you like brandy?"

"No, thank you. I must make my visit brief."

The captain unstopped a glass decanter and trickled brandy into a glass. "What keeps you from spending time with your old friends this time, eh? You are too wedded to your duties, as always."

"This time it is a woman I will be wedded to. I marry tomorrow."

The glass slid out of Gainesborough's hands and splintered on the carpet. "Marry?"

Austin nodded. "Her name is Miss Clemens. She was a passenger on the *Aurora*."

"Good heavens." The broken glass crunched beneath Gainesborough's boot as he crossed to Austin and dropped into a chair.

"You do not seem overjoyed, sir."

Gainesborough glanced at Austin quickly, then shook his head. "Forgive me. I'm happy for you, of course. But I'm much surprised. I remember your marriage to Catherine."

Austin steepled his fingers. "As do I. But this time it will be different."

"Who is she, this Miss Clemens?"

"An Englishwoman. From Gloucestershire."

Gainesborough came alert. "She is English?"

"Yes. She tired of England and her family and decided to find a new start here."

"Well, well. That is interesting."

"I assure you, she is well resigned to giving up her English ways and living here with me."

Gainesborough waved this away. "Yes, she will no doubt adapt to life in the colonies. Who are her connections?"

"No one anyone knows. Her stepfather is a country gentleman, as I understand, not given to politics or society. Her mother is content to follow her husband's lead. Evangeline was quite willing to leave."

"Poor child. Well, we must do better for her here."

"I shall."

Gainesborough smiled. "God help us all when you get that determined look, my boy. I hope for your sake that the marriage prospers." He set down his brandy. "Now for other matters. What delayed you? Trouble?"

"An interesting adventure."

Austin leaned back and began narrating what had happened to him since Evangeline appeared in his cabin and started to seduce him. He skimmed over parts that might embarrass her, such as when she'd washed herself off in his cabin upon her return to the ship, but his face warmed. Gainesborough sat transfixed, his hands curled on the arms of his chair.

Inwardly, Austin's emotions tumbled. He wasn't certain he'd guessed right, and every minute brought him rushing closer to the truth. And it was a truth he did not want to acknowledge.

In the whole of the voyage, only Albright had attempted to steal the papers. And a clumsy attempt it was. Albright had not thoroughly searched the cabin, and he had been caught in the act. The enemy, whoever he was, had not been desperate enough to send a professional to retrieve them. As if the feeble attempt at theft would satisfy Austin's suspicious nature. As if the enemy knew he would have his hands on the papers eventually anyway.

Austin had given over Albright to the magistrate. This morning he'd learned that Albright was no longer in the magistrate's jail.

He finished his story. He tapped his fingers together, keeping his expression neutral.

Captain Gainesborough reached for his glass of brandy. "Well. That is quite a tale, my boy. The partners will be agog. They envy you your adventures, you know."

Austin shrugged. "After this, I will sit in my warm house with my wife and hear of others' adventures."

"Indeed. I look forward to spending more time with you. We can dine together and reminisce like two old men." He smiled. "You are to be commended for keeping the papers safe at all costs."

"I did my duty."

Gainesborough sat forward. "It is more than duty, my boy. The men on that list represent the best chance England has to regain a hold on the colonies. Interesting that Lord Rudolph Wittington is in Boston now, as well. I hear he has the ear of the king."

Austin inclined his head. "He does. He confessed as much."

"Hmm. We may be able to use that to our advantage. Now, my boy, you have the papers with you?"

Austin reached into his coat and slowly withdrew the oilskin packet. His heart hammered as he leaned forward and handed it to his mentor.

Gainesborough took it with a nod of thanks. He sat back and untied the string that held the packet together. Austin held his breath as Gainesborough drew out the three sheets of foolscap, and unfolded them.

Gainesborough glanced up, his face puckered in a frown. "I don't understand." He turned the papers over so Austin could see them. "These sheets are blank."

Chapter Twenty-four

Austin regarded him without moving. "Yes."

"I do not understand. Did you think it too dangerous to bring the papers to me?"

"I did, yes."

Gainesborough raised his brows. "You are right to be cautious. Did you mean to trick whoever might be following you into thinking you'd given the papers to me?"

"Not quite."

His mentor tossed the papers and oilskin packet aside. "Where are they? At your house? Shall we adjourn there and retrieve them?"

Austin shook his head. "We should not go to my house."

"Your ship, then?"

"No."

Gainesborough's frown turned sullen. "What game

are you playing, Austin? Where are they?"

Austin's blood raced. He forced his voice to remain cool. "This morning I had them delivered to a high government official. To be delivered to the president."

"You did? Why?"

Austin said nothing.

Gainesborough stilled. Every movement of his body halted, his breathing, the flicker of his eyes, the twitch of his mouth. Motionless, he stared back at Austin, his disingenuous look fading.

In the corner, a clock ticked monotonously, slicing away moments of time. The fire crackled, oblivious to the somber air in the room. Austin could smell the change, moving from the warm meeting of two old friends to cool, suspicious distrust; and his own fear.

Gainesborough spoke. "You know, then."

A muscle in Austin's jaw tightened. "I guessed. I hoped I was wrong. I did not know until just now."

A relieved light entered Gainesborough's eyes. "You did not give them to someone in the government, did you?"

Austin shook his head.

"Excellent. You can still bring them to me, then."

"No."

Gainesborough rose. Austin watched him, a droplet of sweat trickling down his spine.

"Austin, my boy, this country is weak. It will never last. I thought it right when we broke away from the rule of England, but I see now what a mistake that was. Each day brings some new disaster that the young government cannot face—unless it becomes as much a tyranny as we thought England was a dozen times over.

The United States was founded on lofty ideals that have never been tested. England has a proven ruling system, and it is to England that we must return."

"You wish to fight the war again?"

Gainesborough paced. "Of course not. If we go about things the right way, no blood will be shed. These men listed can use all their power and influence to invite the king to reign again over these shores, as he does the Canadian provinces to the north. We can still be an independent governing entity, just a provincial government."

"With all due respect, sir, I fought the English. I killed men, I narrowly escaped death myself. I believed the American states would be better off because of it, and I still believe that."

Gainesborough swung around. "You spend much time at sea, my boy. You do not see what happens here. The little rebellions in the remote colonies; the disregard of any kind of laws; the shortage of grain; the dangerous state of the banks. The government has no money and little power. I see it every day."

Austin broke in. "And every gentleman listed on those papers had power and wealth under the old regime. They have little under the new. Small wonder they want to get it back."

"I cannot expect you to understand. You have never learned anything of politics and what a dangerous game it is."

"I have learned enough. Enough to know that I cannot give those papers to you."

Gainesborough's tone softened. "We need men like you, my boy. You have experience and intelligence.

Once the English are invited back, you can expect a high position with them. You say this girl you are marrying is English. She will be most pleased."

"Evangeline is sensible enough to see through a foolhardy scheme. If the English regain their hold, both you and I will no longer be important."

"You wrong them."

"And your fears goad you. Someone has fanned your fear until you no longer remember what it was like before. But I remember. The arbitrary laws that favored the English-born over the colonial-born. The sudden arrests for the flimsiest reasons, the soldiers destroying homes and villages without apology because they were drunk. I do not want to see that happen again."

Gainesborough's face darkened. Austin watched him carefully. He wondered at his own fear; his mentor was an aging man, no match for Austin's strength.

"Such days are over," Gainesborough snapped. "This argument is foolish. I want the papers."

"And if I refuse to give them to you?"

Gainesborough crossed the room to stand above him. "Please, do not refuse, Austin. I love you like a son. You know that."

"I'm sorry. I must refuse."

A look of profound sadness crossed his mentor's face. "Then I must kill you."

Evangeline paced the music room, her eye on the clock. It grew later and later, and still Austin did not return. Outside, clouds had gathered, and a cool summer rain pattered against the windows.

"You should go to bed," Lord Rudolph said. He lingered at the pianoforte, picking out a soft tune.

"I cannot sleep." Evangeline about-faced, and paced back the length of the carpet. "I did not like the look on his face when he left. He knew he was walking into danger. And yet, he went anyway."

Mr. Seward lounged on a divan, the newspaper he had been reading at his feet. "A brave man, our captain. Cool as frost, he was, over Miss Adams and her pirate."

Lord Rudolph looked up. "What did he say to you before you shot the noble Sebastian? I heard him murmuring, but my ear did not catch it."

"He never blinked an eye. 'Make it look real, lieutenant,' he said. 'I have a pistol in my coat. I pray to God you are a dead shot.' "

"It was handsomely done," Lord Rudolph offered.

"I am a dead shot. Always have been."

Evangeline again heard the roar of the pistol, smelled the sharp scent of gunpowder, saw Sebastian's scarlet blood raining to the carpet in Austin's sitting room. She closed her eyes.

When she opened them, Lord Rudolph stood by her side. He touched her arm. "We should not have spoken of it. Come, sit down."

He led Evangeline to the divan that Mr. Seward hastily vacated. The young man hovered over her in concern. "Shall I bring you another glass of brandy?"

"No, no. I am all right."

Evangeline sank down on the divan and plucked at her skirt. She sensed the other two exchange worried glances and forced a smile. "Truly, I will be all right. It was frightening, but we are all unhurt." Her gaze traveled to the clock again. "I wish Austin would return."

Lord Rudolph sat down beside her. "He should not have left you tonight."

"He had to. Delivering the papers is more important than looking after me."

Lord Rudolph caught her hand. The kid of his glove was smooth and cool. "Don't be so self-sacrificing. He should have entrusted the papers to us and remained with you, instead of the other way around."

Seward looked troubled. "I must agree."

Evangeline shook her head. "I am not a wilting weed, and he knows that. He knew I would be safe here. He is facing the greater danger by himself, and that is why I wish he would return."

"He should be here planning his wedding. He had no right to take a risk when he is marrying in the morning." Lord Rudolph closed his hand over hers and looked into her eyes. "The offer is open to return to England with me, Evangeline. You do not have to marry him."

Evangeline said nothing. She thought of Austin, blindly determined to marry her, blindly ready to turn his back on his beloved way of life.

Lord Rudolph moved closer. "I can take you to friends tonight, a family who will keep you safe. Then we can slip on board ship in the morning and sail for England. You can save yourself from a marriage you do not want. My family will welcome you."

His handsome face hung close to hers, his warm breath on her fingers. He offered her a choice. She could leave the Americas forever. She could leave Austin free to pursue whatever life he wanted, prevent him from marrying her out of duty.

She thought of England, of the cool green swards of the Cotswolds, of the gentle rains, the slow pace of life. She thought of the barely veiled dislike her stepfather held for her, the weakness of her mother, who never raised objection to her husband's treatment of her daughter. She thought of Harley, who had betrothed her simply to make himself a respectable marriage. She thought of her narrow, lonely life, and the narrow, lonely person she had been.

The visage of Austin swam into her vision, his dark hair burnished red by the setting sun on the high sea, the flash of his dark eyes, angry at something she had said, his warm touch on her flesh, the weight of his body bearing hers to the carpet of Mrs. Milhouse's drawing room. She thought of his wickedly handsome smile, the glint of interest that had appeared in his eyes the night she had walked into his cabin to distract him from the mutiny.

He had taken a frightened, ignorant spinster and changed her forever, not just by bedding her, but by showing her a whole new world inside herself.

She thought of the Evangeline Clemens of England, and she thought of the Evangline Clemens she was now.

She gently withdrew her hands from Lord Rudolph's. "I will remain here and marry Austin. I thank you for your kind offer."

Seward unclenched his fists and sank into a chair.

Lord Rudolph's mouth turned down. "Very well, but I think you make a mistake. The offer stands, Evangeline. If you ever need me, write to me, and I will make arrangements to transport you to England."

"I will be Austin's wife. I have decided that. But," she said briskly, rising to her feet. "You have given me an idea. Can you find out for me where all the ships that sail from the harbor in the next few days are going?"

Lord Rudolph raised his brow. "I can. Where do you want to go?"

"I am not particular. The farther away, the better. Mr. Seward, do you have the direction for Mr. Osborn and Mr. Lornham? All Austin's officers, actually."

Seward frowned. "Yes. Why?"

"I need to write some letters."

She snatched up a candle and moved quickly across the music room and out into the echoing hall. Booted feet clattered on the marble as Seward and Lord Rudolph tramped after her.

She yanked open the double doors on the right side of the hall. "Do not worry, gentlemen, I am only going into the library."

The musty smell of books assailed her as she glided into the room. It was warm here, since its windows had faced the afternoon sun. A large globe sat in a stand near the window. No doubt the landbound Austin had often spun it idly, contemplating far-off lands as he waited for his shore leave to end.

The large desk reposed in the center, strewn with books and maps and notes Austin had been making that day. She moved them carefully aside, clearing a space, then seated herself in the hardwood chair. The desk dwarfed her; she would make the small writing table she had found upstairs her own after their marriage, leaving this monstrosity to her husband. When he was home.

But the desk upstairs was empty, and Austin's was well-stocked with paper and ink. She pulled open the top drawer.

She reached into it, then stopped. Her brain clicked a for moment or two longer, finally discerning what her eyes saw.

Folded papers reposed on top of the stack of clean foolscap, folded papers she had seen before. She touched the dry leaves, her fingers trembling, then she drew them from the drawer.

The handwriting was the same, the names were the same. The folds had creased, slicing ominously across the name *Mr. Howard Langdon.*

But she had seen him remove these sheets and tuck them into an oilskin packet—a packet which he had slid into his coat, before departing the house in search of the man to whom he planned to relinquish the documents.

Austin Blackwell would not make such a mistake. Austin Blackwell would not leave the papers, unlocked in a drawer in his library for Evangeline, or Mr. Seward, or Lord Rudolph to find. Without a reason.

"What is it?"

Lord Rudolph's breath touched her neck, his hand reached around her. She turned quickly, pressing the papers to her chest.

His eyes held only concern. "Evangeline, what is the matter?"

She looked up at him, her emotions rolling and tumbling. Behind Lord Rudolph, Mr. Seward stared, the same concern on his face.

She dragged in a breath. "Austin left the papers behind."

"He took them. I saw him."

"No. They are here."

Slowly Lord Rudolph reached down and slid them from her grasp. She bit her lip as she let them go.

He moved away from her, turning the sheets around. He read them, his expression bemused. "Good God. My cousin George is on this list."

Seward started forward, his young eyes alarmed.

Lord Rudolph sidestepped him and swung away, never taking his eyes from the paper. "If my cousin is part of this, you know it is a damned foolish scheme. Cousin George is an idiot. No wonder Blackwell wants to stop this." He looked up. "Where did he say he was going?"

Evangeline laced her fingers. "He did not. He mentioned his mentor, but I do not know who he is."

"Captain Gainesborough," Seward said.

The other two swung to look at him.

"Who is he?" Lord Rudolph asked.

"You do not know of him? He was a war hero. Captain Blackwell's commanding officer. The captain speaks of him often. They were as close as father and son."

Lord Rudolph tapped the papers to his palm. "Either he did not wish to involve this captain in the danger, or he did not want the man to have the papers for some other reason."

Evangeline pressed her hands together, her voice going quiet. "Austin is in danger, isn't he?"

"He is a sensible man."

"But a stubborn one. You know he left us here because he did not want us to be hurt." She thought a moment. "Perhaps he left the list for us to find, so that if he did not come back—" her heart squeezed in fear—"then we could take it safely to the right people."

"He's a damned fool."

Seward clenched his fists. "He should have taken me with him."

"That he should have, lad. Do you know where this mentor of his lives?"

"The captain?" Seward scrunched up his face. "My father used to know him, blast where was it?" He opened his eyes. "I have it. Charles Street. I remember now; I visited the house with my father years ago."

Lord Rudolph folded the papers and thrust them into his coat pocket. "I hope you remember which house, boy, because your captain may not leave it without a fight."

Evangeline's heart thumped. He meant that Austin might be trapped, held prisoner, perhaps no longer even alive.

Seward rose to his full height, his childlike face taking on a glow of excitement. "I'll lead you right. Do not worry Miss Clemens. We will bring him home to you."

Lord Rudolph grinned. "In plenty of time for your wedding. Seward, do you still have that pistol?"

"I do, indeed."

"Load it, then."

Evangeline planted herself in front of him, her hands on her hips. "You are not leaving me behind."

"This is men's work, Evangeline. Wait at Mrs. Milhouse's. We'll bring him straight home, I promise."

Evangeline stuck out her jaw. "I will not wait here with my hands folded not knowing what is happening. I cannot. I will wait outside in safety if necessary, but please do not ask me to stay behind."

Lord Rudolph let out an explosive breath. "I do not blame Blackwell for wanting to lock you in the cellar. You have a fervent disregard for peril, my dear."

"I do not care about that. I have to know if he is all right, and if he is not—" She bit her lip. "I want to be near."

Lord Rudolph studied her a long time. Her pulse raced, her palms grew slick, and her knees trembled. She tried not to picture Austin lying who-knew-where, cold, dead, alone. She wanted to be with him, to hold him, to comfort him, to tell him that she loved him.

"You care for him, don't you?" Lord Rudolph said softly.

Evangeline's throat worked. She nodded.

The hope that had underlaid his gaze since he had asked her to return to England with him died. "Lucky sod. Well, I suppose I will have to face my demons by myself." Without explaining that cryptic remark, he went on. "All right, Evangeline. You may accompany us."

Seward exploded. "What? No, she must stay here. Where she will be safe."

"She will only follow us if we do not let her. Besides, I have an idea, and we'll need her for it."

He bent his gaze on Evangeline again. Even in her relief and triumph, a dart of uneasiness pricked her.

* * *

Pain beat at Austin's temples and pounded through his head. He peeled back his eyelids. Black and white stars shot across his vision and he groaned.

He could not remember where he was or how he got such a pounding headache. He was not on board ship because the familiar rocking was absent. On land then, inside a house. His cheek pressed something prickly that smelled of wool, but it was also hard. A carpet, rather than a blanket.

Whose carpet? His vision still spun sickeningly, and he could make out nothing. He was warm enough, so he must be in a well-kept house, and he could smell the sweet scent of burning logs.

Over the roaring in his ears, he heard a voice. It was a familiar voice, one he trusted. Hope leapt in his heart. Perhaps he'd been robbed in the street and this person, this friend, had brought him in his house to mend.

But why was he lying on the carpet?

"He's coming 'round," said a voice Austin definitely did not like.

The familiar voice answered. "Thank heavens. You hit him too hard. You might have killed him."

"You said you didn't want him to run away."

"Yes, but I need to ask him questions."

Austin's vision cleared enough for him to see the blue and red pattern of the carpet on which his face rested. The pain narrowed to one dull point on the back of his neck.

A knee in satin breeches lowered to the carpet beside him. Hands, trembling and cold, lifted his head. "Austin."

Austin looked up into the worried face of a thin, graying man. Captain Gainesborough.

At once, the memory of the events poured over him. Austin had tried to rush Gainesborough, to prevent him from taking the pistol from his desk. He'd heard a sudden noise behind him. He'd tried to turn, then the burly fist of Gainesborough's six-foot-five footman had connected with his skull, sending Austin stumbling to the floor.

He remembered reasoning that Gainesborough was only one, small, elderly man. He'd forgotten that small men might have large servants loyal enough to attack on command. He wondered dimly what had become of his own footman.

"I apologize, Austin," Gainesborough said. "You must promise me you will sit quietly, or Jeremy might hurt you again."

Jeremy's huge boots came into view. Austin lay still, realizing it would be prudent to feign himself more hurt than he truly was until he recovered enough strength to fight the huge man.

"Go to hell," he said between his teeth.

Gainesborough regarded him sadly. "I am so sorry it has come to this, my friend. I never should have assigned you the task of retrieving the papers. But I knew I could trust you."

"You could trust me to bring them straight to you? You should have thought again."

"I wish you would not do this."

"Hold to my convictions? Let myself be easily swayed from what I believe right? I'd think you'd have more contempt for me if I did suddenly sway to your side."

"My boy, I thought myself right for a long time. But I have been persuaded by events that I was wrong. I only ask that you consider what I have said."

"Or your tame footman will trounce me again?" Austin sat up, pretending to wince.

"I wish you would join me. I do not like the alternative."

"Killing me, as you threatened? You would go that far?"

Gainesborough hesitated, his dark eyes troubled. Then he nodded. "I must."

"Then I will be the first casualty in your cause."

He rubbed the back of his head. The footman had moved back a few steps. His beetling eyebrows met above his nose, and his lower lip stuck out like an unruly dog's.

"I do not wish that."

Austin calculated the distance between himself and the footman, and between himself and the door. The stretch of carpet to the door looked long. Austin reasoned he could take three steps before the footman caught him. He would have to fight. But he was seasoned, and he was strong. He might just win.

"I am—"

A sharp *rat-tat* from the outer hall interrupted him. Gainesborough started. The footman glanced up warily.

"Were you expecting a visitor?" Austin asked.

"They'll go away," the footman said.

Gainesborough shook his head. "It would be odd if we did not answer when the house is lighted. See who it is and put them off."

Jeremy shot Austin a wary glance. "What about him?"

Austin cradled his head in his hands and gave a little moan.

"It is all right," Gainesborough snapped. "Go quickly."

Jeremy scowled, but shambled out the door.

Austin rubbed his head, at the same time coiling his muscles and subtly shifting his weight, readying himself to spring. He could easily overpower Gainesborough and make his exit out the window before the footman had time to return.

Jeremy's heavy tread died away into the distance. Then came the sound of the door scraping open, and Jeremy's inquiring tones greeting the uninvited guest.

A light, feminine voice answered him. "Good evening. I believe my fiancé, Captain Blackwell, is here. It is urgent that I speak to him at once."

Chapter Twenty-five

Evangeline.

Curses raged through his head. Wittington was a dead man, and Seward, too.

Austin rapidly changed his plans. He could not flee and leave Evangeline to Gainesborough's mercy.

The footman answered her. "The captain ain't seeing anyone, miss. Good night."

"But Captain Blackwell left some papers behind, and I know they are very important."

Gainesborough hurried to the sitting room door. "Jeremy. Let the young lady in."

Jeremy did not answer. But he must have opened the door for her because Evangeline said politely, "Thank you."

Her light step sounded in the hall. Austin drew his knees to his chest and circled them with his arms, his body tightening. Gainesborough stood in the doorway, swaying slightly, as if his legs trembled.

Evangeline appeared in the dim hall. "Good evening. Are you Captain Gainesborough?"

Her blue-gray skirt moved slightly in the draft, as did the ringlets of hair that peeped from her cap. Her voice, soft and musical, wrapped his senses, comforting him, even in the danger.

The captain cleared his throat. "Good evening, Miss Clemens."

"Captain Blackwell seems to have left something behind. I thought it important enough to intrude upon you—oh, good heavens!"

Her eyes widened as they rested on Austin. She ducked under Gainesborough's arm and hurried to him.

"Austin, what happened? Are you hurt?"

Gainesborough loomed behind her. His gaze pierced Austin. "He slipped and fell. He will be all right."

Evangeline dropped to her knees beside him. Her sleeve rustled like spring leaves as she reached out and touched his face.

"I will be fine," Austin said, his lips tightening. "You should go home."

"I thought it important to come."

She gazed into his eyes, her expression fixed. As she leaned forward, she gave him the slightest, barely perceptible, wink.

Austin bit back a groan. She had not come in the belief he had left the papers behind by mistake. She had come to rescue him.

She leaned closer. The clean scent of her almost melted him.

Gainesborough strode quickly forward. "You brought the papers? That was kind of you, my dear. You may give them to me. Austin meant to bring them for me."

Evangeline rose. Austin studied the brocaded slippers that hugged her slender feet, mesmerized by her delicate femininity. He wanted to reach out and trace the fragile bones of her ankle, to press his lips to the top of her instep.

She strolled across the room toward the fireplace, turning her back on Gainesborough. "The papers he left are just a list of names, as far as I can see. Are you sure these are the right documents?"

The captain followed her slowly, his eyes intent on her slim back. "Indeed, my dear. They are very important."

She turned. The sheets of foolscap rested in her hands. "They do not seem important."

Gainesborough stopped. He smiled, though his eyes remained tight. "They might seem unimportant to a lady, but I assure you, they are the right papers." He held out his hand. "You may give them to me."

Evangeline regarded him silently. Then, quick as thought, she swung toward the fireplace and held the papers just above the flames.

"Let Austin go."

She spoke sternly, but her voice held a note of hysteria. The hand that held the papers trembled.

"My dear, what are you doing?"

Austin sprang to his feet. "Evangeline—"

The bulk of Jeremy filled the door. He growled and

started forward. Evangeline moved the papers closer to the flame. Gainesborough gasped and frantically waved Jeremy still.

Austin strode to the fireplace. "Evangeline, give those to me."

"No. Not until they let you go home."

Gainesborough's pallid flesh filmed with perspiration. "Of course he may go home. He only came to deliver the papers. You may go home together."

Evangeline glanced from Gainesborough, to Jeremy, to Austin. "I am afraid I do not believe you. Allow Austin to leave the house, unmolested, and I will hand these papers to you."

And iron hand clenched at Austin's stomach. "I am happy I am marrying you tomorrow, because my first act as your husband will be to beat you black and blue for this."

Evangeline's spectacles shone red and gold in the firelight. "Then I am glad we are not married, now."

Gainesborough's chest rose and fell in rapid breaths. "He is right to punish you, girl. Do as he tells you."

Anger trickled through Austin's hot fear. Gainesborough had known Austin for fifteen years, and yet he took Austin's words for truth. He believed Austin could hurt someone as fragile and helpless as Evangeline.

Well, perhaps not *fragile* and *helpless*.

Her indomitable spirit radiated from her, and some part of him stood back in admiration. She had faced down pirates and mutineers and Spanish prison guards and English frigates. She'd braved fire and sea and storm, and now she stood braving certain death because she thought she could save him.

309

And he loved her for it.

"Evangeline, put down those papers and go home."

She narrowed her eyes. "You go home."

Gainesborough's face went gray. "For God's sake. Jeremy. Get the papers."

Jeremy moved fast for a big man. Austin stepped in front of him. Jeremy's arm shot out, and Austin caught it.

Evangeline dropped the papers into the fire.

The flames swallowed them with a hungry crackle. Gainesborough's shriek rent the air. He stumbled toward the fireplace, falling to the hearth, clawing for the papers as they crumpled in on themselves.

Austin shoved Jeremy off of him and grabbed the poker. He raked the documents, charred and burning, onto the bricks. Gainesborough snatched them up, careless of the flames, trying to beat them out with his hands. Bits of blackened paper floated lazily to the carpet.

Gainesborough wailed. "They're blank! These are blank. God help me!"

Relief and rage ripped through Austin. He would have to install a brig in his home and lock Evangeline in every night to keep her from these damn fool escapades.

Roaring, Jeremy charged. Austin swung the poker, connecting with the big man's shoulder. Jeremy howled, knocked the poker aside, and continued his attack.

Glass shattered, wood splintered, and two men hurled themselves into the room. Austin, fighting for his life, did not look around, but he knew they were Seward and Lord Rudolph Wittington. Two more he would lock in his brig.

They charged Jeremy. Austin, breathless, stepped out of the way in time to keep Seward's wild, swinging fist from connecting with him instead of the footman. Wittington approached Jeremy from the other side. The two men planted punches, one on either side of the footman's head, at the same time. Jeremy squeaked, like a mouse caught in a cat's deadly pounce, and fell to his knees.

Wittington grabbed Jeremy's hair, tilted his head back, and delivered a clean punch, done in the correct English boxing style, to the man's jaw. Jeremy slumped forward, crashed into the carpet, and went still.

Seward laughed shakily.

Wittington wrung his hand. "Damn, the brute has an iron jaw."

"Austin."

Evangeline's voice snapped Austin's attention to her. She sat on the floor, cradling Gainesborough's head in her lap. The old man had his hand pressed to his chest. His breath, shallow and fast, wheezed out between gray lips.

Austin dropped to his knees beside him. "Sir."

"My boy." The voice rasped from his trembling mouth, and spittle flecked his chin.

Austin clasped his hand, which was cold as ice. "Lie still. Seward, send for a surgeon."

The younger man nodded once and sprinted away.

Gainesborough reached up and pawed at Austin's arm. "It is too late."

"A surgeon will be here, soon. He will save you."

The blue lips curved into a smile. "Always were damn stubborn, weren't you?"

Austin gently parted his mentor's waistcoat. He placed his palm over the old man's heart and massaged his breastbone, as he'd seen ship's surgeons do.

Gainesborough's gasps eased a little. "Austin, burn the papers. Do not destroy those good men. They only want what is best for this country."

Austin did not answer. He stroked the old man's chest, wishing he could pour his own strength into him. This man had taken him, a green lieutenant, and given him the courage and conviction to rise to command. He had comforted Austin when Austin's brother had died, had given him silent sympathy when Austin's estranged wife had passed away. And this night he had threatened Austin's life, and he would die an enemy.

His own heart throbbed and hurt. He had wanted to come home to peace. To friends, to domestic life. Perhaps what he wanted did not exist.

"Promise me," Gainesborough whispered. "Do not have those men and their families humiliated and executed. They can do no harm if they are not united."

Evangeline's hand touched Austin's. He looked up. Her gray eyes behind her spectacles were full, her mouth twisted with sorrow.

He was struck by how well she understood him. Her sorrow was for the dying old man, but also for Austin. She knew, somehow, what he was losing.

He smoothed the hair from his mentor's brow. "I will do my best, sir. No blood will be shed over this."

Gainesborough relaxed slightly, and his eyelids

drooped. "Your wife has great courage. She is nothing like Catherine."

Austin hid a smile. His first wife had been a frail, rather helpless thing, who had to have lackeys to do even the smallest task for her. Evangeline, in only her chemise, faced down prison guards and rescued stranded Englishmen.

He looked into her tear-filled eyes. "Go home. Wittington, take her."

"Yes." Lord Rudolph moved forward and held out his hand to her.

She gazed up at him, that stubborn look coming to the fore. "I cannot leave Austin."

"Yes, you can," Austin said wearily. "Wittington, I give you leave to bind her hand and foot and drag her back home if you have to. Take her to my neighbors and make her stay there this time."

Evangeline shook her head. "Austin—"

"No. I will be all right. I want to be alone."

Evangeline looked down at the dying old man. She touched his shoulder. "I am sorry."

Gainesborough opened his eyes. "Bless you, my dear."

Austin slipped his arms beneath Gainesborough's torso, gently easing him from Evangeline's lap. Evangeline got slowly to her feet. Austin cradled his mentor in his arms, holding him firmly, while he returned to massaging his heart.

Running feet sounded, and Seward pounded in again, followed by a sleepy-looking man in an unbuttoned frock coat. Austin recognized him as a surgeon who'd served many a naval man. Doctors sneered at

Jennifer Ashley

him, but he had saved the lives of enough seamen that Austin knew and trusted him.

The surgeon took in the scene, and his face went grim, telling Austin what he already knew. Gainesborough would die.

A feather touch, soft as a breeze, brushed his shoulder, followed by Evangeline's sweet scent. He heard her footsteps pattering alongside Lord Rudolph's heavy tread, leaving him to face his demons alone. As it should be.

Seward gave him a look of quiet sympathy. The surgeon knelt beside him, and unlaced Gainesborough's shirt, continuing the massaging that Austin had started.

An hour later, Austin still held his mentor in his arms. Then Captain Gainesborough, a hero of the Revolution, closed his eyes, and died.

Evangeline sprang awake when she heard Austin's step in the hall. She lay on the divan in the library, where she'd had Austin's footman make up a fire. The footman sported a black eye and still shook from the sudden violence at Gainesborough's house. Jeremy had knocked him down then gone to assist his master in detaining Austin. Gainesborough's footman, he told her, had been dragged away by Seward and Lord Rudolph to a magistrate.

She rubbed the sleep from her eyes. The window was gray with false dawn, and despite the fire and the blanket she'd found upstairs, she was cold.

"Austin."

She heard him hesitate, then the slow thump of his boots as he turned toward the library. He pulled open the door. The lights from the hall silhouetted him, sharply outlining his broad shoulders and narrow waist.

He stood motionless, regarding her, his face in shadow. He would grow angry any moment, demand to know why she was there instead of at Mrs. Milhouse's where he'd sent her, command her to return there.

Slowly he left the doorway and moved to the divan, his tread weary. She sat up, pulling the blanket around her.

Austin unbuttoned and pulled off his frock coat, letting it slide carelessly to the floor. He sank down on the divan next to her, not even looking at her, his arms and legs limp.

He said nothing. The look on his face was blank, uncaring. She had never seen him like this before. Always Austin Blackwell was vibrant and alive, his whole body alert, his dark eyes snapping. The life had gone from him, and that frightened her more than all his anger and arrogance ever had.

She touched his shoulder. "Austin."

He turned his head and looked at her. His brow puckered, as if he were just noticing her beside him.

"Austin, I am so sorry. I know he must have been like a father to you. Mr. Seward told me about him, and some of the stories of how you fought together, and how you revered him—"

Austin pressed his fingers to her lips. His black stare was filled with anguish and loss and torment too old and deep to understand.

Evangeline touched his sleek hair. The smell of sweet wood smoke and the night air clung to him. Two gray

315

hairs, incongruous among the dark red, twined together at his temple.

Swiftly, suddenly, he gathered her to him. He buried his face in her throat and locked his arms about her. She thought he would weep, but he remained very still, holding her in his vice-like clasp. She closed her eyes and pressed a kiss to his mist-drenched hair.

He held her for a long time. The clock in the corner struck the quarter hour, then the half. False dawn gave way to true light, faintly golden.

She smoothed her hands down his back. "You should sleep. I will return to Mrs. Milhouse's. She does not know I am gone. I slipped out because I could not sleep and I wanted to see you. But I will return, if you wish it."

She babbled softly, in whispers.

"No." His head came up. His face was flushed, his eyes sparkling with unshed tears. His thick fingers furrowed through her hair. "Stay. I am so damned tired of being alone."

His gaze held her, paralyzing her. She managed a very faint nod.

"Stay with me forever. If I have to be on shore, I want to be with you."

"Yes," she whispered. Her mind danced with the plans she had made with Lord Rudolph before he had left her at the Milhouse's the night before. She had no doubt that he and Mr. Seward would carry out her instructions to the letter.

Austin kissed her. His lips were possessive, the kiss fierce and strong. He tumbled her hair, loosening it from its pins. She clutched the placket of his shirt, holding it hard while his tongue circled hers, ravishing her mouth.

She groaned softly. He released her. His eyes were dark with passion, his breath hot. He scooped her into his arms and rose. Evangeline clutched the blanket as she was whisked up with him, for some reason needing to hang onto the wooly folds.

He carried her from the room and across the empty hall. He mounted the stairs, cradling her against his chest. The hard thump-thump of his heart echoed through her own body, the movement of his breath against his ribs pushed her own chest, as if she breathed with him.

At the top of the stairs, he turned, carrying her through the darkness to the room at the front of the house from which she'd pilfered the blanket. It was dark there, too. No candles or firelight softened the shadows, and only a faint sliver of light filtered through the closed drapes.

Austin carried her to the bed. He held her close while he dragged back the covers, then he deposited her on the sheets. He rested one knee on the mattress, and loosed the hooks and laces that held her clothes together. His hands roved swiftly, precisely, removing her bodice and sleeves, her stays, her skirts and underskirts, stripping off her slippers and stockings. He unlaced the chemise with steady fingers and tugged it off over her head.

Evangeline lay back in the cold sheets, her hair tumbling around her, her hands finding purchase in the blankets he had shoved away.

Austin stepped back, then began removing his own

317

Jennifer Ashley

clothes with the same unemotional precision as he had hers. She fixed her gaze on him hungrily. He tossed aside his waistcoat and drew his shirt off over his head, breaking the ribbon that held his hair back. His dark hair tumbled forward, brushing his massive shoulders. Muscles rippled in his torso, hard outlines touched by the tiny light that leaked into the room.

He slid off his boots and stockings and breeches. He came to the bed, naked as a god, his organ standing out hard and ready. She sensed there would be no teasing seduction tonight, no soft words of passion, no slow caresses. He needed her, and he was coming to take what he needed.

His need frightened her. She could never hope to be enough for a man like Austin Blackwell. He was complex, with deep passions that she did not understand. She wanted to reach what was behind his dark eyes, to soothe it, to love it, but she knew he would forever hold himself from her.

Now, he needed her, and she knew only one way to help him. She lifted her arms to him, inviting him to come to her.

Chapter Twenty-six

He did. Austin climbed onto the bed and gathered her to him, pressing her cheek to the hard line of his shoulder. His hot touch slid to her back, kneading and stroking.

He kissed her, as fiercely as he had in the library, lowering her back to the sheets. His hands caressed in long strokes, teasing her breasts to tingling hardness, gliding between her thighs to touch her womanhood and bring it to life.

His fingers slipped inside her, and she whimpered. Her own hot moisture stung her thighs. Her fear vanished, and she wrapped her leg around him. She cradled his face in her hands, touching the hard bones of his jaw, his brow. She leaned forward and kissed his lips, letting her tongue trail to the prickle of his unshaven chin.

He made no sound at all. He pulled his caressing finger from her and parted her thighs, then rose up over her and entered her in one long, hard stroke.

Evangeline twisted her head to the side, sighing her pleasure, crying out to the pillows. Austin rested inside her for a long moment, his eyes closed, his shoulders bunched. Perspiration shone on his upper lip.

Then he began to love her, swiftly, cleanly, again making no sound. Evangeline writhed beneath him, lifting her hips to his, wanting this joining. She twisted the sheet in her hands, thrusting wantonly to him, aching for him.

He loved her silently, the anguish in his eyes never diminishing. She wrapped her arms around him, trying to give, her heart tearing. She loved his man of strength and tenderness, of great kindness hidden beneath his arrogance. She longed to make him happy, and she did not know how.

"I love you," she whispered. "I love you."

He released a deep groan, his eyes closing, and then he came. He kissed her with his climax, his lips hot and wet, kissing her brow and eyelids and face and hair.

Then he collapsed onto her, his weight crushing her into the mattress. He kissed her neck, her throat, her shoulders, as he withdrew himself. He lifted himself from her and crashed down beside her, panting as if he'd swum for miles and at last had reached shore. He lay there for a long time, his glittering gaze fixed on the draped canopy above them.

She lifted herself on her elbows. "Austin?"

He looked at her. The stark grief and anger in his face broke her heart. Gone was the barrier between them, and his raw emotions poured over her.

She touched his face. "My love."

He rolled onto his side, and pushed her to face away from him. Then he gathered her against him, his chest to her back, his large thigh sliding between her legs. He held her there, his arm tight about her waist, not speaking, not sleeping.

As the sun rose to touch the city, Evangeline slept, secure against his hard, warm body, his arms sheltering her even as his tears wet her shoulder.

Feather-light kisses on her flesh woke Evangeline. She stirred, wondering where she was. A prickly woolen blanket covered her, and her head rested on soft pillows. Behind her lay the solid, warm bulk of Austin. He lifted her hair and let it trickle back down to the bed.

"Good morning," he whispered. "It's our wedding day."

Evangeline gasped and sat up. Someone had opened the curtains, and sunlight streamed into the room. "Good heavens. What time is it?"

"Ten o'clock in the morning."

His still face held a fixed smile. The emotions of the night before had vanished, and she wondered if she had imagined them.

"When will the ceremony be?"

"This afternoon at two. I have arranged everything."

No doubt he had. She had arrangements of her own to make. "I must go back to Mrs. Milhouse. She wants to alter a dress for me to be married in."

"What is wrong with the one you wore yesterday? You are beautiful in it."

She gave him a pitying look. "It is not something a man would understand."

"Apparently not."

She bit her lip. "Austin."

"Hmm?"

"What will you do with the papers?"

His expression went somber. "I have not yet decided. They are still in my desk?"

"Yes. I thought they would be too dangerous to carry about."

"They are." He raised himself on his elbow. "And if you ever try to rescue me like that again, I will lock you in my cellar for certain. In chains. And throw you crusts of bread."

"I was so afraid for you. If I had not gone, he might have killed you."

"He might have."

She clenched her fists. "You say that as if it is no matter. You might have died."

"Then the papers would have found their way to a higher official. I left Wittington instructions to take care of you if anything happened to me. All would have been well."

She picked up a pillow and swatted him with it. *"Well?* All would have been *well?* You would have cheerfully died and left me alone? You selfish, arrogant—"

He snatched the pillow from her. "I thought you would be well rid of me. You have tried every argument to keep from marrying me."

Evangeline kicked back the covers and scrambled out of the bed. She stood up, planting her hands on her hips. "You understand nothing. I do not want you to die."

A thoughtful look crossed his face. Evangeline looked down and realized that she was completely naked.

She pulled her chemise from the pile of garments on the floor and yanked it over her head. Lying naked with him had seemed the most natural thing in the world, but now her face scalded and she fought the urgent desire to flee.

He watched her with an amused glint in his eyes. She snatched on her stays, trying to fasten them. She turned in circles, attempting to catch the hooks in the back, grunting in frustration.

Austin put aside the covers and rose. Evangeline stilled. Naked, the glow of morning sunlight haloing his body, he was magnificent. Shadows played on the sculpted muscles of his arms and thighs, light touched the down of dark hair on his chest.

Good heavens, she was about to *marry* this man. She gulped. If all went as she planned, she would sorely miss him.

Austin silently held out her spectacles. As she shoved them onto her nose, he took her by the shoulders and turned her around. Swiftly, expertly, he fastened her stays. He fetched her bodice from the floor and slid it over her arms, drawing it together and fastening the hooks in back. He continued with her skirts, dressing her as if she were a doll. He bade her sit on the damask chair before the fire, while he knelt, still naked, and slid her stockings over her calves to her thighs. Heat streaked through her, starting at his warm palms and hurrying down her spine.

He stood up again and kissed her brow. "Go down to the dining room and have breakfast. I bade my staff prepare it for you."

"When did you do that?"

"This morning. While you slept like a baby."

"Good heavens." She straightened the lace on her sleeves. "Mrs. Milhouse must be frantic with worry. I must go to her."

Austin shook his head. "She came early this morning, having missed you. I told her you were well."

Evangeline's face heated. "She must think me a hopeless wanton."

"She is so ecstatic that I am to marry you, she is in a very forgiving mood. She teased me about true love and other nonsense."

A chill touched Evangeline's heart. Nonsense? She dimly remembered whispering in the dark that she loved him. She hoped he had not heard her.

She forced a smile. "Yes, she is quite romantic."

"Go on and have something to eat. You must be hungry."

He stood there, arms folded, the light playing on the planes of his unclothed body, as if he were still the captain on his command deck, naked or no.

She bit her lip and turned away. At the door she stopped. Her heart beat swiftly, aching with each throb.

"Austin."

He raised his brows.

She took a deep breath, steeling herself. "Love isn't nonsense."

She blurted the words, then fled.

* * *

They were married in a small and simple church down the hill from Austin's house. Evangeline walked there on Austin's arm, with the Milhouses strolling behind them. The vicar waited at the church that Austin called Anglican, explaining to her that it had been a Church of England until the war.

Lord Rudolph, Mr. Seward, Mr. Lornham, Mr. Osborn, and other officers from the *Aurora* waited there also. Austin swept them a look of surprise, then arranged his face in blank lines again. He had not invited them. But Evangeline smiled secretly. Mr. Seward had done well.

Austin had donned his formal uniform, replete with medals from the war. The deep blue of his coat set off his dark hair and black eyes. He stood straighter in the uniform, she thought, as if the coat stiffened his backbone. The sensual man who had dressed her with gentle hands this morning had vanished.

Austin marched her straight to the altar without any preliminaries. His expression was fixed, as if he thought the sooner it was done, the better.

Since she had blurted the idiotic statement about love, he had spoken little to her, and then only to give orders. The captain had returned, pushing aside the man.

The vicar read the service, and she and the others murmured their responses. When Austin bothered to join in, his baritone rumbled to the corners of the church. At last, they were to say their vows. Austin repeated the words that would bind them together, his voice firm and uninflected. Evangeline stammered a little over hers.

And then they were married. Austin bent to kiss her. Evangeline lifted her face, her lips parted, waiting for him. He pressed a brief kiss to the corner of her mouth and turned away.

He led her out of the church again, barely acknowledging the congratulations from his men. He did not stop at the door, but strode on into the street, dragging Evangeline with him.

Halfway up the hill, Evangeline tugged on the arm that propelled her along. "Stop. Please."

He halted, staring at her. Evangeline panted to catch her breath. "You are walking too fast. The others will not catch up."

"Why would we want them to? I married you, Evangeline. I am anxious to begin my domestic life."

"They are all coming to tea."

"They are?"

"Yes." She lifted her chin. "I arranged it."

"In my house. Without telling me."

"In *our* house. Yes."

He gave her a steady stare, then turned away without a word. Evangeline raced to catch up with him again, a little fear growing in her heart.

Not much later, she stood in Austin's front drawing room with the guests from the church, wishing she could eat some of the lovely cakes Mrs. Milhouse's cook had produced. But her stomach fluttered and her mouth was so dry she knew she'd never choke anything down.

The only women in the room were Mrs. Milhouse and Evangeline's cousin, Beth Farely, who had arrived in time for the ceremony. Cousin Beth was, like her letters, prim and upright. She seemed surprised at Evangeline's marriage, but pleased she had made a wealthy connection.

The two women were Evangeline's only female acquaintances now. But, she thought as she sipped a cup of sweet tea, she would have ample time to make new friends. If all went as planned, she'd have all the lonely time in the world.

Her throat worked, and she swallowed tea hastily. She must remain resolute. And above all, she must not let on to Austin what she planned to do. The scheme would work only if he were in the dark until the very last minute, when it would be too late.

"Congratulations, Evangeline."

Lord Rudolph stopped beside her and bent his one-eyed gaze upon her. He went on softly, "My felicitations."

"Thank you."

Austin appeared at her other side. "You will be taking ship for England shortly, will you not, Wittington?"

Lord Rudolph glanced up, his eye holding a sardonic light. "In the morning. Now that you have won the game—and quite fair game it is—I will be returning home. The black sheep returning to the fold."

"You insult my wife," Austin said quietly.

Evangeline's heart fluttered. The way he said "my wife" in such firm, possessive tones sent shivers up and down her spine.

Lord Rudolph bowed. "Forgive me. I forgot myself."

"It is quite all right," Evangeline said quickly. "Surely you will be happy to return home after all this time. And after your stay in that ghastly prison."

Jennifer Ashley

"It had its bright moments."

Austin grunted. "No doubt England will rejoice at your homecoming."

"There will be a few who do not, and unfortunately, those few have the power to make my life miserable."

He always spoke in riddles. Austin gave him a cold stare. The camaraderie the two men had shared the night before seemed to have vanished.

She broke in. "You must write to us, Rudy."

His lips twitched. "Of course, my dear. I will address the letters to your husband, as is proper. Perhaps he will even read them out to you."

Austin's look turned thunderous. "Perhaps you could catch a boat tonight."

She stepped between the two men. "Good lord, I meant to write my parents about our marriage. They will have no idea, and heaven knows what my step-brother will tell them."

Lord Rudolph inclined his head. "I would be happy to carry a letter home for you."

Austin plucked a glass of wine from a nearby table and raised it to his lips. "I already wrote them."

"You did?"

"Yes. When we docked. I gave it to an outbound ship. I explained that I would marry you and have the keeping of you from now on. And that I thought they had dealt with you most abominably."

Evangeline stared. "You wrote that to my stepfather?"

"I did. Their behavior over that cub you jilted was appalling."

"Did you tell him that, too?"

"Yes."

328

She bit back a wild laugh. "Oh, good heavens. My stepfather will never speak to me again."

"We can hope not. I will take care of you now, Evangeline. You will want for nothing. Yesterday, I altered my settlements to ensure that you will have a healthy income both as my wife and my widow."

Lord Rudolph raised his brows. "How romantic of you."

Evangeline looked up at her husband, her heart full. "You are so kind to me."

"Protecting his investment," Lord Rudolph said cynically.

"No, you wrong him. Austin has always been kind. He could have hung my stepbrother and thrown me in his brig, and cared nothing for what happened to me. He's helped and protected me every step of the way."

The hard glint in her husband's eyes softened. "Stop looking at me like that, Evangeline."

She blinked back tears. "Why?"

"Because it makes me want to kiss you, and I cannot with Wittington looking on."

Lord Rudolph grinned. "I do not mind."

Austin set down the glass of wine. He gazed down at her, letting his eyes move to take in her lips. He reached up and traced them with his finger.

His voice roughened. "Evangeline, ask me to kiss you."

She swallowed. "Will you kiss me? Please?"

He leaned down and brushed his lips over her mouth. Frissons of passion slid down her spine to gather at the join of her thighs. An ache stabbed her there. She would miss him. Oh, how she would miss him.

A feminine sob from Mrs. Milhouse sounded over the soft applause and guffaws of the males.

Austin straightened up, a smile of triumph hovering around his mouth.

Evangeline flushed. "Goodness. I must see to my guests."

She ducked away under Austin's arm and fixed a smile on her face as she marched toward her cousin. She looked back. Austin watched her, heating her with his gaze.

The only flaw to her plan was the presence of her cousin Beth and Mrs. Milhouse. Neither lady had been privy to it, and it would be much too hard to explain. Evangeline whispered to Mrs. Milhouse for a moment, then that good lady brightly invited cousin Beth to step next door with her and sit comfortably in her sitting room. Evangline promised to join them soon.

She saw the women out to the front hall, then returned to the sitting room, now filled only with males. Her heart beat swiftly, her stomach twisting in knots. She had to do it. She'd planned it; it must be done.

She looked at Austin. How splendid he was in his dark coat and kid breeches. The restrained lace at his cuffs fell over his strong hands, hands that had stroked her so gently as they lay together in his bed. The same hands had aroused her to soaring desire, awakening her to womanhood.

His sleek hair was pulled back into a severe queue as usual, its red highlights shining in the sunlit room. His dark eyes, quiet now, had spoken last night of such heartbreaking anguish. Last night, she had wanted nothing but to make the whole world better for him.

And now she could, in her own small way.

She pulled the double doors closed and stood before them. Across the room, Mr. Seward caught her eye. She nodded slightly, and he swiftly stuffed the canape he held into his mouth and wiped away the crumbs.

"Gentlemen," she said in a clear voice.

Conversation ceased around the room. The officers and men and Lord Rudolph focused their attention on her. Austin watched her, his brow creasing.

She drew a deep breath. "Now!"

As one, the body of men turned toward her husband. From out of pockets and from under coats came lengths of rope, coiled and ready. Seward snapped an order, and the whole roomful rushed at the bemused Austin and bore him to the ground.

Chapter Twenty-seven

"What the hell?"

Austin's breath left him as he fell, hard, to the carpet. Osborn's knee drove into his chest. He gasped, flailing, then he caught Osborn's leg and flipped the man neatly onto his back.

Austin scrambled up in time for Seward to launch himself at his captain once more. The young man had all the zeal and energy Austin had lost in ten hard years of life at sea. Austin barely blocked Seward's flailing arms. Seward kept at him, determination burning in his face.

Someone grabbed Austin from behind. Austin butted him with his head, and he heard Wittington grunt. The damned Englishman held on. Another man leapt in, seized Austin's arm, and twisted it around his back. Rope burned Austin's wrists.

What the hell was going on? As he fought, he dimly sensed Evangeline hovering on the edge of the crowd, her hand pressed to her mouth. She had given the signal for the men to fly at him. Was she, and Wittington, and all Austin's crew part of Captain Gainesborough's conspiracy after all?

His heart tore, even as rage boiled up inside. Had he found the woman of his dreams, only to discover his dream a sham? He might have known that peace would be too hard to come by. His mentor had betrayed him. His aching heart had barely stood that blow. To have Evangeline turn against him as well made him bleed inside.

Wittington looped the rope fast around Austin's wrists. Austin shifted his balance and landed a quick, but brutal kick to Seward's stomach. The young man's eyes widened, and he made a whooshing sound as he gently folded over.

Austin curled his fingers around the rope, sliding it from between his hands. Wittington held on, but Austin spun, breaking away, his wrists working constantly. He kicked Osborn again, in the hip this time, as the man rushed him.

The ropes grew slack and fell. Osborn was wearing an ornamental sword, part of his dress uniform. As he struggled to regain his balance, Austin ripped the sword belt from his waist and backed into a corner.

The sword rang as he drew it out. He held it in front of him, the long, thin blade glittering.

Wittington took a step forward. Austin aimed the point at him, ready to drive it home. He tasted bile and the salt tang of blood. Scarlet drops spattered the crisp white lace of his cuff. The men eyed him warily.

Evangeline clasped her hands. "You must take him by any means necessary, gentlemen. You promised."

Austin leveled the sword. "The first man who comes within my reach dies."

The men, except Wittington, shuffled back uneasily. A few other officers wore swords, but none made a move to draw them. Seward clenched his bit of rope, as if determined to use that weapon or none at all.

Austin switched his gaze to Evangeline. She stood, agitated, a little way behind the crowd, her eyes round.

He kept his voice deadly quiet. "You arranged this."

She nodded. "It is for your own good, Austin."

"You are my *wife*. You do not decide what is good for me."

One of the older petty officers rolled his eyes. "You have not been married long, sir," he muttered.

Rage churned inside him. "What is for my own good? Prison? I asked you once a long time ago how long it would be before you spat me out. Do you remember? Now, I know."

Evangeline bit her lip. "It will not be a prison."

"Execution, then? Clean and swift, I hope."

Seward spoke up. "We are only taking you to the ship."

"Ship? What ship?"

"The *Christina Marie*, sir. She sails this evening."

"For where? England?"

"China, I believe," Wittington said mildly. He looked amused about something.

"Damn you, Evangeline, why do you want me locked up on a ship bound for China?"

"The captain agreed to release you once the ship was well to sea."

"Best of luck to him," Osborn muttered, rubbing his hip.

"The captain will be putting to shore in the Indies, to stay with his family. You will take over the ship from there."

Austin's eyes narrowed. An ache itched just behind them. "Why should I take over another man's ship? I have retired."

"Because you cannot retire. You must return to the sea, Austin. It is the only way you will ever be happy. Not here, not tied to me and a staid and unchanging life."

Austin slowly lowered the sword. "Oh, my God. Is that what this is all about? You do not believe I want to stay with you?"

"You might want to stay, now. But later you will grow to resent me. You will hate me for tying you to a life you despise. And you will leave."

Tears wet her cheeks. They spilled out from under her spectacles and dropped from her lips.

He gentled his voice. "And how is this better? Why are you sending me away if you are afraid I will leave?"

"Because I do not want to watch you grow more discontent with your life as the days go by. Now that we are married, you do not have to feel guilty about taking care of me. You have taken care of me. You can go about your own business."

Austin balled his fist. "Do you think that is all this marriage is to me? Guilt?"

"And pride. You did not want Lord Rudolph to take

care of me. You believe no one can do it as well as you."

He nodded. "That is true."

She brushed at her tears with the back of her hand. "You see?"

"Damn you, Evangeline. Do you think I chased you all the way to Havana to get you away from that villainess because of guilt? You think I felt guilt when you stood in my cabin in your chemise trying to wash off the gunpowder? Do you think I cared anything for pride that first night when you came to my cabin and let me kiss you? No. I wanted you. Damn, but I wanted you. I burned for you. I would have taken you, but I was interrupted by a mutiny. Anything short of that, and you would have been mine that very night."

Lord Rudolph was grinning widely. The other men pretended to be elsewhere, except for Seward, who watched the drama, looking close to tears himself.

Austin came forward, brushing past Seward and Lord Rudolph. "Do you think I chased you up and down the Atlantic coast, and fought for my life, and held you in my arms because of *pride?*"

Evangeline gulped. "Yes."

"You little fool. Why do you think I hurried home, ready to settle down at last?"

"B-because you thought you should."

"Because I love you."

She looked up, eyes widening, tears streaming. "You do?"

His heart tore. "I do, dammit. I've loved you since you charged into my cabin and started unbuttoning your dress. I loved you when you laughed at the wind and the sea and I kissed you. I loved you when you held me and made me forget the waves that tried to kill me. I loved you when you burnt those papers under Gainesborough's nose, even while I wanted to break your neck for doing it. I loved you when you let me make love to you on Mrs. Milhouse's carpet."

Evangeline went scarlet. Her hands flew to her cheeks. "Austin. Good heavens."

He reached her. "And I love you now."

Her eyes were gray pools of anguish. "But how long will that last? How long until you blame me for taking the joy out of your life?"

He laughed. "Evangeline, you put the joy *into* my life. I know now I never truly loved another person before, because I've never felt like this."

"You love your life at sea," she whispered.

He touched her chin and tilted her face to his. "Do you not understand, yet? I turned to the sea to distract me from my loneliness. But as long as you are with me, I do not care if I am on land, or at sea, or on top of a mountain. It is not the sea I need, Evangeline. It is you."

Behind him, Seward gave a little sob.

"If you can be on land or at sea," Evangline stammered. "I wish you'd choose sea. Just in case."

Austin traced her cheek. "Seward, what time does this *Christina Marie* leave port?"

Seward sniffled. "Six-thirty tonight, sir."

He locked her gaze with his, wanting to hold it forever. He loved this woman of strength and courage, who was willing to sacrifice all happiness for him.

"I will be on it. On one condition, Evangeline."

"Wh-what is that?"

"You will be on it with me."

Hope dawned in her eyes. "With you?"

"If you force me to sea, I will drag you with me. You love it as much as I do. If you want me to sail that be-damned ship to China, I will. But you will be there beside me. You will look down the throat of morning with me, and you will watch the stars with me at night."

She smiled, her tears shining, and her voice caught. "Oh, Austin, please."

"No please about it. You are my wife; you will do as I say."

A stubborn light crept into her eyes, one that boded no good for his future. But she gave him a brilliant smile and a shaky salute. "Aye, sir."

"Now, kiss me."

The laughter from her lips sounded anything but obedient. "I love you, Austin," she whispered, then she opened her arms, like angel's wings, and came to him.

Lord Rudolph snorted. "About time."

Starlight filtered through the small square window in the captain's day cabin, which had been converted to a sleeping cabin for Austin and Evangeline. Evangeline sighed, happy to the tips of her toes. The bulk of her husband lay next to under the blankets. He was not asleep. He'd buried his face in her neck when he'd collapsed next to her after their fierce lovemaking, and now he wound her hair through his large fingers, idly letting it trickle from his hands.

Beneath them, the ship rose and fell on the waves, rocking the bed like a cradle.

Evangeline studied the constellations as the window

drifted back and forth over them. After six weeks at sea, the familiar Big and Little Dippers, the Three Sisters, even the North Star, moved closer and closer to the northern horizon. Soon, Austin had said, there would be new constellations and she'd see the Southern Cross.

He lifted his warm hand to her breast. "I am pleased to see your bout of seasickness left you."

Evangeline smiled in the dark. "Yes." She would wait a few more days before she told him her condition had nothing to do with seasickness.

"What are you thinking of?" he asked softly.

"I was wondering if Lord Rudolph had reached England yet. If he's made his peace with his family."

"He'll be in London by now." Austin sounded uninterested.

"He told me before we boarded why he did not want to go home. He is engaged to be married."

"Is he? Then why the devil did he ask you?"

"He is trying to think of ways to get out of it. The marriage was proposed when he was a child, and he says the girl has grown into a harpy. She does not want the marriage, either. But I think when he returns and she sees him, she will come to her senses. He is quite handsome and dashing."

Austin raised up on his elbow. Tension radiated from him. "Were you ever tempted to marry the confounded man?"

She smiled. "No. I always knew I could not. He will be a marquess one day. He does not need a wife like me."

His dark brows drew together like thunderclouds. "Is that the only reason?"

"No." She stroked his sleek hair from his temple. "But I like to tease you. You should not be angry with him. He did save your life."

"That does not mean I have to like him."

She rose up on her knees, slipping one leg over his torso. "I did not marry him because I knew, deep in my heart, that I should marry you."

"Damn right you should."

His warm lips found her shoulder. Desire fluttered in her belly. She leaned forward.

"Are captain's wives allowed to give orders?"

"That depends on what the orders are."

She put her lips next to his ear and whispered what she wanted, taking time over the details. His body went rigid under her, and the sheet between her legs rose the slightest bit.

He said in a choked voice, "I think that I can carry out those orders."

"Then please do, Mr. Blackwell."

"Aye, ma'am."

He caught her shoulders and rolled her down into the bunk. She fell, laughing to the pillows. He did not laugh. His eyes dark with passion, he slid his palms up her body and proceeded to obey each and every one of her requests, adding a few of his own that she hadn't known were possible. The ship rocked gently beneath them, carrying them together to whatever exotic lands and adventures awaited.

Epilogue

My very dear Miss Pyne:

You may be surprised to learn that I write to you from the far-off country of China. Yes, I sit in a house in the city of Peking, the residence of a foreign merchant, who is an acquaintance of my husband. How different it all is from Gloucestershire! We are waited upon by a Chinaman with a long pigtail and silken trousers, and given tea that is black and bitter but quite soothing.

I have found the Chinese people to be kind and courteous, if given to making a great din. There are firecrackers and paper dragons everywhere and lanterns and streamers, and everyone is in brilliant clothing. My husband tells me it is the New Year here; in February, is that not strange?

I have given my husband a New Year's gift then, a small boy with dark red hair and black eyes. The Chinese say he is very lucky to be born now, of all times. But my dear Miss Pyne, should the happy day ever come to you, I do not recommend delivering a child during a gale in the middle of winter in the middle of the Pacific Ocean. I do not know what my husband worried about more, me or losing the ship.

I told him, of course, that if the ship were lost, it scarcely mattered what happened to me. Besides, women have been about this task for centuries. For a midwife, I had a gnarled, hardened sailor, his skin so brown and smooth I cannot tell his age. But his wife has born him fifteen children, just imagine, many times with only his help. I felt quite odd giving myself to his care, but he was as gentle as a mother, and told me funny stories to keep me cheerful.

I wept at the sight of my child, but I wept for joy. My husband easily pulled the ship through the storm, as I knew he would, but when I laid his son in his arms he stood as one stunned, and I fancy I saw a tear in his eye. Gentlemen, my dear Miss Pyne, as I am now in a position to know, are very curious creatures.

Where I shall be when this letter finds you, I do not know. I follow my husband about this great, large world of ours, and there is a new place and new sights every day.

Oh, my dear teacher, did you ever imagine your young pupil would rise to such bliss? I know you happy in your single state, but if the day ever comes you wish to exchange that state for the married one, I recommend boarding a ship in Liverpool bound for America.

If you can throw in a mutiny and a pirate or two, so much the better.

I remain,

Your fondest student,

Evangeline Blackwell